"Emerson's eccentric characters, vividly specific Seattle settings, witty dialogue, and complex but impeccably credible plot combine for a delightful and satisfying reading experience."
—*Booklist*

"Earl Emerson writes with the richness and grace of a poet, evincing a quality of phrase and nuance that elevates the genre."
—ROBERT CRAIS

"A delicate combination of action, suspense, and fine character development . . . A great night-by-the-fire book."
—*Globe and Mail* (Toronto)

NERVOUS LAUGHTER

Earl Emerson

BALLANTINE BOOKS • NEW YORK

A Ballantine Book
Published by The Ballantine Publishing Group
Copyright © 1986 by Earl Emerson

All rights reserved under International and Pan-American Copyright Conventions. Published in the United States by The Ballantine Publishing Group, a division of Random House, Inc., New York, and simultaneously in Canada by Random House of Canada Limited, Toronto.

http://www.randomhouse.com

Library of Congress Catalog Card Number: 96-95365

ISBN 0-345-42945-1

Printed in Canada

First Ballantine Books Edition: October 1997

10 9 8 7 6 5 4 3 2

"The boys with their feet on the desks know that the easiest murder case in the world to break is the one somebody tried to get very cute with; the one that really bothers them is the murder somebody only thought of two minutes before he pulled it off."

—*Raymond Chandler*

1 THE HEADLINES READ: NORTHWEST TY-
COON SHOOTS TEENAGE MISTRESS,
SELF, IN BIZARRE SUICIDE PACT.

It was the sort of tacky emotionalism the papers gulped down whole, no matter how much they belittled the supermarket checkout tabloids for trashing people's lives with the same bludgeon of publicity.

The front page of the Seattle paper was loaded with pictures: a photo of the underage girlfriend swilling beer with her poorly dressed friends; a three-year-old photo of the ill-fated businessman grinning disarmingly as he accepted an award from the mayor.

The biggest picture was a ghoulish snapshot of the bodies being trundled out of the Trinity Building into the sunshine—one to the morgue, one to the emergency room at Harborview.

Several days earlier the instructions had arrived in a cheap white envelope, handwritten in an effortless, flowing cursive I decided was that of a woman. After the building had emptied for the day, someone with a flair for the dramatic had poked the envelope through the mail slot of my cramped office in the Piscule Building.

It was early—a Friday morning in May.

Mr. Thomas Black—Investigator:

Don't be alarmed at the quasi-outlandish nature of this offer, but I am more than a little embarrassed about this whole affair and wish to manage it with the least amount of fuss.

Your name was mentioned by mutual friends as one who could be trusted implicitly.

I have no idea what your rates are or how far this money will take you. Until it runs out, please follow Mark Daniels and report on his movements.

He spends a great deal of his time in the office on Harbor Island, both before, during, and after the regular business day. He is a fanatical Mariners fan and he has a cabin on Lost Lake which he may visit from time to time.

There is the possibility that he is seeing women. Please report on this. Send your report to Post Office Box 3751. Thank you for your time and trouble.

P.S. We don't need pictures or legal proof, just reasonable certainty.

The note was unsigned. My guess was that a woman had written it. It might have been his wife. His mother. Mistress. Whoever she was, she smelled positively angelic. The envelope retained a whiff of thick and fragrant perfume intermingled with the unforgettable aroma of freshly minted legal tender. Paper-clipped to the note were five one-hundred-dollar bills, the notes stiff and unwrinkled.

Thumbing through the white pages in the phone book

confirmed that a Mark and Deanna Daniels resided in town, at a plush location on Queen Anne Hill.

It had been a queer deal from the beginning.

It smelled like trouble. It smelled like a corny case from one of the old *Black Mask* stories. It smelled like a scorned woman or a jealous business partner or some other incredibly jumbled and messy domestic intrigue. I should have bundled the bills up, licked some stamps, pasted the twenty-cent darlings on and mailed the hodge-podge to Box Number 3751.

I didn't.

Early the next morning, Saturday, I hopped into my '68 Ford pickup and drove to the address on Queen Anne Hill, parking on a side street on the south slope. There were only two houses on this short, cobbled dogleg of a street. Each of them sported a view some people would kill for.

The residences were uphill and thus higher than the street, but even from the roadway I could see the entire Olympic Mountain Range, Elliott Bay, the hump that was West Seattle, Harbor Island, and most of downtown Seattle, including the Space Needle and the bustling water-front. To the east, the Cascade range was clouded over. It was enough to suck the blood right out of your heart.

Most of the neighbors were still knocking the sleep seeds off their faces when Mark Daniels emerged from his house and wedged himself into an ebony Volkswagen Rabbit parked in the circular driveway. I wondered why he didn't take the new Cadillac sitting beside it.

Slewing from side to side, the Rabbit skittered down the hillside on the twisty streets—streets damp from spotty morning showers.

Thoroughly familiar with his nimble little car as well as his labyrinthine neighborhood, he dropped me twice on the way down the slope. He finally jumped onto the Alaskan Way Viaduct and proceeded south. Only because traffic was skimpy and because I had a fair idea of where he was heading did I manage to stick.

I had done no preliminary research on this cat, so I didn't realize until I read it in the papers the next day that the mammoth building he drove to on Harbor Island—a building with attached warehouses and a dog food factory abutting it, a building that took up the better part of four full city blocks—was one that he owned half interest in.

A rustic wood-burned sign on the corner read Trinity Building.

Harbor Island is a vast flat tract of industrial area at the south end of Elliott Bay between Beacon Hill and West Seattle. It was an island only because the Duwamish River poured into the Sound on either side. It had once been miles and miles of tideflats and marshlands. The Indians had fished and clammed out there.

Reclaimed from the sea by overzealous landfill engineers, much of the city's deep port activity was handled from its banks. The ground rumbled ominously when heavy trucks rolled up the streets. Some scientific wag once claimed the lead content in the air down there—heaviest in the state—was enough to kill a congressman.

Daniels parked in a vacant lot that had been landscaped by professionals, festooned with young birches and dotted with rhododendrons in full flower. The stick-on clock on my dash said 7:45.

In his late thirties or early forties, Mark Daniels wore wool slacks and a pin-striped dress shirt without a tie, the sleeves rolled into wrinkled doughnuts just shy of his elbows.

Maintaining cover in that area was difficult because I was in a pickup truck—an old pickup truck. So I parked a hundred yards away and spied on Daniels through a monocular. He locked the Rabbit and disappeared into the complex through a side door. It was going to be a wait.

Of average height, he had a pudgy face, hefty forearms and a great solid paunch that rode over his belt. His wavy brown hair was short and styled, molting into a fashionable gray at the temples. Like a lot of men these days, he sported a neatly trimmed beard, the mustache shaved away. He had the walk and picky, avoid-the-mud-puddles air of a man who hadn't done any physical labor in twenty years. Or maybe ever.

Thirty minutes later as I thumbed through the paper and settled into the funnies, a late-model Mercedes sports coupe pulled into the lot. A tall, gray-haired man got out and shuffled into the building, disappearing through the same door as Mark Daniels. He left the motor of the Mercedes running. After a while, in the undisturbed and deadly still morning air, I could smell tendrils of diesel exhaust from the Mercedes drifting up the street.

Looking drunk, the gray-haired man bumbled out of the building, sidestepped into the lot, squinted down the road, then hastened back inside the brick building. Nobody could get drunk that quickly. He was a man out of sync with the universe—waiting impatiently for something that couldn't come fast enough.

Along with the exhaust, something else began drifting in the still morning air: the distant wail of a siren. I spotted the genesis in my rear-view mirror and watched the speck of flashing red light in the distance gradually evolve into a boxy aid car from the Seattle Fire Department.

Cutting its siren, it raced up the deserted street and screeched to a halt in the lot of the Trinity Building.

As if on cue, the old man blundered out a second time and distractedly propped the building door open while the two men from the fire department fetched their equipment in large black suitcases from the back of their vehicle. They hustled along behind him into the building.

Soon another white and red boxy fire department van pulled into the lot—the paramedics—and two more men hefted their suitcases of equipment into the Trinity Building.

It was only when I spied the blue ping-pong lights from a prowl car half a mile behind in the rear-view mirror that I clambered out of the truck and hustled into the building. The cop may only have been coming in for a blood run, but if it was for more than that, this would be my last chance to rubberneck.

Inside I found a long fruitwood receptionist's counter that had accommodations for two receptionists and a switchboard operator. Nothing was there but a coffee cup with lipstick on the rim that somebody had abandoned in Friday afternoon's melee. Beyond that, the room opened up into an enormous atrium that could have held four or five hundred people in a pinch. Huge fig trees grew in concrete planters. Ferns dangled from perches built high into the walls. Colorful tulips grew in concrete planters along the walkway. There were three levels, open aisleways fronting the atrium in a rectangular arrangement, offices off each level.

Today's business was all being conducted second floor center.

Standing in the doorway, the old man was pale and sweaty and rigid, his back pressed up against the blond wood of the door. I skipped up the open stairs two at a time. It's funny what you can get away with if you act like you belong.

I strode through the doorway past the old gummer directly into the office.

The old man spoke to the firemen, "Is he going to live?"

"Don't know, Pops. You know who he is? You got a name and address? Next of kin?"

"Sure."

"He related to you?"

"You might say that." The old man swiped at his brow with a balled-up handkerchief. "He might as well be."

Intermingled with the smell of perfume, sweat, and urine, I could still detect a whiff of gun powder.

The office was neat and spacious, with Danish furniture and brushed steel fixtures, though the six bodies inside made it look smaller than it ordinarily would have. Four of the bodies were living, breathing firemen. One body was that of Mark Daniels, fresh blood streaming out of his scalp and down the side of his head, pooling on the carpet in a thick, goopy puddle. He had been shot in the temple. Three firemen were perspiring over him, inserting needles, taking hurried blood pressure readings, and chattering on their portable radios to a doctor at Harborview.

The sixth body was that of a girl who I guessed was about eighteen. No, make that sixteen. She was lying on the floor on her back.

One of the firemen stood apart from the others, gawking at her.

A dishwater blonde, she was short and chesty. She was naked except for thigh-length black silk stockings. Or maybe they were nylon. I couldn't tell without touching them and I wasn't going to touch them.

"I guess she's dead," said the fireman, without looking away from the spectacle.

"Appears that way," I replied. If you looked carefully you could see where the bullet had dug into the side of her skull at about the hairline and done a lot of damage behind her eyes, both of which were open. Cornflower blue. The left one was slightly blown.

A minute later two uniformed cops came in and the party began.

KATHY BIRCHFIELD INSISTED ON chauffeuring me. The car was new, a smart little apple-yellow two-seater, an import from over the water, and the payments had her on a stingy budget.

"I asked you out," she said, "so I'll pick up the tab."

"Like hell you will."

"I will. And don't be such a grouch. And thanks for coming, Thomas. I know how much you abhor parties and chitchat and 'too much silly talk about too much nothing,' as you call it. You don't know how much it means to have you for my escort when I need you. Really."

"Forget it."

I stared out the window at the houses we were passing in the twilight. Dressed to the nines, we were screwing up our eyes looking for an address on Queen Anne Hill only a matter of blocks from where I had picked up Mark Daniels over a week earlier. I was in a double-breasted suit Kathy had insisted on helping me select a year ago. The stiff collar of the shirt chafed my neck.

Kathy was poured into a slinky gold lamé dress that I had only caught a glimpse of through the folds of her full-length fur coat, a coat she had bought years ago at St.

9

Vincent DePaul and redone—long before they had come back into fashion. Kathy had two bedrooms in her new apartment, one for herself and one for her clothes.

"This must be it," she said. "See all those cars?"

"I thought you said this was going to be a small gathering. There wouldn't really be anybody important here."

"Don't go getting scared."

"I'm not scared."

"You sound scared. More than five people in the room and you go bananas."

"I'm not bananas."

"Don't be a grouch. You'll love it."

"Oh tish." It was how her three-year-old niece, who had a longshoreman for a stepfather, said, "Oh shit." We used it between ourselves to show disgruntlement.

She reached past the gear shift knob and squeezed my thigh, making a superb mockery of Mae West. "Ooooooooooooo."

"Tish."

It was a tall colonial, with white pillars bracing the front, antique lamps in the drive, a doorman—the whole bit. I knew the neighborhood vaguely from a case I'd worked when I was still with the city police. Across the street lived a retired United States senator whose maid raked in more money in a year than I ever had.

A conservative guess pegged the house as capable of holding two hundred people. We parked in the first available spot, which was four blocks away, and crossed our fingers that one of the spring showers that had been clobbering the city all day wouldn't drench us. They had valet parking, but Kathy wasn't going to trust her new car to some gawky college kid in coveralls.

Inside, we were introduced to the mayor, a couple of

city councilmen and their wives, a city councilwoman and her husband. It was a political gathering having something to do with a sister city in Japan. There were some round-faced Japanese. I recognized several reporters from the local TV stations, all shorter than they appeared on the tube.

"Oh, Thomas Black," Kathy whispered in my ear when we got a breather from the initial flurry of introductions. I could tell from her tone that she was going to mock me. "You look so big and handsome in that suit. I'll bet half the women here are dying to go home with you."

"Flattery will get you everywhere," I said, spotting a voluptuous blonde across the room.

Strawberry-blonde, really. She was in her mid-twenties. Several times I caught her looking at me. There was something about her—a certain twinkle in her sad eyes when she looked about, as if she were mildly amused by the world—and in love with it. My guess was she had a vivacious personality that for some reason was subdued tonight.

In her childhood her hair had probably been red. Time had transformed it to the fascinating shade of sun-ruined straw. We held each other's eye until one or the other of us broke—and my palms began to get real slippery. I had to meet this woman. Half the knowledge of the universe seemed to pass between us when our eyes met, like an electrical charge. There was a chemistry in the air and we both knew it.

She turned away and spoke deliberately to a sober-looking man at her elbow, a chubby chap who had been pried into a gray suit and strangled with an evangelical collar. After her escort answered her, she erupted into a low-pitched laugh. She had a laugh that flowed like water sloshing in a wooden tub. I could have listened to it all night.

"Kathy? You wouldn't mind terribly if we went home separately, would you?"

"Of course not. You know the deal. Suit yourself."

"You're a peach."

I moved across the room toward the blonde. Halfway there, Kathy apprehended me, grabbing my elbow and standing close, avoiding my face and talking at my arm like a spy.

"You're not making a move on *her*, are you?"

"The blonde, yeah. She's smitten with me. I don't really want to, but I feel it's some sort of duty, you know? Look at her. She's smitten."

"Thomas, she's with a clergyman."

"I'm with an angel. That doesn't mean anything. We can talk about relations—trade relations."

"You don't go to an affair like this and then samba over and try to pick up some society matron who is with a clergyman. Thomas?"

I looked over at the blonde. "It's not that I want to. Or even that I need to. It's an obligation, really. Do you understand what I'm saying? We're talking civic obligation here. My debt to the city."

Kathy smiled patronizingly. I had seen her use the same sorry smile over a gravestone once.

"Thomas! Why don't you wait awhile? Maybe that's her husband. Besides, isn't he Sam Michael Wheeler, that preacher who's on the television all the time?"

"She's head-over-heels in love. Can't you see the way she's been mooning over me?"

"She's not, Thomas. You must look like somebody

she knows or something, somebody she doesn't recognize in this context. Maybe you look like her dentist. Her sanitation engineer. The guy who snatched her purse last week."

"Funny."

Kathy shook her head. "Believe me, she's not in love with you."

"Do you know who she is?"

She shrugged. "I might have met her."

"Well, she's fallen hard for the kid. Married or not, I'm going over there sometime this evening so I can at least pat her hand and console her."

For the better part of ten minutes the pneumatic blonde and I flicked hot glances at each other. She meandered around the gathering beside the Reverend, and I meandered around beside Kathy and then alone when my date began discussing politics with some of the local pompous and elected. Drinks were served. Canapés were munched. Jokes were told and acknowledged with polite tittering.

Everything was genteel except the blonde.

Her looks grew hotter and lingered longer than they had a right to. The more I thought about it the more I knew she couldn't be married, or even seriously interested in the Reverend.

When the Reverend left her side to fetch refreshments, I waded through the crowd toward her. When I turned around, Kathy was giving me a funny warning look from between two short Japanese gentlemen, one of whom was himself having a hard time tearing his eyes away from Kathy's liquid gold gown.

"Good evening," I said.

Without really being a part of their group, the blonde

had been listening to a conversation between several women standing in a nearby doorway. She was sitting on a shiny sofa under an oil painting. When I spoke she turned her head. The movement made a straight line of tendon run down her neck and into her blouse.

"I understand you work for some security outfit," she said.

"You've heard of me? I'm surprised."

"Somewhat."

"I work for myself." I sat beside her. Up close I could see that she was a large-framed, firmly built woman. She wore a black skirt and a silk blouse in a shade of blue that looked like something on a swallow. Her legs were crossed and one calf was swollen from the pressure of her knee beneath it. Her greenish-brown eyes played over my face.

"Security work. That must be very exciting."

"Mostly it's just work."

"I can't help but think there must be an awful lot of adventure to it."

"About once every ten years." I was thinking about a pair of hoodlums who had tried to teach me to breathe underwater six weeks before.

"You don't know me?" she asked.

"I'm sorry."

"Haven't you been reading the papers?"

"After last Sunday I didn't have the stomach for it. I've been tossing them into the fireplace all week."

"That's right. You were involved in the investigation. You were mixed up in that shooting, but you didn't give the police anything. They were going to arrest you."

"I spent two nights in jail."

"Did you? I'm sorry about that."

I laughed. "It wasn't your fault. So what do you do?"

"A little sculpture. I dabble, really. I was an art major in college."

Across the room Kathy scowled at me and shook her head. It wasn't an admonishment, but an order. She was commanding me to leave this woman. I couldn't believe it. I winked at her.

When the Reverend tried to ford across the room, Kathy intercepted him, detaining him for my benefit. She was, I thought, going slightly overboard.

"You here with your husband?"

"No. No. My husband has been . . . ill. He couldn't make it."

"Sorry to hear that." So, Kathy was wrong. She wasn't married to the man in the collar. She was out for a fling, had chosen me, and Kathy was making a fool of herself.

"I suppose that's your girlfriend in the gold?"

"A friend. She needed an escort tonight. She's going a little goofy right now."

"Just friends? That's hard to understand. She's ravishing."

"It's a long story. By the way, so are you—ravishing."

Her eyes smiled without the rest of her face helping any, and I noted how much green there was in the circles around her pupils. We were going to get along just fine. We both knew it, like some sort of cosmic inference.

Kathy and the man in the ecclesiastical duds reached us and stood over the couch. Kathy said, "Perhaps we should all adjourn to another room. The host has graciously made the library available."

Slowly swinging my eyes away from the strawberry-blonde, I said, "Kathy, I don't believe this."

"No," said the blonde, picking up my hand by the

thumb, standing and pulling me to my feet. "She's right. Come along."

Kathy gave me a look. I gave her a harder look. The blonde towed me away, the others trailing behind. It wasn't until we got to the door of the library that she dropped my hand, which had begun perspiring in her grip.

All four of us walked into the library. The lights were already on. The clergyman closed the door and stood against it and the four of us exchanged looks.

3 THE BLONDE SEATED HERSELF AT A small, round table and switched on a Tiffany lamp, handling the valuable antique as carefully as if she knew what it was worth, as casually as if she owned it. There were five of the obstacles in the book-lined library, and I moved so as not to blunder into one of them.

Diffused lamplight played on her face, and I noted for the first time that her cheeks were splashed with washed-out freckles.

They peppered the backs of her hands and arms and crept down her neck into the swallow-blue of her blouse. As a child, she undoubtedly had been one of those milk-skinned redheads. Her twenty-five or so years on the planet had dimmed the freckles and leached most of the reddish pigment out of her hair. Piled on her head and secured with whalebone combs, it was an entrancing hue of gold. It seemed to change color with the light.

Hands balled into fists and rammed into my pockets, I bided my time and waited to see how Kathy was going to get her foot out of her mouth.

Kathy said, "Most of us know each other."

I glanced around. The clergyman nodded. The blonde

17

gave me a vaguely nervous smile. It was the first time she had looked at all anxious that evening, no doubt disturbed that our smoldering yen for each other would soon be publicly exposed.

"Leech, Bemis and Ott is representing the case," Kathy said. "I'm doing the preliminary background work. Thomas Black, the gentleman by the door is the Reverend Sam Michael Wheeler. The woman he is escorting is Deanna Daniels."

It took a few seconds for it to hit me.

Kathy prodded my memory. "Mrs. *Mark* Daniels."

Smiling, Kathy reached over, picked my hand out of my pocket, and fondled it maternally. Crumbs of comfort.

"Sorry to do it this way, but Mrs. Daniels wanted to look you over before she hired us."

All that eye play in the other room, the staring I had mistaken for hot blood, for good old American lust, had been nothing but a good old systematic professional evaluation. Good teeth. Nice coat. Fetlocks healthy. Pack the animal into the van, Roger. I looked around for a rug to crawl under.

"From what we've been told," said Sam Michael Wheeler, strolling across the room to Deanna Daniels and draping his arm heavily across her shoulders, "from what we've been told, in a situation like this the investigator is almost as crucial as the lawyer. Of course, we're no experts. This is the first time Deanna has been involved in something of this sort. I've had experience in civil litigation. And, of course, I was in the military for ten years."

I cut him off. "Comparing the military to a murder

case is like saying you know what an artichoke tastes like because you once ate a piece of celery."

"Thomas . . ." Kathy lowered one of her looks on me.

The Reverend continued, "Deanna just wanted to . . . check you out without any pressure. Don't you see?" He gave me a glance that was partial smile, partial patronage, and partial obsolescent aristocratic hauteur. It was a lethal look that might work on a cowed congregation. In his forties, he had a full head of mustard-brown hair and a chubby face that couldn't be called anything but boyish.

I turned to Kathy Birchfield. Since passing the bar a year ago she had been working at Leech, Bemis and Ott, a well-known firm of attorneys in Seattle. The invitation to work for L, B and O had been a coup, and since she was the only one in the prestigious house who wanted to sink her teeth into criminal cases, by default she was getting those cases when they presented themselves. While I wasn't considered their official investigator by any means, the two times before that Kathy had needed someone, she had called upon me.

"Well," I said, removing my hand from Kathy's grip and folding my arms across my chest. "Did I pass muster?"

"I'm sorry," said Deanna Daniels. "We weren't trying to belittle you . . . or anything. I just felt uncomfortable hiring a firm without . . . I mean, I've heard wonderful things about you. It's just that I had to see you. I go on my gut instincts a lot. It's how I am. Now that I've met you I feel silly. Of course you'll do."

Kathy said, "Thomas does work for Leech, Bemis and Ott on a case-by-case basis, Deanna. We'll have to lay it out for him and see."

Deanna bit her lower lip. "Sure. I remember you explained that at the office."

Pacing around the room, Kathy outlined the situation. I couldn't help noticing that for a clergyman, Sam Michael Wheeler's eyes lingered a little too long on the shimmering gold dress. Maybe I was watching him too closely. But then, he was only human. Even Deanna was looking at it.

"A week ago Emmett Anderson, Mark Daniels' long-time business associate, dropped by the Trinity Building to pick up some papers. You were outside, Thomas.

"When he got upstairs he heard somebody groaning in Mark's office. The door was locked from the inside, but he had a key. You know what he found in there. You saw it. Mark Daniels has been in a coma at Harborview ever since. The doctors don't know when he might regain consciousness. Or even if he will. Meanwhile, the Seattle Police Department has built a case on him. If he lives . . . they prosecute for murder."

Kathy glanced across the room to see how Deanna Daniels was absorbing this narrative. The Reverend rubbed the back of her shoulder in a comforting motion, and she laid her hand on top of his, both their hands massaging lazily in unison. Despite her voluptuousness, I couldn't help noticing how thin her hand was.

"If he dies, Deanna stands to lose a good deal of insurance money. Life insurance doesn't pay off on suicides. And she may lose part of the business to boot."

"How does she lose part of the business?" I asked.

"Emmett Anderson and my husband have been together for years," said Deanna, clearing her throaty voice and avoiding my eyes. "They were very close when they first started out, and they did most everything without putting any of it in writing. Some of the ventures Mark owned outright. Some Emmett owned. Most Emmett owned. We've only done a little investigating, but it would take an army of accountants to straighten things out if Emmett decided not to assist. I know that's hard to believe, but they started off small and most of the money in the beginning was Emmett's. When they got bigger they didn't see any reason to change . . ."

Kathy finished for her. "Legally, he could choke off the Daniels estate with next to nothing. At least we think he could. So far we're having a difficult time pinning him down on what he is planning to do. And Mark had run up some bills. He's behind on his child support. He bought a custom-made sailboat for a small fortune. He is up to his ears in debt. If Deanna doesn't get the insurance money and doesn't get any of the business, she'll be out on the street."

"You could sue for your share of the business."

Kathy shook her head. Deanna said, "I'll have to declare bankruptcy. Going to court would take years. I could never pay it all off."

I looked at Kathy. "What do they have downtown?"

"The girl's body. The gun. It is registered to Mark. The fact that he knew the girl. She worked at the plant for three months last summer. And the note."

"What note?"

"He left a suicide note in the typewriter in his office."

I hadn't seen it, but there had been a lot of confusion that morning, a lot of other things to look at. Though I had searched, I hadn't seen the gun either. One of the paramedics had surreptitiously laid his coat over it until a uniformed officer showed up.

"Do you have a copy of the note?"

"We know what it says," said the Reverend Wheeler. "It was a family courtesy to provide it for Mrs. Daniels. Detective Crum was kind enough to do that."

"Ralph Crum?"

"I believe that was his name." The hand-on-shoulder business wasn't stopping and it was beginning to wear me down. "Do you know this Crum fellow?"

"What did the note say? Better yet, do you have a copy with you?"

"If you know this Detective Crum, it might make things more expedient. We weren't aware that you had contacts with the police."

"The note?"

Deanna stared at a Flemish tapestry hanging on the opposite wall. She quoted from memory in a voice flatter than a student saxophone.

" 'Deanna dear. Forgive me. So much of my life has been lived apart from you that now when you require so much of me I find it so very hard to give. This is something that's been coming on for a long time. Don't feel bad for me. Just forgive me. I'll love you forever. Mark.' "

"That's it?"

"That's it," said the Reverend Sam Wheeler, his voice a bit more chipper than I would have liked. I noticed he wasn't wearing a band on his left hand. Perhaps his plump ring finger had outgrown it.

"Mark didn't write that," Deanna said, springing up and moving toward me. The Reverend followed, grasping her by one elbow, acting as an anchor on her fervor.

"How do you know?"

"Because Mark didn't try to kill himself. He wouldn't. He just wouldn't."

"Was the note signed?"

"Typewritten. His name at the bottom."

"What about the girl? Do you think he shot her?" Tears began trickling down Deanna's cheeks. I was pouring salt into old wounds.

The Reverend took advantage of Deanna's momentary confusion to hug her to himself, a self-satisfied look on his mug. Any moment I expected him to start purring.

"Of course he didn't shoot her. Mark wouldn't shoot her."

I looked past the couple in front of me to Kathy who was watching the three of us, an indecipherable look marring her liquid violet eyes.

"No woman thinks her own husband would shoot anybody. Yet it happens every day. Tell me specifically why you think Mark wouldn't do such a thing."

"Aren't you being a little hard on her?" interjected the Reverend Wheeler. "This lady has had quite a week. She may lose everything this life has seen fit to give her. Her husband is lying half dead in a hospital bed in a coma that he may never wake out of. She only came to this party because I talked her into it. It's killing her to sit in the hospital alone and wait. Lord almighty, man, can't you see it's killing her?

"She's been almost a week without any real sleep. She needed to get out by herself, if only for a few hours. I practically forced her to come and meet you here. And now you're giving her the third degree like some sort of police-state baboon."

"It's okay," said Deanna softly.

"No, it isn't," continued Reverend Wheeler. "What do you think it was like for Deanna coming to this party where everybody knew what happened—to know that everybody was whispering behind her back? Answer me!"

"No," said Deanna. "No more, Sam. It's all right. In fact, I want to answer him. If I can't, then he's right. I don't have any right to hire him."

The bluster Wheeler had worked up seemed to sizzle away like air out of an old tire. He walked his hand from Deanna's shoulder to the back of her bare neck, where he cupped his meaty thumb and palm around the base of her skull and left it there like a man cradling a melon. She didn't seem to notice.

"Do you have reason to think Mark couldn't have done it?" Kathy Birchfield asked.

"That note. Mark had the typewriter in his office, but he only used it for business. Whenever he wrote anything personal he used a fountain pen. It was just his way. He loved fountain pens. He never would have typed a note like that. And those words—they just aren't his. I can't quite put my finger on it, but there was something clichéd about the way that note was written."

"Did you tell the police?"

She nodded. Kathy looked from Deanna to me and said, "We'll talk to them later, Thomas. Ralph Crum said he'd talk."

"Just one item before you get too wrapped up in this," said Wheeler, unctuously. "We understand from the news media that you were involved in some sort of mysterious activity out on Harbor Island . . ." He let it waft in the air, awaiting my—he thought—compulsive explanation.

I watched Deanna's eyes turn to mine and grow reflective. Chances were she had hired me to follow her husband. She uncrossed her legs and smoothed the skirt over her thighs. She was a large woman and had the look of an athlete, a swimmer or an avid tennis player.

"That is to say, the day Mark was discovered by Emmett, you were there. You were apparently working on something. But you wouldn't tell the police. Is that correct?"

"You got it."

"What were you working on?"

I flicked a piece of lint off my left sleeve. I straightened my cuff. I looked at Wheeler, at his hand resting on Deanna's neck. I looked at Deanna. "I've got rules, Reverend Wheeler. One of them is not to compromise a client."

"Are you saying you were out there working on a case? For a client?"

"I'm not saying anything."

"We have a right to know. After all, Leech, Bemis and Ott are Mark's attorneys and they're hiring you to look into this. His life may hang in the balance. At the very least, his reputation. We have a right to find out just how much you're hiding."

Something in the green-brown of Deanna Daniels' eyes told me she wasn't exactly sympathetic with Wheeler's line of inquiry. Contesting it was a feat she didn't have the requisite energy for. Neither did I.

Wheeler continued, "We're paying your bills, fella. Now, cough it up. You can't hold out."

"Watch me."

When he got tired of glowering at me, which took longer than I thought, he turned to Kathy Birchfield for succor. She shrugged and said, "Thomas is very good at what he does. If there's something more to be found out about this case, he'll find it."

Deanna gave me a look that might have been gratitude—but was both melancholy and inquisitive in turn.

Wheeler walked to the door and turned around, the knob in his fist. We could hear people conversing in the hallway. "Coming, Deanna, honey?"

"In a minute."

"I'll meet you outside," said Kathy, following the glances that were passing between Deanna and me. I no longer wanted to think there were sparks, not with her husband five miles away in a coma, so I thought it was something else. Something primordial, something about a knight in shining armor, something about a man with a rope in his hand when you were sinking in the black night off the side of a ship. I had seen the look before—a dangerous situation which left a distinct and bitter aftertaste if things didn't pan out.

Chatter from the corridor grew louder through the half open door. Deanna stood, walked to me, raised her hand as if she were planning to touch me, dropped her hand and said, "There is one thing. How did the girl get there? And how did he have enough time to get into the mood? I mean, suicide is a big step. You don't just wake up in the morning and say, 'Okay, bang.' Do you? Also, the note said he had been thinking about it for a long time. He never mentioned anything about suicide. Never ever. You'd think he would have said something. Maybe once when he was drunk."

"Did he get drunk?"

"Not a lot." She avoided my eyes. "Once or twice a month maybe."

"You don't love your husband anymore, do you?"

Her words were clipped, almost angry: "Not anymore. Not for a long while."

She heeled around and walked out of the room. Outside in the hallway a young waiter in an ill-fitting white coat longingly watched her walk away, swept up in the perfume of her being. Me—I was going to need an inoculation against her witchery. Along with several booster shots.

WORKING AN IMITATION ANTIQUE crank phone in the hallway, I dialed Ralph Crum. He said he was plowing through some paperwork, but would meet us in twenty minutes at a café on Third Avenue. It was a seedy greasy spoon and Kathy was going to draw a lot of looks in that liquid gold.

"I'll take a cab," I told her when she met me at the front door.

"I don't think so, big fella."

"Hey Pancho."

"Hey Cisco. I go weeth you."

"Okay. But keep your coat buttoned." On the assumption that I was kidding, she playfully closed a fist and rapped me on the shoulder.

Two angry rain showers doused us on our short journey, but the street was dry when we parked on Third Avenue. Seattle was like that. If you don't like the weather, stick around five minutes.

We commandeered a table by the window so Kathy could keep an eye on the grifters and panhandlers on the sidewalk—and on her new car.

"Sorry about the ruse," said Kathy. "I know how embarrassed you were."

"Nothing to it." I buffed a nail on my sleeve. "I wasn't embarrassed."

Kathy Birchfield looked at me as if I had just offered to work a variation of the pigeon drop on her favorite aunt. "You were, and you snapped at Wheeler because of it. He's a powerful and very influential man in this community. Besides, he's done an awful lot to improve life for certain segments of society in this town. I wish you didn't take such a sudden dislike to certain people."

"Naw, I wasn't embarrassed."

"Okay." She held up both open palms. "Thomas, I'm sorry. I just wanted you to know that Mrs. Daniels was very specific. You weren't to know anything about what was going on. Don't ask me why."

"I think I know why."

"You do? I've been wondering all evening."

"Forget it."

"I didn't want to embarrass you."

"The pinnacle of your emotional life is embarrassing me, Kathy, and you know it."

I looked away from a pair of middle-aged lovebirds necking in a back booth in time to see Kathy wiping a smirk off her face with an open hand. "Don't feel bad about it, Thomas. Deanna's always been the kind of woman men get brainsick over."

"Brainsick?"

The smirk returned in spades and above it her eyes were as amused as if I'd done a jig on the tabletop in a fig leaf. "You have to admit, you were a little green around the gills."

Kathy sipped at a Dr Pepper and watched two men in ragged coats pushing a broken-down Dodge up Third Avenue, one of them steering through the open driver's window. Cars beeped. A lady Metro driver with a per-oxide mop manhandled her bus around them, honked and flipped them off.

"Why is Crum talking to us?" We both knew it was almost verboten for a homicide detective to talk to defense attorneys about anything. They made their case and handed it over to the D.A. The D.A. might want to talk to us. Never the dicks from downtown.

"Ralph Crum figures the case won't get to trial and he wants to save us some grief."

"Why won't it go to trial?"

"Because of Mark Daniels' physical condition."

"You mean Daniels isn't going to wake up?"

"The doctor I spoke with gave him one chance in ten of regaining consciousness. At that, he may be a vege-table. In fact, they haven't even taken the bullet out yet. They feel it's much more likely that he'll just linger on for a few weeks, or months, and then die."

"Does Deanna know this?"

"We haven't discussed it. She may. She probably does."

"How much life insurance are we talking about?"

"Oodles. Three or four separate policies. I think it's over $600,000, all told. And his business holdings are worth more than that—if Anderson decides to do the decent thing and split it down the middle. The problem there is Anderson was real close to Mark's first family. He was disappointed when Mark divorced Helen and married Deanna."

"I bet a lot of people were disappointed the day Deanna got married."

"Funny. By the way, who were you working for? Were

you following Mark, or the old man, Emmett Anderson? Or the girl?"

"Deanna asked me where the girl came from. Good question. She didn't drive there with Mark and there weren't any other vehicles around."

"You're avoiding the question," said Kathy. "Who were you working for?"

"Maybe later," I said, as Ralph Crum stormed through the front door of the café, spotted us and clumped over to our table. He shook off his trench coat, unsnarled an argyle scarf from around his neck and meticulously laid both items across a nearby chair. He scooted into the booth beside me, so that he could gaze across at Kathy. It was May and not as cold as he affected it was.

A small, blue-eyed, balding man, Ralph Crum was punctilious and invariably polite, even when he was arresting you for an axe murder.

"Sorry about last week," he said, piercing me with his wet blues. "I know a couple of nights in jail ain't no picnic. It wasn't my idea. The boss gets a little heavy-handed. I think he's becoming political or something, and this case has a lot of people watching it. I been interviewed more than two dozen times this week."

"Free board and lodging for two nights? All the pinochle partners I could ask for? Are you kidding? I should have been paying you guys."

Crum looked at me for a second, trying to discern how much was acid and how much was leg-pulling, then broke into a tiny wry smile. He took out a pipe and began working with the fixings. Crum was married, had four children, and fell in love with Kathy every time he saw her. Maybe he forgot about her when she wasn't around, but when she was there, he was definitely in love. It was the only reason he was being so helpful.

"What do you want to know?" he asked, dipping a match into the bowl of his pipe and sucking.

"Everything you can tell us."

"You're wasting your time. He's not going to live. If he does live, he'll be a rutabaga. We can't try a vegetable. He'll just lie in bed somewhere and round-the-clock nurses will feed him intravenously and wipe his behind and clip his nails. And he'll wither away. If by some miracle he does live and he's not a rutabaga, we've got a case on him that is airtight."

"What makes it airtight?"

Ralph expelled darkish blue smoke out the side of his mouth in spurts. "First, the girl worked for him last summer. He met her there, began sleeping with her, got upset about how things were going, and knocked her off. Then himself. He's got debts coming out his ears."

"You have witnesses that he was sleeping with the girl?"

"We're getting to that. It was his gun. A .357 Magnum firing .38 specials. Two empty shells in the cylinder. She was shot from about two feet away. The barrel was only an inch or two from his head when he got it. The lab tests show the gun was in his hand when it was fired. In his right hand. He's right-handed. He wrote the suicide note and left it in the typewriter."

"That's all?"

Crum gave a snort. "What else do you need? Hell, even I'd plead guilty if they had that on me. Okay. There *is* one more thing. He's a type B secretor. The girl had sex with a type B secretor sometime that morning. That's the icing on the cake right there."

Kathy said, "What's a type B secretor?"

"Approximately eighty-five percent of the population secretes their blood type in other bodily fluids. So even though we don't have a sample of blood from the man who had sex with her that morning, we know he was blood type B. And that he was a secretor. He could have been a type B non-secretor. Or a secretor type A. Understand?"

"And Mark Daniels is a B?"

Crum nodded. "And the man the girl had sex with is too."

"The fact remains," I said, "that Deanna Daniels does not think her husband did it."

"How many wives of suicide victims want to admit that it happened, Tom? Not many. Most of them think of it as some sort of indictment of themselves. As if they've failed somehow."

"He was only in there a half hour," I said. "You think she was waiting for him, he screwed her, then shot her, typed a note and drilled himself? All in thirty minutes?"

Crum shrugged. He didn't care if a man could do that in thirty minutes or if he could do it in thirty days. His case was airtight. We all sat there and mulled it over for a few moments. Crum ordered coffee and doughnuts from a young waiter growing a mustache that looked like dirt smudges. Outside the gritty booth window a pair of pigeons fluttered to the sidewalk and began strutting around in search of treasures.

"Who was the girl?"

"Nobody seems to know. According to papers we found in her purse, she was Debby Crowley, but last summer, when she worked in the Trinity Dog Food plant, she went under the name of Beatrice Hindenburg.

We've been trying all week, but we can't find anything on her."

"Not even where she lived?"

Crum shook his head. "She's probably a runaway. Maybe from out of state. How do you trace a thing like that? She could have come from anywhere. Chances are her folks haven't even bothered to contact the authorities. We thought Daniels might have been stashing her up at a place they keep on the lake, but we checked and found nothing. She was referred to the Trinity Dog Food plant for temporary work by the Downtown Runaway Center. But their records are never what they should be. We couldn't get any name on her except Beatrice Hindenburg. No current address. No relatives. Nobody seemed to know where she came from. Maybe Alaska. We're getting a lot of runaways from ice country."

"You think Mark Daniels was keeping her in an apartment somewhere?"

"Could be." Crum didn't seem real interested in the conjecture.

"But you haven't been able to find it?"

"Hell, we don't need it. We've got that rutabaga nailed to the wall. Screwed, blued and tattooed. He couldn't weasel out of this if he hired a thousand lawyers and ten thousand detectives."

"It seems to me that if you found out who the girl was, you might learn a lot of interesting things."

"Mmmm. Like what?"

"Like whether or not she had a jealous boyfriend. Like whether this was a long-term affair or a spur-of-the-moment thing. And where did the girl come from that morning? How did she get to the plant? You find a taxi or whatever that took her there?"

"Nope." Crum popped his eyebrows twice, acknowl-
edging that I had a point, but that the point wasn't going
to spur any untoward activity downtown.

Kathy turned from the pigeons on the sidewalk and
glanced from Crum to me and back to Crum. She wanted
to say something. That was obvious. But she didn't.

Sliding out of the booth, Kathy said, "Thank you for
your time. Hope you don't get into Dutch telling us all
this."

"Don't even think about it." Crum stood and let me
out, eyeing Kathy as if to memorize the details of her
face. We didn't shake hands. He plunked back down,
took a long gander at Kathy's dress through the folds of
her coat, and said, "Open and shut. Don't waste your
time."

"There's more to it than that," I said.

Crum popped his eyebrows again.

I said, "You ever get the feeling that all people are
good for is filling up graves?"

Dunking a piece of doughnut into his coffee and shov-
eling it between his thick lips, Crum said, "Why, yes. I
get that feeling quite often. How 'bout yourself?"

"Once in a while."

Kathy drove me back to the party, rolling the window
down in her car so the night breeze would expunge
Crum's pipe smoke from her fur coat. Though I looked,
Deanna and the Reverend Wheeler had already left. We
stayed late, very late. Kathy drove me to my house off
Roosevelt Way, gave me a sorry look and an even sorrier
peck on the cheek.

I skipped up the steps and went into my house, turned
on the TV for company, thumbed open the phone book
and scribbled Deanna Daniels' number. It was only

natural Deanna would swear her husband was innocent. But some of the facts were skewed. She had a point about that. We would see.

I put the pad beside my bed. Then I undressed, brushed, took a leak and trotted into the living room to flick off the set. Sometimes I used the electronic blabber like campers used the dampening sound of a nearby river or waterfall. White noise. I slept fitfully thinking about pneumatic blondes and giant rutabagas.

5 THE NEIGHBORHOOD SPARROWS HAD just begun their morning serenade when a breeze rattled a tall forsythia against my window and dragged me up from a dream about a man trying to hang me.

I crawled out of bed, showered, shaved and pulled a week's worth of newspapers out of the basket beside the fireplace, scanning them to see how much yummy scandal I had missed.

The Daniels case was the biggest scoop to hit this town in five months. I perused carefully, examining each page for peripheral articles. The only scraps I culled were some flimsy background items they had printed on Mark Daniels, how he had battled from the bottom of the pack to evolve into a corporate giant.

I snipped the articles out and left the clippings on the table.

It was eight-thirty when I slid into my pickup and drove to the Daniels house near the crest of Queen Anne Hill.

Anticipating the pall Deanna's presence—her unattainability—would cast over my psyche, I deliberately tuned the truck radio to one of those elevator-music stations that slowed down your blood.

The gray Cadillac was in the drive with a yellow personalized license plate that read DeeDee.

The ebony Rabbit I had tailed eight days earlier stood beside the Cadillac. A third car, a new Chrysler, was parked behind the Caddy. I walked over to it and stuck my hand out over the hood. Heat rose from the engine block. It crackled tinnily under the hood. I climbed the concrete steps, thumbed the buzzer and wheeled around to look at the world.

An Indonesian freighter steamed across the glassy sound toward the huge bright orange loading cranes on Harbor Island. Below on the hill, church bells pealed and ripped open the crisp morning air.

"Nice view, eh?" The voice was deep, much deeper than mine, and mellow enough to soothe the video hordes.

I turned around. Sam Michael Wheeler, replete with natty black suit and evangelical collar, smiled gamely at me. His collar wasn't strangling him like the one last night had. He wore them a size smaller for parties where he might turn up a sinner or two.

"Deanna in?"

"Morning. You have an appointment with Mrs. Daniels?"

"Nope."

Wheeler pursed his lips twice in succession, looked me over—I was wearing jeans, a polo shirt and Pumas—and, by way of answer, swung the door wide, beckoning with a sloppy yet flamboyant wave of his forearm for me to enter.

The odor of chlorine and the stifling humidity of moist

warm air trampled my senses. Instead of a living room in the front of their house, they had an indoor pool, turquoise light radiating around the terra-cotta walls, marbling the ceiling. A determined swimmer could do laps. The surface was somewhat roiled, as if someone had been splashing recently. Small, puddled footprints on the walkway confirmed my hypothesis.

Piloting me past the pool into the house through a set of triple-insulated sliding glass doors, Wheeler, without turning around, gestured for me to sit. He then progressed through the room and out the far end.

The living room sported a wall-to-wall view of the pool area out the sliding glass doors, and—out another set of windows—a view of the bay and the snowcapped Olympics. Across the Sound, a rain squall lashed Bremerton. The furnishings were all new, all neutrals, Danish and modern, lamps bobbling off the ends of curved brass poles. It was the kind of house somebody trying very hard to be chic had spent a lot of energy on.

Wheeler came back first, walking all the way across the room to the couch, and stood inches from my knees so that I couldn't have risen without bumping him. He had a duck walk, feet aimed northeast and northwest.

"Going up to the hospital this morning," he announced, a single note of glee buried in the carefully orchestrated bland harmony of his tones. "It's a trial. A real trial. But Deanna's holding up well. The woman has courage. You have to admire the woman. And poor Mark. It isn't often when you visit a man in the hospital that you've already written the funeral service. Half the state'll be there. I'll say one thing for Mark. He had friends in high places."

Sam Wheeler savored hospitals and tragedies and graveyards a little more than he should have. But then, why not? It was his business.

He smiled down at me. I curled the edges of my mouth up at him. He pivoted and swaggered across the room to a bank of family photos on a low table. Of medium height, he was a heavy man who seemed propelled toward blandness. His success in television ministry baffled me. But then, the camera often arbitrarily magnified one personality quirk and dwarfed the others.

"You, uh, have some business with Deanna this morning?" he asked, without turning away from the photos.

"Sure do."

"May I ask what it is?"

"Thought I'd get keys to the Trinity Building."

"I doubt if she has them. You planning to give the place a little inspection tour?"

"I might poke around."

"This morning?" Wheeler cocked his head around and riveted his dark eyes on me.

"Whenever."

The Reverend picked up a gilt-framed photo of Deanna in her high school days and fingered some dust specks off the face. He set it back, deliberately altering its position, although the setup had been very deliberate to begin with.

"You get the keys, I'll go with you," he announced.

"Not necessary."

"I know that building well. Years ago I worked out of there when my folks used to run a little mom and pop store. Bought ice from Mark. Nuts, they got a freezer big as a barn. I'd pick it up in my old truck and drive it out to Issaquah where my folks ran the junction store."

"You've known Mark a long time then?"

"Years and years. We went to school together. Been friends ever since."

"What is he like?"

"Heck of a man. Good head for business. Sharp, friendly, loyal. A good husband. Good father. The best. And generous too. I've got maybe ten, eleven suits and sports jackets he's given me. We're the same size and when he gets tired of something he gives it to someone. Some have never been worn."

"He play around?"

"You mean with other women?"

"Yeah."

"Mark was a complicated man. His minister is more than likely the last man he would have confessed indiscretions to."

"People have glimmers though. We know things without being told."

Deanna walked into the room before he could reply. Her hair was bundled in a towel.

As she sailed toward me, Wheeler docked with her and looped his right arm over her shoulder. She did not object.

Barefoot, her toenails painted the same rusty rose as her fingernails, she wore a pale lilac silk caftan. Faintly diaphanous, it was plain she wore nothing underneath. I thought Wheeler hadn't noticed because he was looking at an opposite wall, but when I followed his gaze, I saw he was watching her in a mirror.

"Thomas. How nice to see you. What can I do for you?"

"Honey," said Wheeler, squeezing her shoulders, "Mr. Black would like to borrow Mark's keys to the Trinity Building. I think he wants to do a little sleuthing." Wheeler chuckled, patronizing the child in the room— me. "Why don't you just give me the keys and I'll open it up for him? I know where just about everything is. All the revisions on the old buildings."

I stood up. "I'll go alone, if you don't mind. You must have a service this morning, or something."

"Obviously you don't know show business. My sermons are all taped. In fact, Sunday is my least busy day. I'd be more than happy to show you around. I can show you things you'd miss otherwise."

"Alone," I said.

"I insist."

"Sam," said Deanna. "I think Thomas wants to do this by himself."

"But I'll save Black some time. A great deal of time."

Deanna turned and padded off to fetch the keys. On the way out she caught a glimpse of her reflection in a full-length mirror. When she came back, she was wearing a terry robe over the caftan. Sam Wheeler reached out and palmed the keys before she could deliver them to me.

"We can drive in my car," he said, lurching toward the door.

I looked at Deanna. "You have another set?" I asked, coolly.

Wheeler turned around, a hurt look impinging his boyish face. He spoke peevishly, disbelieving. "You really don't want me to go, do you?"

"I work alone, Reverend Wheeler."

Pulling his heavy lips into a pout, Wheeler tossed the keys at me. Clinking in the space between us, they shot across the room and would have struck me in the face if I hadn't caught them. It was a good way to hurt someone and make it look like an accident. I looked down at the simple steel ring which held about thirty-five keys.

"Sorry," said Deanna, folding her arms across her chest. "I wish I knew which ones were for what, but I never could keep track."

"I'll make out."

"You should be okay on a Sunday morning. Nobody works on Sunday. The only person you might run across is Emmett Anderson. Just explain who you are and I'm sure he'll agree to let you look around."

"I'm working for Mark's attorney," I said. "He doesn't have the right to object."

"I guess not."

"Learned a little humility the other day," said the Reverend Wheeler, rolling on the balls of his feet, riding his paunch forward in front of himself like a pregnant woman. "I was watering the yard when I saw a cat under a rose. This was a particularly pesky cat who's been bothering us for years. I hissed at him but he only glared at me, glared at me like the very devil himself. I hissed again. Stamped my foot. He still didn't move. So I sprinkled him. He didn't move. Gave me the evil eye. Then I turned the hose on him full force."

Deanna cocked her head and listened attentively. I stuffed the bundle of keys into my Levi's pocket.

"When the cat was fully drenched, he started to crawl away. Only his front two paws worked. The hind legs were broken—he'd been run over by a car." Wheeler held a plump thumb and forefinger up to the light. "I felt about that big."

"That's awful," said Deanna.

"There is a point though, my dear. Things aren't always what they seem. Are they, Black? If we act humbly, we'll be on the right side every time. We get a little persnickety, why, things can go awry." His boyish smile was almost disarming. People didn't thwart his will every day. When they did, they listened to a sermon.

Deanna Daniels looked at me. I winked and walked past Sam Wheeler into the pool room. Sam did not move for me to pass. It was hard to tell if he thought I already had enough room or if he was being persnickety.

"Nice pool," I said on the way out.

"You'll have to come over and use it sometime." Deanna followed me to the front door. "This is a sun roof. It opens up mechanically when the weather's nice. We'd love to have you up here."

I searched her smoky eyes for some evidence that my folly of last night was remembered, saw none, nodded, and descended the steps. She was still watching me from the doorway when I got into the truck, a longing in her eyes that I might have mistaken for personal interest if the circumstances had been different. When I got to the corner I looked back and she was still in the doorway, still watching.

I drove down the cobbled street. The Reverend Wheeler's story about the cat would have been a lot more impressive had I not heard a comedian tell it on TV the night before while I was looking up Deanna's phone number.

The Trinity Building parking lot was just as abandoned as it had been when Daniels parked in it last Saturday. I left my truck in the same stall he had used, ear-marked Daniels—President.

After six or eight stabs with different selections from the weighty key ring, I got the side door open and went in, past the receptionist area and up on the open carpeted stairs. If you looked closely, you could see the blood-stains in the carpet. They could have been marked *his* and *hers*.

The typewriter was gone, no doubt confiscated by the police. The carpet had been vacuumed and the desk combed through. Except for a pair of unused tickets to a Mariners game last Thursday evening the place was sterile.

No address book. No list of appointments. Not even a package of chewing gum in Mark's desk. All personal items had been confiscated. All except a glossy eight-by-ten portrait of a smiling Deanna on a rustic-looking lakeshore dock. She wore shorts and a halter-top and looked a few years younger. I turned away from it. I was already overdosed.

I spent half an hour wandering through the maze of offices, nosing around, fumbling through people's desks. I found a paperback novel about half-naked slave women from another planet in the bottom drawer of one of the secretary's desks. That was it.

The huge office complex was joined to a cold cement-floored warehouse stacked high with cases of canned dog food. It held maybe four truckloads, with pallets and space for eight more.

I shambled through the dark warehouse and out into the dog food factory through an enormous sliding fire door. The whole place smelled like machinery and some sort of soapy antiseptic.

High windows along all the walls filtered in enough daylight so that I could see without groping for the light switch. A man was standing in front of me.

He was small and dark and Asian.

A needle-sharp meat hook glittered in his fist.

Behind him four other short Asian men stood in a broad semicircle, as if they had been waiting for me. Presumably they were about to pluck and butcher a big chicken. This bird was about six-one and weighed around one-eighty.

"Morning," I said, giving a small beauty-queen wave.

Nobody blinked. They were like statue targets in a pinball game, frowns painted on their brown faces. Behind the leader with the meat hook, three of his cohorts held short lengths of lumber. The fourth had doubled up his fists into tight little roots. A tic festered in one dark eye.

"Morning," I repeated, smiling and nodding. I was doing a lot of nodding. "Nice day. I'm an emissary for Mark Daniels' lawyer. I'm working for Mark Daniels. You guys must work here. Nice place to work?"

The man in front, the one with the hook, stepped forward in snakeskin cowboy boots that had five-inch heels. They were tiny enough to be women's boots. He was a foot shorter than me. All of them were. When he got just out of arms' reach, he began slashing at my face with the meat hook, advancing a step with each swipe.

I kicked out at his knees and missed. He lashed to and fro with the meat hook until it sang in the air like a birch switch.

The men behind him fanned out and scurried toward me, soldiers following their platoon leader.

I thought they were merely trying to unnerve me until

the leader snagged a piece of my polo shirt and ripped it with the hook. He took a small, very painful snip of my chest with it. He was quick. Quicker than shit.

I COULD FEEL BLOOD SLUICING DOWN
my belly and into the rim of my jeans.
My guess was each of them knew six different brands of
karate.

They advanced. I was gunless and getting scared.

Like a nerd in his first self-defense class, I leaped up,
yelling and gesticulating with all the absurd menace I
could muster.

"Yah!"

Startled, all five of them hopped backward a pace.

The fire door behind me had slid shut on its weight, all
avenues of escape gone.

Ripping a forty-pound dry chemical fire extinguisher
off the wall, I jerked out the pin. I held the handle and
body in one hand, the hose and nozzle in the other, ready
to press the trigger with the heel of my palm.

They looked at me as if they had never seen a fire
extinguisher.

"What is this? A Tupperware party?" Each of them
took a step forward. "I'm working for Mark Daniels'
lawyer. Do you understand?" Each took another step
forward.

The hardest-looking of the lot was the leader. He bore

the bleak, scarred face and dead eyes of a skilled mercenary—no—of a torturer. The four chaps abetting him looked like farmers from the Mekong Delta, recently emigrated with enough English to get them a basket of Bok Choy at Safeway and a tank of unleaded at the local service station.

Dangling the nozzle, I reached into my snug jeans pocket, used two fingers and tweezed out the lump of keys.

"These," I said, "were given to me by the wife of your boss. I didn't break in. I have keys. You do work here, don't you?"

Without taking his black, otherwordly eyes off me, or even blinking, the leader spoke in a birdlike Asian dialect. Two of his pals grunted in reply, nodding. All of them were nodding.

"Beautiful," I said. "I'm off the hook . . . so to speak? Everything is hunky-dory? You understand? Comprende? Friend?"

Stepping forward, the leader flailed the meat hook at my face. He swung at me six or seven times in quick succession. I yo-yoed my head backward each time he swung and felt the tiny spurt of air from the hook on every swipe.

In unison, they moved toward me in tiny mincing steps. They were closing in. I backpedaled to the fire door and tried to elbow it open so I could squirm through. It was too heavy.

Then I thought of a great trick.

I flicked the keys at the leader. They struck him across the bridge of the nose and clanked on the concrete floor. Flecks of blood appeared on his nose. The trick worked just great. He didn't bat an eye, just whipped the meat hook again. Whoosh. Whoosh.

Ducking backward and upward, I knocked the back of my head on the steel fire door and crushed the firing mechanism of the extinguisher at the same time.

It wheezed for a split second before it coughed a cloud of ultra-fine powder into his face. The swirling dry chemical mixture caught him wrong because he began hacking right away—must have aspirated some of it. I cocked one leg up and kicked him square in the sternum.

He went reeling, knocking one of his soldiers down with him.

Two unlaced Kmart jogging shoes with the heels crushed down stood where the second man had been.

The man on my far left ran at me, whirling the piece of board in his hand high over his head. He didn't realize how tall I was, how long my legs were. Back braced against the steel fire door, I kicked at him sideways, striking him across the ribs and sending him sprawling. I heard the meaty sound of ribs cracking. These men were tiny.

The two men in the middle were getting very nervous. Glancing at each other they came at me together, one swinging his timber high, and one low, hoping teamwork would succeed where individual initiative had withered. I blocked the low one with the extinguisher as I sprayed the upper one with a burst of whitish dry chemical. It blinded him. I bashed the low man on the skull with the bottom of the extinguisher. He went down fast.

The man I had kicked made his way to his feet, grimacing, limping and clutching his fractured ribs. The leader got up, clopping his cowboy boots on the concrete floor, white powder drifting off his body in tiny clouds.

"Give up," I said. "No more fighting? Somebody will get hurt. Nobody wants to get hurt. You get hurt. I get hurt." The leader flicked open a gleaming seven-inch switchblade and passed the meat hook to his other fist. "*I* get hurt."

Three of them came at me while a fourth—in whiteface, his ears plugged with the gunk—tried to knuckle the powder out of his eyes.

"Hey, listen guys. Tell me what the problem is. I'm not trespassing. Do you think I'm trespassing? I'm not. Talk to me." But they didn't talk, only moved in. "You want a free *Watchtower*?"

I emptied the dry chemical extinguisher, but they knew it was coming and winked against the spurts of suffocating powder, choking and blinking, but refusing to be intimidated.

I grabbed the extinguisher in both hands and used it as a shield, kicking at them below it. I caught one in the knee and he backed up. I booted another square in the solar plexus. He did a reverse rumba and tumbled out of the fray.

They poked, slashed, swung at me. I fended them off.

My old mutt had been in a position like this once, warding off a pack of neighborhood dogs, battling them to a standstill and then snarling at them for forty minutes until I found him and pelted the bastards with rocks all the way back into their yards.

We must have remained there, the five of us—one was unconscious at my feet—for a good two minutes before the steel fire door behind me slowly slid open, making ominous grinding noises.

A tall, stooped old man—the man I had seen last Saturday, the man who had discovered Mark Daniels and the dead girl—stepped through the opening and took a good long look at all of us.

"What the hell is going on?"

The Asians looked confused, then shamefaced. The leader glanced at the old man and back to me, his face ranging through a variety of nervous mannerisms.

"I asked you a question, Hung. What the hell is going on here?"

It took the leader awhile before he could tear his inky eyes off me and reply. "Man here fire this building."

"What?"

"Torch. He is hired torch. Fire up this building. Enemies have hired so Hung is out of work."

"Whose enemies, goddamnit?"

"Hung's enemies . . . from home."

Taller than me, the old man cocked his head back an inch and squinted through the lower portion of his wire-rimmed spectacles. Black spokes in his eyes radiated out of the cerulean blue. "You a hired arsonist?"

"My name is Thomas Black. I'm a private investigator working for Mark's lawyers, Leech, Bemis and Ott."

"Oh, hell. I saw you last week. You was here at the killing."

"I was working on something else then."

"Put that goddamned knife away, Hung," said the old man, strutting through the group as if he were a bowling ball rolling through pins, sauntering past them for twenty yards. Hung folded the blade and pushed it into his pocket, then reluctantly walked over to the old man. They had words for several minutes while the three remaining men picked up their friend and slapped his face.

Stained concrete floors. Corrugated aluminum walls. Three-story ceilings. The building didn't have anything in it but space heaters and various unidentifiable machinery, rollers for assembly packaging and rows and rows of empty shiny tin cans in feeder funnels that ran the length of one section.

The two men conferred, one tall and ashen, the other small, brown, diminutive. When they were finished, Hung heeled around and walked angrily away, avoiding my eyes, his back stiff, his face rigid. The four men in front of me hustled after him, one of them carrying the shoes I had kicked a man out of. A moment later I heard a door clang shut.

"Sorry about that." The old man took the extinguisher and set it in the middle of the walkway so he wouldn't forget to have it recharged. He then slapped away some of the chalky dust that had roiled up onto his slacks.

He stared at the blood on my shirt. "The Nip nipped ya, huh?"

I looked down at the red dappling my polo shirt and shrugged. "Let me get you to the first-aid station. Over here in the foreman's office. Slap a dressing on that. By the way, my name is Emmett Anderson. Folks call me Andy. You might have heard of me. I'm Mark Daniels' business partner."

"Thomas Black," I said, gripping his hand, which was weak, his palm sweaty.

He was tall and thin and old and gangly. He walked in a characteristic bowlegged cowboy slouch. He had been everywhere and done everything and he knew it.

Knifing a key into a windowed door of a cubicle built off the main room of the factory, he switched on the lights and dug a first-aid kit out. I hoisted my shirt while he taped a bandage onto my chest.

"Kind of a nasty gash," he said, stashing the kit away.

"Your man there is kind of a nasty guy."

"Hung? Don't mind him. He made a mistake. Don't know what's going on, really. He told me somebody phoned him at home and warned him some of his old enemies had hired a torch to set this place up so he wouldn't have any job. Nor his brothers. Two of them fellows were his brothers. The other two work here. It's plausible. Why? You wanta prefer charges on him?"

"Not today."

"Couple months ago his uncle got blowed up in Texas in some factory gig. Something to do with Anglo-Asian tensions. So he had cause. He's one of our lead men. A good worker. And he's intelligent."

"You have a lot of Vietnamese working here?"

"Vietnamese, Laotian, Cambodian, Filipino. Most of 'em are direct off the boat. That's why Hung is such a good man. Speaks seven languages. We couldn't get along without him. One of Mark's friends got us into it, hiring boat people. Did it as a favor at first. But hellfire, these people are better workers than most of the whites. And they're loyal. You saw how loyal. So we been hiring almost nothing but. Damn fine workers."

"How'd you happen to show up in the nick of time?"

"You accusing me of something?"

"Just wondering."

"Hung's wife got scared and called me. They know me. I been over to dinner. We have a big company picnic out at Mark's place on the lake every summer. Hung's quite a guy. He was a colonel in the South Vietnamese army. You oughta hear some of the war stories he tells. Used to hunt tigers in Nam. Was an engineer. But he can't qualify here."

"So he works in a dog food plant?"

"We got a fella here was a doctor in Cambodia.

Another was a professor. By the time they learn the language and get their families settled it's five or ten years. Then you're talking another five or ten years of education to qualify for our system. If you're already thirty or forty when you come here, that makes you forty or fifty when you're going back to school. It ain't worth it. Most of 'em stay in menial jobs."

"Who phoned Hung?"

"He didn't recognize the voice. Said it was a white guy, though. Said a guy was going to burn the plant to the ground. He highballed it down here and brought his friends. I don't know what the hell they were going to do to you, but I wouldn't put anything past Hung. Good thing I came along."

"You been having plant troubles? Anybody ever threaten to burn the place down before?"

"Nope."

"Mr. Hung is a pretty dependable guy usually?"

"Mr. Doan. Hung Doan is his name." The old man peeped at me over the rim of his bifocals and smirked. His teeth were long and yellow. He looked at least eighty years old. But he might have been in his sixties and sick. He moved with vigor, but each time he did so he took stock and breathed heavily. "Keep looking for a Hung Low, but all we got so far is a Hung Doan. These people are strange on names. One named a daughter was born last year Snow White. Snow White Bui."

"He's dependable, though? Hung Doan?"

Emmett combed his hair with one knuckly hand and said, "That's a matter of opinion. I wanted to fire Hung, but Mark wouldn't stand for it. We had a young guy come in here applying for a job once. Can't recall his name. Vietnamese. He saw Hung out there on the floor and he about went nuts. After we calmed him down enough so he's speaking English again, why, he told us Hung had killed his mother and father and half his village with a bayonet. Said Hung was some sort of sadistic terror specialist for the South Vietnamese Army, got a kick out of watching people die in the most gruesome manner possible."

"He have any proof?"

"This little guy that accused him, he got out of the country with his wife, five kids and a bag of clothing. Three of the kids died on the trip to the ocean to get a boat. Naw. He didn't have proof. We called Hung in afterward and asked him about it. He got a little shifty-eyed, denied it, but we couldn't really do anything but fire him. And Mark wouldn't have it. He didn't think it was fair to take a man's job on the accusation of a complete stranger."

"What about you?"

"Never have trusted Hung. Mark dies, I'll fire his ass." His eyes got filmy thinking about Mark's death. "There's just something about Hung. I believed every word that little fellow applying for the job said about him. He wouldn't work here. Was scared to. We got him a job over in a fish packing plant on Airport Way. But I believed him. Mark did, too, I think. He just didn't believe it was fair to fire Hung. Not without proof. Told me he was going to investigate Hung himself. Last week they had a couple of meetings. I don't know what about, but Hung didn't look too pleased coming out of Mark's office."

"From what I read, you and Mark have built yourselves up into quite a proposition. You personally hire people to work out here in the plant?"

"This plant is only a fraction of what we've got. Mark and I own a cannery in Tacoma, a wood mill in Everett and a few other things. Whenever anyone is hired or fired, we take a personal interest in it. That's part of the secret of our success. People. We know everybody that works for us."

"You been with Mark long?"

" 'Bout twenty years. Started right here in this plant. I was the manager of a small trucking company. Mark was a junior exec. We always got along famously and when I got some money saved up, enough to take out a loan and start something on my own, why, I asked Mark if he didn't want to team up."

"Sounds like you're real close."

"Up until he got his divorce three years ago. I never did agree with that. Mark . . . Mark was like a son to me. Still is, I guess. When I went in there last Saturday and saw him lying in a pool of blood, I just about cried. I really did." He had cried, but maybe he didn't remember. Or maybe the old buckaroo just didn't want to admit it.

"He have any enemies?"

The old man picked up a rubber mallet someone had left on top of a cardboard box, walked away from me and dropped it into a nearby toolbox. "What are you working on, anyway? You said you was hired by Mark's lawyers?"

"I'm trying to help devise a defense for Mark."

"Defense?"

"If he recovers they'll try him for murder."

His exclamation was drawn out and musical, and the only reason I recognized the word—which took five seconds to say—was because I had heard others mouth it the same way. "Sheeiiit."

"He have enemies?"

"Mark? A jealous husband or two. Mark was a cocksman. Don't know why. He wasn't like that in the early years. He just ... I never did figure it out. He started caring more for that gutwrench in his pants than his wife and two kids. Happens to a man."

"He having an affair with the girl we found dead?"

"Couldn't tell ya. He knew I didn't approve, so he rarely talked to me about other women. Knew he was stepping out when he was married to Helen. I don't know about *this* marriage. Tell you the truth, I don't think the cops know either. We hired the girl last summer. Had to look her name up in the files. Beatrice Hindenburg. But the cops called her Deborah something or other. Couldn't find where she lived. I know they couldn't 'cause they came back askin' more questions about her late as Friday."

"Did Mark know her last summer?"

"Was right over in that room there with me when I hired her."

"You did all the hiring?"

"Took turns."

During our talk we had been strolling toward the rear of the plant. We went through an opening in the concrete wall and into an area that looked like a loading dock. Across the dock area was a large door to a freezer, a freezer big enough to drive a car into. Several cars and a few trucks to boot.

"This is it," said Emmett Anderson. "This is where the whole thing began. I sneaked up to Mark's office one day when we were still at National Truck out in the north end and said, 'I'm quitting, sonny. Gonna start up my own firm. You in?' All he said was, 'When?' Got a streak of wildness in him. A gambler. I put up the money in the beginning, then we turned it into a joint venture."

"Andy, why don't you sit down for a minute?" I gestured at a stack of cartons.

Anderson shuffled over and carefully squatted on a carton. "You noticed, huh?"

"You look a little winded."

Wheezing, he inhaled and exhaled in his own perfected rhythm. After a long while he looked up at me, his eyelids closing down on that cerulean blue, and said, "You know Mark never knew. Years ago he would have known. We were close then. But now, I got maybe six months to live and he hasn't an inkling."

"He might beat you."

"I ain't racing, but he might. Hell of a note. Hell of a note."

I leaned against the stack of cartons. Everything in the plant was neat; everything in its place. The rubber mallet Andy had found was an anomaly. Preciseness in an operation as large as this one didn't just happen. It filtered down from the top.

"Cancer," said Andy. "And don't go feeling sorry for me. I don't mind. We all gotta go sometime. I would rather know when and how than have it spring up on me some night while I'm riding the old woman. I always have hated surprises. Love to gamble, but hate surprises."

"Mark's wife is worried you won't divvy things up fifty-fifty if Mark dies."

Andy took off his eyeglasses and wiped them on his shirt. He inspected them against the light from one of the high windows. They trembled in his fingers. "I'll bet she is. I'll bet she's mighty worried."

"You holding a grudge against her?"

He shook his head, hooked the glasses back around each ear and stood up laboriously. He moved to a large sliding steel door with more agility than I expected. Opening a padlock on the door, he slid the door open. I helped when I saw how heavy it was.

"Let me show you this place. It's my baby. Always will be. It's what made me and Mark. We bought it from a family thought it was the stupidest investment they ever made. Thought they were skinning us. Sold it for twenty-four thousand bucks. Thought they just stole the pants off a couple of hicks from hicksville. Hellfire, the land alone was worth more than double that."

He gave me the royal tour, treating me as if I were an out-of-town dog food manufacturer. I didn't need a tour of a dog food plant, but I was beginning to like Andy, and he was here alone on a Sunday morning and he wanted to show me his baby. So I tagged along after him and gawked, billing and cooing at the appropriate moments, genuinely impressed with his business acumen, with the histories of various machines and processes. He knew it all, every aspect of the business. I was impressed with his baby and the love he had for it.

7

ANDY PARADED ME THROUGH EVERY step of the process. The complex was even larger than I imagined.

Attached to the huge, square, modern office building and its atrium was the warehouse stacked high with cartons of cans. Adjoining that, the dog food factory. Trinity Dog Food: Best in the West. The factory itself had been expanded and augmented like a jigsaw puzzle gone wild until it was more than quadruple its original size. It looked like the inside of a domed stadium. Outside, a hundred feet behind the factory was another huge pink cement-walled complex which the Trinity Corporation rented out to various industrial companies. Sandwiched between the two buildings in the grass lay a set of railroad tracks that ran unobstructed for five hundred feet.

I looked out at the windowless building behind the plant and beyond the shielded strip of tracks. "Seems like someone could drive a truck back here on the weekend and unload a warehouse without being seen."

Andy peered at me over the top of his spectacles. "You're dead right. Coupla those places across the way been cleaned out. Had to install a complete burglar alarm in the building to keep our leases. Cost a bundle."

61

"You don't have a system here?"

"Who's going to hijack dog food?"

"How many entrances are there into the office building where the shooting was?"

"Counting outside where you parked? Six, seven maybe. There are three doors from the parking lot. On the third floor one of the halls has a door that leads here. We never use it, but it's unlocked most of the time. On the main level there must be ... Let's see ... the fire door we used. Two others."

"Kept locked?"

"Not always."

Rail cars hauled the meat and grain to the loading dock at the back of the factory. On one side was a storeroom for the grain sacks, on the other a freezer as big as a house. Andy took me into it. The ceiling was thirty feet over our heads. Ice hung from it like crystal stalactites.

"Colder than a witch's titty, eh? Between thirty and forty below in here. Keep it that way for the fish. Take a deep breath. It'll freeze the boogers right where they be."

"This where Sam Wheeler used to buy ice from you?"

"You know Sam? We got some trays back there we make ice in. Don't use 'em much anymore. Buy? Hell. That sniveling little pissant never paid for a thing in his life. Cheapest bastard you ever met. Mark used to give it to him."

One section of the freezer was hung with beef quarters in racks. The main section was stacked with whole chickens and fish in packages, piled almost to the ceiling in spots.

The old man showed me where they hurled the fish or chicken or beef into bladed machines that gobbled it and spit it out in chunks dinky enough for the smaller machines to digest. They had one machine—a gigantic meat grinder built like a car engine with a huge squarish smooth-sided funnel on top—that could chew up an entire beef quarter, bones and all. He showed me where the grain was cooked, how the meat and grain were mixed, mashed and stirred together to formulate the different recipes. They even had a head chef. He guided me through every step in the process, visiting each machine in turn. I didn't have the time, but hell, he was dying.

"Started off twenty years ago," he said. "Nobody ever heard of Trinity Dog Food. Now we're the leading seller on the West Coast and sliding into the markets in the East."

After he had walked me through the canning process, we sat down in the glass-walled office off the factory floor.

Emmett Anderson offered me a swig from a bottle in a desk drawer. When I declined, he fished out the makings and built a cigarette in his knobby fingers, sealing it with his tongue. It had been a long while since I'd seen someone do that.

"Gonna die," he wheezed. "May as well die with my vices intact."

When he had pretty much caught his breath, I said, "This Beatrice Hindenburg who worked here last summer. How did you come to hire her?"

Andy shrugged, placed his hands on his knees, pistoned himself to his feet and walked over to a battered army-green file cabinet. He riffled through it for a minute, then pulled out a loose-leaf file. "Beatrice Hindenburg. Somebody called on the phone and asked us to look at her. Don't recall who, now. I think that was it. You want the address she gave us?"

"You give it to the cops?"

"Last week."

"If they couldn't find where she's living, I won't either. I'll copy it, just in case. Anybody around here close to her? A co-worker?"

"That I couldn't tell you. Can't even remember where she worked. I'll call Hung. Just lives up the hill. He'll remember." A few minutes later Andy cradled the telephone receiver and said, "Ingrid Darling. Hung says they used to eat lunch together. Maybe even drove to work together."

"She still work here?"

"Nope. Just a summer worker like the other. A young girl. They was both young." Remembering the massacre last Saturday, he shook his head and inhaled on the cigarette which hadn't left his lip.

"Can you get Ingrid Darling's address?"

"I'll show you what we had." It was on Capitol Hill. He also gave her mother's name and street number in Ballard, a section of the city down by the docks.

Before I left I had Andy draw up a list of people Mark knew. The tally was extensive. I had him put a star beside the names of those Mark knew well and two stars beside those he had known for over five years.

I drove to a hardware dealership, waited for it to open and had a disgruntled clerk reproduce every key on the steel ring Deanna had given me. Eyes like slats, the clerk kept gawking at me; thought I was some sort of housebreaker. At the Daniels homestead the Cadillac was gone. No one answered the bell. I poked Deanna's keys through the mail slot.

It took me all the rest of that day to exhaust the list of Mark Daniels' friends. I contacted most by phone, a few in person, and couldn't locate four. Most were business acquaintances, were shocked about Mark's predicament and were far too obliging to a stranger on the telephone claiming to be working for Mark's attorneys. Loose lips sink ships. But the shock of Mark's predicament had shaken loose a lot of things.

The most productive calls were to two of Mark's drinking companions, two men he had known while working for National Trucking. Both still worked for National and once or twice a week during the season they picked up Mariners' games together. Once a month they would get bombed. Both men assured me that Mark stepped out on his wife when the occasion presented itself. One told me he knew for a fact Mark slapped Deanna around from time to time.

"You mean he hit her?"

"Sure. Used to whop Helen all the time, too. That's why she divorced him."

At five in the afternoon I changed clothes, grabbed a basketball and dribbled it three blocks away to the school. Seven high school kids were lounging around shooting baskets and lying to each other, waiting for another body to show up so they would have even teams. We played for an hour and a half. When the clouds rolled in and primped the city in a misty gray, when it started drizzling, two of the boys went home. The rest of us rearranged the teams and played on in the feathery mist. I played until my feet were sore and my legs were rubbery.

Late in the evening I reached Deanna at home. "Deanna. Thomas Black here. How's your husband?"

Her voice was fuller than I remembered. "Thomas.

He's fine. I mean, he's the same. At least he's not deteri-
orating."

"How are you?"

"I'm okay, I guess."

"I need a list of friends Mark knew. I want to talk to
everyone."

She didn't provide nearly as many names as Andy. She
could only cook up three names to place a star next to.
The others she called acquaintances. Only one of the
names was on Andy's list: one of the drinking partners
from National. After cross-checking the lists I was struck
by the fact that the Reverend Sam Michael Wheeler was
on neither.

I called, spoke to people, left messages, and spoke to
more people. It was Monday just before noon when I felt
I had plumbed as far into Mark's life as any of his friends
were going to let me. I had interviewed fourteen people
on the telephone and visited five in person.

I reached Kathy Birchfield at work and offered to take
her to lunch. We met in a small Mexican restaurant on
the waterfront. Juan's. ("Have a juanderful day.") Next
to our window a hulk of a ferry was moored. It bobbed
on the tide as we ate, making us both slightly queasy.

When Kathy sat down she eyed me for a long time
before she spoke. "Hey, Cisco."

"Hey, Pancho."

"You still love me?"

"Always."

"No, I mean after what happened the other night. You
know? When you turned yourself into the court jester to
Deanna Daniels' Queen Guinevere."

"Would you get off that?"

Kathy lowered her voice an octave and imitated my

speech only too well. "I think she be smitten, girl. I really think she be smitten with me."

I gritted my teeth, picked up a spoon and plunged it into my gazpacho. I glared at Kathy as long as I could hold it and then laughed.

Kathy waited a beat and laughed, too. "She's not your type, Thomas. Those big brassy women never go for you. It's the tiny delicate women who find you attractive."

"Like you?"

"Like our waitress. Or haven't you noticed?"

"She's just trying to get a tip. They do that."

"You still think Deanna has a thing for you, don't you?"

"What?"

"Don't give me that jive, Thomas. Once you get your mind fixed, you're jinxed for life. I know you secretly think she has the hots for you. That's what you think, isn't it? Sure, it is. You're even blushing."

"Private detectives don't blush."

"Must be a heat rash, then."

"Want to know what I found out about Mark Daniels?"

"I wanted you to take me with you, Thomas. I thought you were working for me."

"Solo. I work solo."

"Can't I go on part of it? I like to watch you work, and there's absolutely nothing going on at the office these days. Business law is dreary."

"Old man Anderson told me he thought of Mark as a son, but that's not what other people say. Maybe they were like a father and son once, but two weeks ago they got into a knock-down drag-out fight that was so loud one of the secretaries phoned the police."

"A fist fight?"

"Just shy of that."

"Maybe . . ." Kathy picked up a fork and toyed with an enormous tostada. "Maybe Mark was moody enough to kill himself. Maybe he really was moody enough to kill himself."

"Most of the people I talked to were aware that Mark dallied with the ladies. But nobody knew of any current amours. I couldn't find anyone who had ever seen him with Beatrice Hindenburg. Or Crowley. I did talk to a sales clerk at Nordstroms one of his buddies said he had 'planked' a couple of times. She wouldn't fess up."

"But?"

"But you could tell she knew him from the way she evaded my questions. She had an engagement ring on. I believe that might have explained her reluctance to talk about an affair with a married man."

"So he played around. A lot of men play around."

"Mark Daniels beat his first wife. My guess is he beat his kids, too. That's why his first wife left him. He had an explosive temper that flared up and then was gone in just a minute. He beat Deanna, too."

"Thomas, are you sure?"

"According to my sources, the last time was only a few weeks ago."

I SAID, "I DON'T THINK MARK WAS ever depressed in his life. Moody. Angry. Rowdy. Violent, when he thought the time was right. But nobody ever told me he was depressed."

"People don't have to be depressed to commit suicide, Thomas. They could be angry maybe."

"Maybe."

"He beat Deanna? I don't believe that."

"Sent her to the emergency room six months ago. Whopped her so hard he broke one of her teeth. Sprained a wrist. She left him for a week."

"Why did she go back?"

"I really couldn't say."

"She must love him a whole heck of a lot."

I shrugged, remembering what Deanna had confessed to me Saturday night when we were alone. I wondered now why she had confided in me, someone she had only known a few minutes.

"Wait a minute, Thomas. If it wasn't a suicide-murder, what was it? Are you saying Mark had people who hated him enough to sneak in there and shoot them both, to kill an innocent person to get at him?"

"Or the girl did."

"I never thought of that."

"Or it could have been a burglary, something like that."

"But it sounds like Mark probably has a lot of enemies."

"He quarreled, he blew up at people, but he apologized, always tried to make it good. And most of the time he was generous. He never fleeced anybody in his business dealings. I don't think anybody holds any grudges."

"With him in the hospital, who would admit to a grudge?"

"Only a fool."

"But the police said the gun was in Mark's hand when it was fired. How do you get around that?"

"It could be accomplished. Mark and the girl step into the room. Somebody stands behind the door with the gun they found in Mark's office, lets the girl walk in unharmed, then presses the pistol to Mark's head. Pop. They take the gun, fit it into Mark's hand and shoot the girl. It can be done. With luck it'll make a nice neat frame."

"Like this one?"

"If this is a frame, it's as neat as they come."

"Wait a minute. The suicide note in the typewriter. A burglar couldn't have done that. He wouldn't have known Deanna's name for one thing. Didn't it have her name on it?"

"I believe it did. That's a good point."

"And the girl was naked. And Mark wasn't. How do you account for that? Ralph Crum said she'd had sex recently."

"I can't account for any of it right now. Could be whoever shot Mark raped her before he killed her. But that makes the timing even tighter."

Kathy finished her meal without another word. She watched the traffic, both auto and foot, on Alaskan Way. Before we left she slipped a tip under my plate for the waitress.

"That's too much," I said. "Way too much."

Kathy gave me a bawdy wink and wandered out to the cashier. "We don't want her to think all that eye business was wasted."

The co-worker Emmett Anderson had told me about, the friend of Beatrice Hindenburg, still lived on Capitol Hill. She had neither moved nor found another job.

Her apartment was in a shabby two-story building several blocks from the community college. In the street I could smell diesel exhaust from city buses and, from a nearby bakery, the overpowering aroma of yeast and sugary doodads in ovens. I parked illegally in an alley, jogged up the stairs and rapped on her door, which was half-open. I had the feeling it was always half-open.

Ingrid Darling was tall and thin, almost spindly, with good bones. Her rear was tailored for sitting astride a horse. Her blade-shaped face was so pale it looked bloodless. Dull brown and stringy, her hair hung straight down her skull like wet yarn. She wore jeans and a short-sleeve sweater, the fabric speckled with tiny fuzz balls. Looking at the bones she called arms, I wondered how well she had been eating lately.

Without opening the door farther, she stood hipshot in the doorway, swaying to an Oak Ridge Boys album that strained the outer limits of a tinny stereo across the room. "Yeah?"

"Ingrid Darling?"

"Call me Kandy, okay? Kandy Darling. Kandy with a K."

"Sure, Kandy." I handed her one of my cards. She read it, shimmed it into her tight jeans pocket and nodded. "Another one, huh?"

"Can I come in?"

"Suit yourself." She walked away from the door and across the room where she rolled the volume down on the stereo, then hitched across to a single bed, picked up a blouse, surveyed it, folded it sloppily and patted it down into a ragtag suitcase that had seen better days. "Moving out. Been here almost a year, and when you have three roommates in a place this size, I'm tellin' you, it gets on your nerves. So Hazel asked me to move out and I told her that's what I was planning all along. If she thinks I want to stay here with these loonies, she's nuts. I mean, I don't even talk to any of these girls anymore."

"You work for Trinity Dog Food last summer, Kandy?"

"Trinity? What a job. We had to take the bus out there every damn morning at quarter to six. You ever take the bus to Harbor Island?"

"Who's we?"

"Bea and me."

"Beatrice Hindenburg?"

"Um hmmm. Course, working there wasn't too bad, except for the noise. More money than I made anywhere else." She glanced furtively at me. "Almost anywhere."

"She ever call herself Deborah Crowley?"

"She called herself Mickey, and Gerry, and Kiki, and

all kinds of things. I think Deborah Crowley was her favorite. She thought it sounded like a movie star or something. But her real name is Beatrice Hindenburg, and don't let nobody tell you different. I seen her write that on a letter to her mom in California."

"You know her mom's address?"

"Nah. I just seen the one letter. Didn't pay no attention."

"Know what city?"

"Naw."

"What was she writing her mom about?"

"Bea was on the streets, same as me. She just ran farther was all, from somewhere in Southern Cal. She wrote 'cause her little brother was having a birthday and she wanted to give him something. She loved her little brother. Had a few bucks, but she didn't know how to wrap up a present and mail it, you know, so she put ten dollars in an envelope, wrote a note for her ma, and mailed it. Her ma wrote back that she was takin' the money for rent Bea owed her. Bea like to died over that. I mean, shit man, how much rent could she owe? She ran away from home when she was fourteen."

"You know why she ran away?"

"Her old man was hittin' on her. You know."

"Her *dad*?"

"You sound like you never heard of such a thing. I know five or six girls on the street left home for the 'xact same reason. And he wasn't no step-dad either. He was the real shillelagh."

"The cops been talking to you?"

"Why would they? You trying to get me in trouble or something?"

"About Beatrice. Nobody's spoken to you about her?"

"Coupla months ago."

"Don't you read the papers?"

"I don't read so well. My teachers were all a bunch of jerkoffs."

"What about the news?"

"We don't got a TV. We listen to the Boys mostly." She cocked a thumb at the stereo.

"Beatrice is dead."

She stared at me as if I had slapped her across the face. Her gray eyes were like small orbs of a black and white TV on the wrong channel. "What'd you say?"

"She got shot a week ago Saturday. I'm investigating it."

Kandy dropped onto the bed, bouncing, and said, "Oh man. That's gross. That's really gross. I can't believe it. Bea was a nice kid. That's bad. I mean, I finally got my life together, you know, and then I hear all about this. Man, this is rotten. I got this boyfriend . . . I mean I can't tell my mother or my friends about him 'cause they wouldn't approve, know what I mean? He's an older guy. We're movin' in together. Just him and me. It's what I've always wanted. And now I hear this about Bea. Who did it, man? Who would shoot Bea? A pimp?"

"They think it was a suicide pact between Bea and her lover, a man named Mark Daniels. One of the owners of Trinity Dog Food."

"Mr. Daniels?"

"Was he involved with Bea last summer?"

"You mean was he gettin' any off her?"

"Was he?"

"I doubt it. He drove us both home from work once. Bea was staying here then. Took us to a tavern and bought us both beers. Bea got a kick out of that 'cause we're both underage. Didn't faze me. My boyfriend buys me beer all the time."

"Bea lived here?"

"For a few weeks. Then when she quit Trinity she moved downtown somewhere. I never seen her much after that."

"Was she hooking?"

"Come on. A runaway? We gotta eat. Besides, Bea liked the life. I mean, she really likes the streets. Them weeks she worked at Trinity, she was miserable. She missed the street. She wanted to do right, but she really missed the action."

"What about a pimp?"

"Not that I knew of. She was kind of a hit or miss kid. Sometimes she'd work. Sometimes she'd go hungry. Scared of what might happen, if you know what I mean."

"Who talked to you about her?"

"A detective, man. Just like you. Older. Big guy. About your size only he was fat. I got his card here somewhere. He told me to hold on to it and if I thought of something else to call him and he'd pay me. You gonna pay me for this?"

"What'd you have in mind?"

She raised her eyebrows, as well as her voice. "Five bucks?"

I took a bill out of my wallet and handed it to her. She pulled it tight between her two hands and examined it like a child.

Though there had been an indefinable tension in the room since the moment I had stepped in, a personal and sexual tension, she was one of the least sensuous, least sexual people I had ever met. There was an almost sleepy, androgynous quality to her mannerisms and looks.

"You got any more money?" She ran her tongue around her lips in a complete circle and gave me a look she had culled from a movie house down on First Avenue. Her tongue had huge pores on its pink slimy surface.

"Where are you moving? In case I have more questions."

"Can't tell. I got your card. I'll call you in a week or so."

"Can you find the other detective's card?"

She turned, bent over and began pawing through the heap of articles on the bed, finally retrieving it from the pages of a paperback that looked as if it had never been cracked open. The book was titled *How To Name Your Baby*.

The card read: Seymore "Butch" Teets—Investigations–Private.

"What'd this fella look like?"

"Like my father. Ancient and all broke down. Wore one of those goofy hats, you know, like they wear in the old movies. Started pawing me once he found out what he wanted to know. I threw a pot of cold coffee on him."

"What did he want to know?"

"Same stuff you been asking. About Bea."

"Two months ago?"

"About that."

"And the cops never showed up here?"

"Could have. I'm not around much. After today, I won't be around at all."

On the way out the door I turned around and said, "How did you and Bea meet?"

"Don't really remember. On the street, I guess." I suddenly glimpsed some remnants of shame in her eyes.

"How'd you get jobs at Trinity?"

"Oh, that. The Downtown Service Center. In Pioneer Square. The Wheel works there. He got the jobs for us."

"The Wheel?"

"Reverend Wheeler."

"Reverend Sam Michael Wheeler?"

She grinned up from her clothes folding, almost a smirk. "That's the one. Why? You know him?"

"Do you?"

"Naw. He just got us jobs."

Private Detective Seymore Teets catered to clients out of a seedy office off Nickerson. Humming with flies, the place was two blocks from the ship canal.

Tilting a slat-back chair on its hind legs, he sat with eyes glued to a dog-eared Classics Comic—*A Tale of Two Cities*. He was as fat and ugly as a fisherman's cat. A snap-brim fedora was perched on his large head, just like Kandy had said. He was smoking a stogie, pursing his meaty lips and blowing plumes of smelly smoke past the rim of the comic. His hands were big and broken-looking, like an ex-boxer's. On the wrong side of fifty, he looked like he had lived every year twice.

He made me wait while he finished the page.

"Good writer, eh?" he barked, banging his hand down hard on the empty desk. "Eh? That Charlie Dickens could really spin a yarn."

"So they tell me. You Seymore Teets?"

"Call me Butch. What'cha need? I do it all. Strong-arm? Find a lost kid? Tail your wife? Tail your boyfriend? I even catch lily-waggers. Twenty bucks an hour plus expenses. I know, it seems like a lot, but you gotta consider the overhead and the years of experience backing up my every move."

"I'm Thomas Black. I'm . . ."

"Who? Black, huh? I seen your name in the papers." He snapped the brim of his hat loudly with one finger and wobbled the cigar around in his teeth without dropping it. "You don't look so tough. Saw you in court once testifying. Musta been about a year ago. You don't look so tough."

"I've been eating a lot of A-1 sauce."

He teetered backward on his chair, gnawed on his stogie and tucked either side of his jacket back so that he was sure I knew he was wearing a revolver in a shoulder holster. It looked like a .38 snub-nose. They punched holes in you as easy as any.

Broad and fat, his face was corrugated. The creases were deep enough to wedge pennies into. A shock of wavy brown-gray hair peeked out from under the fedora. His piercing brown eyes didn't want to let me look away.

"You were asking around about a girl named Beatrice Hindenburg awhile back. Anything ever come of that?"

Butch Teets got up and walked around the desk, moving like a poorly executed caricature of John Wayne. "Who wants to know?"

"Who do you think? I do."

"Who are you working for?"

"Who were you working for?"

"No, I asked first, smart guy. Who you working for?"

I smiled, but I could see it was a no-deposit smile. He would never return it. "Let's write down the names and seal them in envelopes."

He watched a fly buzz slowly through the air between us, then shot out one meaty hand like a snake's tongue and caught the fly. He crushed it, eyeballing me all the while, then dropped the crisp corpse onto his desk.

"That's quite a trick," I said. "I can juggle a little. Want to see?"

"Maybe you think I'm so old I can't outrun my own farts," he said. "And maybe things aren't what they used to be, but don't underestimate me. I got five submachine guns dumped in different parts of Half Moon Bay. I'm one of the last survivors of the Siskiyou dope wars. A lotta old geezers around today got rheumatism now 'cause they underestimated me. Got it?"

"Tish," I said.

We were belly to belly, mine slim and hard, his round and hard. He had stashed the cigar in a sawed-down beer can he used for an ashtray. His breath reeked of cheap tobacco and cheap beer, too fresh to have been from last night. Sometimes heavy drinkers sweated the beverage. The telltale spiders of a chronic drinker dappled the bridge of his nose and his upper cheeks.

"Listen, punkola," he said, grabbing the lapels of my sport coat so hard that I could hear small pieces of the material tearing. "I ask you a question, I want a goddamn answer. Who hired you?"

I cocked my right arm back and slugged him in the gut. He folded so violently our faces almost collided, then he took a few steps doubled-up, as if he were walking on stilts. I waited to see whether he was going to pull out the gun.

He stood partially upright and said, "Whoo. Boy, I guess I'm outta practice. I really opened myself up for that. You're tougher than I thought."

"Must be the hula lessons."

He hobbled across the floor to a washroom, closing a

door with a frosted glass panel behind him. "I'll be back in a sec," he said. "Gotta spruce up."

Out the window behind his desk I could see the mast on a schooner traversing the locks on its way to the Puget Sound. Somebody was going on vacation. Up to the San Juans for a few weeks of campfires, scuba diving, crab pots, and sand in the socks.

I found a rubber band in his top drawer, along with a blackjack, about forty stray bullets and some nudie magazines. The guy really played the part. Cutting the rubber band in half with a pair of blunt-nosed child's scissors, I turned to the windowsill. By stretching the band tight, sighting down the taut line, edging it close to unsuspecting bluebottles and then letting go one end, I killed four of the buggers in less than a minute. I dropped the rubber band into his wastebasket and spilled the flies onto his Classic Comic.

When he came out, his face was dripping water and soap. He mopped it with a nubby towel that had Munson Motel printed on it.

"Beatrice Hindenburg," he said. "Worked for her father. He's in California. He's still paying child support on her and he's pissed. I hadda find her and prove she wasn't living with her ma in Southern Cal."

"How'd he come to hire you?"

"Used to work out of L.A. Moved up here for my health. Been sorry ever since. This whole state is full of ex-Californians, like a blight. Drive to the end of the loneliest logging road in the Cascades and you'll find a parked car with California plates on it. Hell, I'd rather take the smog than the fungus that grows up here in all this rain."

"I'm working for Mark Daniels. The one in the papers.

I'm trying to find out what I can about Hindenburg and Daniels."

"Yeah, I seen where she got blasted by that guy. Shame. She was just a kid."

Butch Teets meandered around his desk and gaped at the line of dead flies on his comic.

"Can you tell me about it?" I asked.

The dead flies had him confounded. "What all do you need to know?"

"Where did you track her to? And what did you see?"

Teets brushed the flies off the table with the thick edge of his hand, then filed the comic in a drawer in his cabinet, a drawer that contained nothing but comics, dozens and dozens of them.

"A motel out in the North End. Out off Aurora. They used to show dirty movies on TVs over the beds, but they've cleaned up their image."

"You tracked her two months ago?"

"Yeah. About. How did you know?"

"You spoke to somebody named Kandy. She told me about it. Recall the name of the motel?"

"Sure, we'll go out together."

"I'd rather just have the name."

Bracing himself against the desktop on his huge tanned knuckles, Butch Teets glowered at me. "Sure you would. But I know better. You're on a case, clown. And where there's a case, there's money. And where there's money, there's Butch Teets. I want in."

"In what?"

"Whatever you got going. I got caught a little short this month and I need a piece of the pie. Whatever you got playin', it's fifty-fifty."

"I'm working for an attorney. There's nothing more to it."

"Hell, boy. You think I was born yesterday? You're working a flimflam and I want in."

"What'd you see at the motel?"

Butch walked over to a table in the back of the room and rustled through a disheveled stack of newspapers. Finally he came back with a front page of the *Times*, the one with the pictures of Beatrice Hindenburg-Crowley and Mark Daniels. He pointed to the picture of Daniels with a blunt fingertip. "Him."

"What about him?"

"He was with her. Had some sort of love nest set up. What was he . . . forty-five years old? And she was sixteen, seventeen? Wait, her father told me she was fifteen. Can you beat it? If I wasn't the consummate professional, I would have gone in there and beat the tar out of him."

"How long did you follow her?"

"Coupla days. Her father wanted me to tail her a week, but two days was all I needed."

"How'd you find her?"

"Her dad had a letter from the kid he'd stolen from his ex-wife. The return address was a house in the U-district. Hindenburg was using it for a mail drop. I waited around until she showed up for her mail, then tailed her. The afternoon I picked her up, she met Daniels in a little coffee house in the U-district and he drove her out to this motel. They stayed there five or six hours. He went out once for a six-pack and came back. He left her alone there at maybe ten, ten-thirty that night."

"You follow him home?"

"Didn't have to. I was after the girl. Fact is, I didn't

even know who he was till I seen it in the paper this week."

"How many times did you see them out there?"

"Twice. First, I thought she lived there, but she didn't. I never did figure exactly where she was living. Think she just bummed around. One friend's apartment one night. Another the next night."

"You know where any of these apartments are?"

He shook his head.

"What do you know?"

"Let me in on the scam and I'll tell you."

"You talk to the cops about this?"

"Yeah, but they weren't interested in what I had to say."

"Why not?"

"Me and cops . . . we don't get along. Got a history of not getting along."

"Where is this motel?"

"Follow me."

"I'd rather you just drew a map. You got crayons, don't you?"

"Tag along after me or you don't find it."

The fly corpses really had him on the ropes. Before he left he peered down into the wastebasket at them, then opened the top drawer of his desk and flung a handful of dully clinking bullets into his jacket pocket.

He drove a junky old Ford Falcon that spewed so much oily smoke from under its belly I was afraid a cop would stop him before we got there. I followed him across the Aurora Bridge and out of the city. He drove at breakneck speed, a regular California daredevil. I had to run innumerable amber lights to stay with him.

The Galaxie Motor Court Inn had seen better days. It

was a block off Highway 99 in a grimy area of drive-in burger joints and small businesses getting squeezed out by conglomerate stores and bland shopping centers designed by bland technicians. A block away a weary residential section began.

Teets parked his Falcon in a no-parking spot, fiddled with his shoulder holster so every kid within two blocks knew he had it and beat me through the front door of the manager's office.

When I got there, he had a wallet flopped open and a fake badge showing, opposite a pair of cheap handcuffs.

"You're not going to use that?" I said.

"Let a consummate pro handle this, would you?"

We heard the throaty, wall-rattling sounds of a large dog barking. A door ten feet behind the counter in the tiny office popped open and a full-grown German shepherd charged out, barking and lunging at Teets. He ignored me. The dog dashed straight for Teets, as if he'd been waiting all day for him to show. His teeth had been borrowed from a crocodile. They were bared, saliva drooling out between them. This sucker was hungry.

I catapulted myself up onto the counter, pulling both feet up behind me. Teets tried the same thing, but there was only room for one.

 **10** THE LADY WHO LUNGED OUT
of the back room baby-talking
and grappling with the German shepherd had ex-prostitute
written all over her. Let's be generous: ex-showgirl.

In her fifties, she had an hourglass figure—only the
hourglass was plastic and someone had left it in the sun to
warp. She wore snug jeans and a tight magenta sweater.
An unnatural blondish-white, her teased and sprayed hair
looked bulletproof.

Teets peeled himself off the wall and gave her a boldly
appreciative once-over while she ran the dog into the
back room. When she closed the door and faced us, her
mustard-colored eyes inspected the buzzer and bracelets
Teets was flashing.

"Are you the manager?" I asked, but Teets overrode
me in a booming voice.

"Police Department. You run this crackerbox?"

"I own the Galaxie Motor Court Inn, yes. What can
I do for you gentlemen?" A hint of loneliness lurked
behind the eyes.

Teets nudged me and said, "You got pictures?"

I showed her a photo of Mark Daniels I'd clipped from

the newspaper, and one of the girl. The girl wasn't so hot. She had been dead a few hours when she posed for it.

"You know these two?" Teets asked.

Studying the photos for several long beats, she said, "What's this in connection with?"

Teets took out a small notebook and began writing. "You got a name?"

"Olive Peyton."

"And you own this place?"

"My husband left it to me when he died."

"I'll just bet he did. You want to keep it?"

"What does that mean?"

"It means we have questions for you. It means we ask and you answer."

"Excuse him," I said, in softer tones. "His mother dropped him on his head one too many times." Teets glanced at me warily. "We think this man and this girl may have been staying here. You recognize them?"

The bottle blonde looked at me as if she were really seeing something ten feet behind my head. I had the feeling nothing I could do or say would affect her.

"Don't pay much attention to my people. But yeah, I think maybe I do. He pays while she waits out in the car."

"You sure it was these two people?"

"Him, I'm sure of. Round face. The beard. The eyes. It's him. Her? I couldn't be so certain."

"I am," said Teets. "It was her."

I kept my eyes on Olive Peyton. "When was the last time you saw them?"

"Two weeks?"

"How many times have they been here?"

"Don't know. Two dozen maybe. A dozen with her."

"What do you mean by that?"

"He's been coming for years."

"With other women?"

She nodded and patted her coiffure. It moved in one piece, like a helmet. "Always with a woman."

"Know his name?"

"I know what he writes in the register."

"What's that?"

"M. Daniels."

Teets and I looked at each other. "How about his car? You write the license number down?"

"I never bother. Not with the regulars."

"He have a favorite room?"

"Right across the way. Twelve?" She pointed a finger with a nail that had been chewed to the quick. "Give you the key if you like. There's nothing in there. We keep our rooms tidy and we keep them antiseptic."

"Let me look at your register first." I made a list of all the dates when the signature M. Daniels cropped up. In six months of bookings I found it sixteen times, always to Room Twelve, always in the evening or late afternoon, and always one night at a time.

"Tallyho," said Teets as we left, tipping his hat.

Outside in the courtyard I looked at Teets. "You get his license plate?"

He shook his head, eyes on the manager through the curtained window. "Had it once. But my notes are always messy. It's back at the office somewhere. If I had six months, I could find it for you. What's the point?"

I forged across the weedy macadam. Teets lagged, peeping through the curtains. "What's the matter?" I said.

"Think maybe I'll go back in there. That little lady's got an itch I think I can scratch."

"What are you talking about?"

He was incredulous. "You didn't see the way she was looking at me? I thought you were a trained observer. I feel sorry for you if that's how you see things. She needs me to slip her this old bone. You didn't see that? Brother, I feel sorry for you."

"Are you crazy?"

"Hell, man. You got eyes, ain't you? She saw my Smith and Wesson. It gets 'em hot. A man with a gun is something to behold. The fragrant and manly aroma of gun oil is an aphrodizzzzzziac for women."

"You're crazy, Butch."

He gave me a rakish look. "She ain't no great shakes, but she's better than a poke in the eye with a sharp stick. Women worship us comic book heroes."

When I glanced over my shoulder, he was standing beside the manager's hut, peeping through a half-drawn blind. I would be back for him. Even from where I was, I could hear the locked-up shepherd woofing.

The Galaxie Motor Court Inn was laid out on an enormous lot, the single-story buildings constructed in rows and set up in a pattern almost like a Nazi swastika, narrow alleys just large enough for a car to squeeze through alongside each building. My guess was Olive Peyton's husband had died ten years ago; and when she buried him she buried the maintenance schedule in his blazer pocket. The paint was peeling and several shabby doors needed replacing because irate tenants had booted shallow holes in them.

Twelve had a double bed, a shower, a hot plate and a refrigerator that must have been a year or two older than I was. I snapped on a Philco radio that had wood parts in it and waited to see what sort of music the last visitor had preferred. Crystal Gayle crooned a soggy ballad at me.

Twelve was an end unit. I went next door and knocked on ten. This one had miniature cactus plants growing in plastic pots on the windowsill, the curtains drawn and pinned shut. Moisture and a bluish-green mold were heavily beaded up on the inside of the window. A bumper sticker pasted across the top of the door read, "Jesus Saves." Black moss clung to the shaded porch and yellowed copies of the local free Wednesday afternoon shopping news had piled up.

Though I heard movement inside, nobody came to the door. I knocked again. Nothing. I waited a full minute and knocked again. Louder.

"Morning," I said, when the door finally squeaked open on a chain. Her skin was so pale it looked like wax. She was no larger than a child and had matted, close-cropped black hair and a well-established mustache. A geek. In the window behind the cacti a geek man, who looked as if he were her grown son, appeared. "I'm wondering if you live here."

"Who's askin'?"

I handed her one of my cards. She read it slowly and handed it back, handling it with the tips of her long-nailed, dirt-crusted fingers. A fetid aroma began sliding out the door and into the court. Her boy gave me a rigorous and goofy look.

"We live here. Son and me."

"Have you ever seen either of these two people?" I unfurled the newspaper clippings and held them up for her.

"I seen 'em." Her words came out like pellets of hatred. "Come here and raise a ruckus. Play that damn music. Sittin' up all night drinkin' and carousing. Sometimes he'd bring two girls. Satan's work. He'll be burning. Mark me on that. Them guitars is instruments of the devil. My momma told me that and I ain't never forgot."

"He play a guitar?"

"Just the radio. Radio play the guitars."

"Country-western music?"

"That's it. Satan's work. We seen 'em. And we heerd 'em through the wall."

"What'd you hear?"

The door began inching closed. "You ain't from Satan yerself? Is you?"

"Me? No, ma'am."

"You an angel of God?"

"You couldn't really call me that, no."

"Git."

"If you remember anything about what went on in there, would you call one of the numbers on this card?"

"Git." The door slammed in my face. I pushed the card under the door. In the window her son was scratching the nits in his crew cut with dangling fingers like a chimp, flashing me the goofiest grin I had received all week. He disappeared from the window, as if he'd been yanked. Mother and son. Geeks.

All was quiet at the manager's hut. I opened the door and glimpsed Seymore Teets standing in the back room, the door ajar. So—he had gotten all the way into the back room. It looked like a rather strange courtship ritual. Long teeth bared in a tall and unnatural grin, Teets appeared to be debating whether to go for his gun. I couldn't see anybody else in the room with him.

When I got closer and hung the key on the wall rack, I

spotted the dog, inches from his crotch, fangs exposed, mouth slavering, body poised to leap and rip, giving Teets a simple but effective lesson in comportment. Some canny trainer had apparently taught this pooch to go straight for the nutsack.

I found Olive Peyton in another room off the manager's cubicle, blithely stuffing laundry into a paint-chipped Maytag. "Your animal is causing some real concern to Mr. Teets," I said.

Olive Peyton gave me an icy look, then went back to punching laundry into the machine. She switched the machine on and sashayed out a back door to the complex.

I found my way back to the detective.

"Teets? What was the address of the mail drop Beatrice Hindenburg was using in the U-District?"

Whispering, he gave it to me.

Detective and dog were still doing their tango when I left. Neither looked to be enjoying the siege, but then, I doubted if either of them knew how to break it off. I certainly wasn't in a mood to lose fingers trying. The last I saw of them, they were still drying their teeth at each other.

"Have a nice afternoon, comic book hero."

I drove to Queen Anne Hill and rang the chimes on the Daniels place. Nobody was home.

Parking at Harborview was scarce. I found a spot around the south side next to the boarded-up windows of the county medical examiner's office and went up to the second floor. Deanna was in the waiting room off the intensive care unit, thumbing through a magazine. She wore a plain skirt and, under an open sweater, a purple leotard top that clung like a membrane.

"Thomas." Whipping the magazine aside, she stood,

rushed me, snaked her arms around my waist and hugged her face against my heart.

"How's Mark doing?"

"The same." She released my chest but kept hold of my wrists, looking up into my eyes. She was a touching kind of person. She touched both men and women when she spoke to them. I wasn't used to it. "I'm so glad you came here. I feel so alone. And . . ."

She was warm and soft and fragrant and more vulnerable than any woman I'd been around in a long while. I was a perennial sucker for vulnerable women.

"Are you all right?"

"I'm bearing up."

"Mark and you weren't getting along so famously, were you?"

She examined my eyes for a while. "No."

"You left him?"

She nodded, reluctant and a trifle embarrassed.

"He beat you?"

"You know about that?"

"I know about a lot of things. Mark isn't such a nice guy. I found a motel this afternoon where he took women, lots of women. Beatrice Hindenburg in particular."

"That means he was seeing her." I nodded. "Then maybe he killed her?"

"Who knows?"

Deanna sagged against me and murmured heavily.

"Deanna, do you still think Mark couldn't have done it?"

She hesitated. "He was wrong sometimes. But this whole deal is screwy. I know he didn't do it. Suicide just wasn't in Mark. I could believe almost anything else. I believe he had the girl. That he had other women. I might even believe . . . if the circumstances were right . . . that he shot that girl. I found out after I married him two years ago that he got divorced because he couldn't keep his fists off Helen. He even hit the kids. I could believe a whole lot of things, but not suicide. And not that note."

"I obtained a list of dates that he was at the motel. Never on a weekend. My guess is he used the office on weekends. Was he gone a lot?"

"Sometimes we might not cross paths for days. But I had a busy schedule, too. I was taking some courses. I was sculpting. We were both busy." I had her look at the dates. They didn't mean anything to her. "In our hectic routines, I doubt if I could trace down one of these. Neither one of us kept an appointment book."

"Someone said you have a boat."

"Mark ordered a sailboat—for over a hundred thousand dollars. We haven't seen it yet. Teak decks. It was extravagant."

"Where'd he get the cash?"

"I'm beginning to find out Mark was an expert when it came to juggling funds from one project to another. He borrowed on our house and then hocked some of my jewelry for the down payment. He wanted the boat for me. At least that's what he claimed. Said we needed someplace we could go together to get away from the worm races. That's what he called it. Worms racing for dollars. Now that I think about it, maybe he just wanted it as a place to take his girlfriends."

"Where else might he have gone with a woman?"

Backing off my chest where she had been mumbling into my jacket, Deanna leaned back and peered into my eyes. My inquiries, this entire discussion, was stinging her, whittling down her strength.

I apologized. "We'll talk about this some other time."

"I don't think I'll have the fortitude some other time. He might have gone to the lake. In fact, I can't believe he would bother with a motel. Our place on Lost Lake is less than an hour from here. Why didn't he go up there?"

"Maybe he did."

Deanna looked at me, her greenish-browns as chagrined as greenish-brown could get. Then her look turned steamy. Or I thought it did. Maybe I was only wishing. Looking at her invariably caused my mind to wander. I was reminded of a wacky divorce I'd done some investigating for, in which each partner slept with the other's best friends, all of the other's best friends, just to get even. It had been the sexiest case of the year. Until now.

Brushing my cheek with her fingertips, Deanna laughed a giggly, nervous laugh that made me want to drop all my reservations and give her a buss on the tip of her nose.

"How do I get to this lake?"

"I'll take you. You'll never find the place on your own. We've given directions, sketched maps. Only one in ten finds it."

"Maybe I'm one in ten."

"I'll take you. If you want, we can have dinner up there. The freezer's always stocked. There's a microwave we can use."

She lowered her eyes. I couldn't believe the sheen from the windows on her blonde hair done up in a sweeping pile. Sometimes it looked golden, sometimes strawberry, and in some lights it was almost ash-colored.

Before we left, Deanna and I walked arm in arm into the ICU ward, one of her breasts pressed into my elbow.

Some women you could caress or hold when they were in trouble. Other women you couldn't touch without the touching becoming something else. For me, Deanna was one of the latter. I began to sweat a little.

We sauntered down one hall, up another. All the rooms were open, and most had patients in them— patients with tubes inserted into various parts of their bodies. I was surprised that most of the occupants were elderly. I had expected a lot of young trauma patients.

We stopped in front of a room that had three or four machines hooked up to a bearded man in a white hospital gown. The patient was Mark Daniels, his head twice its normal size swathed in layers of white gauze. His skin looked ashen, almost yellowish. A bag of clear silvery-looking liquid was suspended over his body, dripping something through a line in his arm at the inside of his elbow.

Deanna held back at the doorway, gnashing her lip. I went in and gazed down at him. He had tubes in both arms and one down his throat. A Bible lay next to his bed.

"Sam Wheeler leave this?"

"I never saw much of Sam until this. But he's been a good friend. I'll never forget him for the last week. He's been with me almost every day except today."

Mark's doctor wasn't in the hospital so I spoke to the floor nurse, a jolly woman wearing a short, mannish haircut and horn-rimmed glasses. "He say anything since you got him? Anything at all?"

"No. The Reverend was in here talking to him for a long time yesterday, but as far as I know he didn't answer back. You know the Reverend?"

I nodded.

"He has a theory about talking to head cases so they

can hear you. I don't know. Maybe there's some point to it. He was in here babbling for over an hour. As far as I know, nothing came of it."

"What about when the patient first came in?"

She shrugged. "You might want to ask downstairs in the emergency room."

Deanna waited while I went downstairs, where I bumped into a helpful nurse in the emergency room. "This is the shift that was working when he came in. You might want to talk to Danny—the one across the aisle with the mustache. He's a doctor's assistant down here from Alaska getting some experience. I remember he worked on him."

Danny was short and pleasant and looked for all the world like a young doctor. It was an appearance they cultivated: the mustache, the beguiling mixture of innocence, dedication, bookishness and eyes that tried to say I've-seen-it-all, and somehow failed to say anything. He rubbed the black hair on one of his arms as we spoke.

"The guy upstairs with the bullet in his head?" I said. Danny nodded. "I understand you were here Saturday when he was brought in?"

"Yeah, I worked on him. The medics intubated him, but they didn't do a very good job. We had to do it over. Wasn't really much for us to do on that one. I'm still waiting for a good accident where we can crack the chest and do some open heart. Have they cut him yet?"

"Not yet. I was wondering if he regained consciousness while he was in here."

"He mumbled a bit."

"You remember what about?"

"I remember it well. It kind of got to me. Not right

then. We were all busy at the time. But it hit me later when I had a chance to think about it."

"What was it?"

"He said, 'The Lord is my shepherd.' He said it three or four times. Said it almost like he was trying to convince somebody of it, you know? 'The Lord is my shepherd.' "

Lost Lake was situated just across the border of King County, in lower Snohomish. We drove in my truck. Deanna seemed out of place in a 1968 Ford pickup, but only for a minute. Her perfume reminded me of something, another time, or place, or maybe another woman, but I couldn't quite put my finger on it.

If we had dinner together up there, it would be dark before we returned to the city. She was distraught and vulnerable and I wasn't sure if I was ready for what might happen at the lake.

11 BOUNCING ALONG IN THE BEGIN-
nings of the rush hour maelstrom,
we braved irate truckers and errant bus drivers. We
talked only about inconsequentials, but there was something about Deanna's vivacious prattling and laughter
that made me stop and think. I liked it—I liked her—but
I couldn't figure her out.

The lake lay past Maltby on a bumpy macadam road.
Lost Lake Road. Quaint.

A dinky thing, only a few dozen acres, Lost Lake was
shaped like an egg, was sunk into the earth, trees tow-
ering along its banks. In some states they would call a
puddle like that a sinkhole.

A narrow roller coaster of a road circumscribed the
basin. The Daniels' summer house was on the southeast
corner of the lake, couched in a stand of alders. She had
been right. I never would have found it on my own.

We parked in the sloping graveled drive and she
climbed out my door behind me.

It had been sunny and pleasant when we left Seattle,
but we had driven into a blanket of fog. A cool, fuzzy
drizzle, almost too faint to see, wafted through the air.

"It's really not that much," she said, looking up at the

weather. "It belonged to Mark's grandmother. Two bed-rooms. He's left it pretty much the way it was when she passed away. What makes it neat is the lake. It's all private except for that little strip of public fishing across the way. There aren't any strangers down here. Except us. We don't come often enough to know anyone real well."

It was early afternoon and the local flora looked lusher and more verdant under the oppressive fleecy haze than it would have in sunlight. Even the sky itself seemed to be cast in a greenish tint. The clouds were a uniform gray, low and melded into one big suffocating umbrella. A musician from Florida had once told me he had never experienced drizzle before coming to Washington. It was so fine it feathered your eyebrows like overspray on a careless painter and you could stand in it an hour before you actually got wet.

She gave me the royal tour. The house was plunked smack in the middle of an acre and a half of trees, only a hundred feet from the water. The unpretentious front lawn sloped down into the lake, clumps of tall weeds dotting the shoreline. A small homemade raft was anchored fifty feet out, buoyed by fifty-five-gallon drums. Inside an old shack tacked onto the side of the house, I spotted a red canoe and paddles.

I saw half a dozen houses surrounding the lake, each spaced a football field or more from its neighbors. The surface of the water was unmarred by wind or tide. Near the base of the Daniels' lawn a fish broke the mirror effect with a lazy flip of its tail.

"Trout," Deanna said, reading my mind. "The locals plant perch, too. It's really idyllic. Wish we came up more often." She keyed open the front door and we went in.

Slinging her purse onto a hutch near the front door, Deanna scurried around checking the utilities, inspecting the refrigerator, cracking the kitchen window an inch or two to air the place out. The living room smelled of cheap perfume and beer, as if we had just barged in on a pair of illicit ghost lovers.

"You and Mark are going to get a divorce," I said, "aren't you?"

"I wouldn't say this to anyone but you . . . If he lives, yes, I'll divorce him. I hope he's not . . . I hope he doesn't recover and need constant care. People will think I'm running out. Yes. We're through. He's . . . he's not what I thought he was. He lied to me about why he got divorced from his first wife and he's been lying ever since. He used to hit me. I was so shocked I didn't know what to do."

"I'm sorry."

"Then there were the other things. This sleazy man came up to me in the hospital and told me he had worked for Mark. Said Mark owed him over twenty-five thousand dollars. Mark always told me he didn't owe a dime to anybody. He was always bragging about that. I believed him. I thought the house was almost paid for."

"It's not?"

"After he went to the hospital I called the mortgage company. We owe four months of back payments. Twenty-seven hundred a month. Can you believe that? He wanted me to think he didn't have a care in the world, that nothing had ever gone sour for him. I think I might have loved him more if a few things had gone sour."

"They're sour now."

Her mouth twitched so that I thought she might cry. "Yes."

Deanna took a deep breath, gathered her resources, looked at me, then waved her hands. "Live and learn, I guess. Only trouble is, I never seem to learn." She sat down on a sofa that had frayed arms. "When I was in college I worked in a shoe store in Ann Arbor. The dictum was, one shoe at a time. Don't let anybody try on two shoes at once.

"You know me. Dumb Deanna they call me. One day this couple walks in, both well dressed, obviously moneyed people. They asked for matching alligator shoes. His and hers. Dumb Deanna, I bring out the shoes, fit them each with both shoes. Then the lady turns to me sweetly and asks if I can't get one size smaller so she can see if it fits better. She could hardly squeeze into the ones she had, but I figured the customer is always right. I walked all the way into the storeroom before it hit me.

"Pow. Right out the door, lickety split. You never saw a couple run so fast. When I got out onto the sidewalk, they must have been two whole blocks away. They took my job with them. One shoe at a time. A little common sense. A little perspective. But that's never been me. It was the same with Mark. I gave him both shoes. Dumb Deanna. The story of my life."

She scrunched her hands into shoe shapes and wriggled them.

Was she giving me both shoes, too?

I stood over a cherrywood cabinet stereo, opened the top and picked up an album cover from a Loretta Lynn record. Two other Lynn records were on the turntable. "Mark liked country-western, eh?"

"Mark? He didn't care for any kind of music. Never

listened to the radio, even." She cupped her hand to her ear when she said listened, miming, then laughed when she caught me observing the signal.

"This must be your album, then?" I flagged it at her.

Deanna shook her head, looking grave but unflappable. Then she realized the implications and jumped up. "Never seen it before!"

"It's not Mark's?"

"Mark never bought an album in his life. Country-western is the last thing he'd buy. In fact, none of the punch buttons on his car radio were tuned to anything. He didn't like excess noise, he said."

"When was the last time you or Mark were up here?"

"About a month. Unless Mark came up . . . you know, with another woman."

"Mind if I look around?"

She assisted, pawing through the belongings in the house, squeamishly but thoroughly inspecting the bedding in both bedrooms, peeking into the closets, while outside the wintry cloud loomed over the house and lake. It took ten minutes. Nothing seemed amiss.

"Somebody's been in this house." Her nervous laughter bubbled out of a quaking chest. I went to the doors and checked the locks. There was no sign that anything had been forced. I went around and inspected the windows one by one. Nothing.

"I smelled beer and perfume when we came in."

"Did you?" Deanna said distractedly, pulling pots out of a cupboard. "What do you want for supper? You have to excuse me. When I get stressed out like this I have to be busy. Chicken or steak?"

"Chicken is fine. They were careful, though."

"Who?"

"Whoever was here. They didn't want anyone to know. The beds have been carefully remade with fresh linen. They only left the albums. It was almost like somebody cleaned up in a hurry and forgot them."

"It's creepy," Deanna said, setting about fixing supper, using the motion to ward off thoughts about her husband with other women.

All I could think was that Mark had been up here with Deborah Crowley-Hindenburg or someone else, apparently a country-western fan. Nothing else made sense.

While Deanna fried up a batch of chicken and talked to me over her shoulder, I stared out the kitchen window at the lake and the lushness surrounding it. This was what they meant by lincoln green. Sherwood must have been this color before the air pollution and the wars and the condo developments.

On the far side an old man sat in a webbed garden chair, concentrating, a fishing pole dangling out over the water. A boy younger than school age drove small wheeled things in the sand at the old man's feet, as intent on his traffic as the old man was on the motionless cherry bobber.

I lifted a set of 8-power binoculars off the windowsill, removed them from their case and scanned the opposite shore, slowly working from one end of the lake to the other. A trio of mallards paddled around in the shallows at the bottom of the Daniels' lawn.

Before I got to the end of the lake something warm and soft and aromatic leaned down against me, nudging my cheek. When I turned my head, Deanna ran her hands slowly down my shoulders and languorously across my chest. It was a big move for a woman to make on a detective when her husband was in a hospital bed and she wasn't quite sure how the detective felt about her. But then, maybe I had inadvertently given away some of it with my eyes. Or a lot.

"You're not married, are you?" she whispered.

"Nope."

"Been?"

"Not in this lifetime."

"Why not?"

"Came close a time or two. Things didn't work out."

"What about Kathy Birchfield?"

"What about her?"

"I thought she . . . I mean, you get on so well. You seem like you've known each other for ages. I thought you were living together. Or something."

"Kathy and I have a platonic relationship. Always have had."

"Are you seeing anybody, then?"

"Not a soul."

"Would you mind seeing me, maybe, a little bit?"

"I've been thinking about that since the first time I saw you."

"You sure?"

"I like you, Deanna. When this is over, yes, I'd like to see you."

"Why do we have to wait until it's over?"

She bent over me and kissed me a sideways kiss, long and steamy, tasting of the salt and radishes she had been munching. I felt like somebody had dropped a bowling ball on my head. If I slept with her, I'd probably stroke out and wake up with half my body frozen and nerveless.

"What was that for?"

"Just 'cause."

I twittered my eyebrows in my patented Groucho

imitation. She gave me a quicker, tidier, less serious kiss and backed away to tend the dinner. "You must think me an awful vamp to do that when Mark is . . . hooked up to all those machines."

"I don't know if I do or not."

"Tell me when you make up your mind. I want to know the instant you make up your mind." We looked at each other so hard the windows started fogging over. Humming to a popular tune on the radio, she looked away.

Things looked brighter and bluer in the field glasses, the optics of the glasses screening out much of the green in the air. I could see the mist drifting like particles of smoke in a projection room. I skimmed the lakeshore one more time and then focused on the surface of the water.

I spotted it out by the homemade raft. It wasn't very noticeable and if I hadn't been the suspicious type, I wouldn't have thought anything about it.

Whoever had been in the house had left two items, not one: the album, and what was out in the water.

"Does that canoe in the shed keep your feet dry?"

Deanna half-turned and shot me a quizzical look. "Sure. Take the paddle with the blue tape around the handle. The other one's cracked."

I barged out the back door, clumped through the damp grass and pulled open the rickety door to the shed.

The canoe was beautifully constructed, wooden, forty years old and much lighter than it looked. I hoisted it up and carried it on my shoulders Indian fashion. When I jogged back up for the paddle, I could see Deanna's strawberry-blonde head bobbing in the window preparing dinner.

I poled off, took two short, powerful strokes and glided

out to the raft. If I hadn't grabbed hold of the rough, unfinished boards on the raft I would have glissaded all the way across the satiny surface of the lake. I maneuvered around, peering intently into the glassy depths. Without a light, without sunshine at my back, I could see only about four feet into the bluish-green.

It was right where I had seen it in the binoculars, only now it was deeper. I rolled my shirtsleeve up and plunged my arm to the shoulder socket, dangerously tipping the canoe. My face was so close I could smell the surface of the water. Ducks. The cold water caused me to shiver.

My fingertips grazed something. It felt airy, like undulating corn silk. Or floating hair. Yes, that was it, hair throbbing back and forth gently in the almost motionless water.

Even holding my breath and dipping my head and shoulder into the lake, I couldn't quite get hold of it. Nor could I pierce the murk enough to see what it was, but my heart was racing.

**12** PADDLING BACK TO SHORE,
I nosed the canoe into the base
of the lawn where it thumped hard, screeching against
the gravel and jolting me. I raced up the lawn to the shed.

Hunched inside the musty, cramped shed in the mono-
chromatic murk of the afternoon, I scavenged some
rusted fence wire, worried a three-foot piece off and
angled one end into a needle-sharp makeshift grappling
hook. I slogged back to the canoe and stroked out to the
corn silk. Piloting around in circles, it took me awhile to
detect it this time. The mass seemed to be sinking deeper.
In another few minutes we would need scuba divers.

I dipped the hook into the water and finagled, jigging it
around in the depths. After about two minutes I snagged
something. Jerking, I set the hook. The wire wasn't very
stout and the hook on the end was feeble at best, so I
hauled it up slowly, reeling it in like a careful fisherman
working up a hundred-year-old sea turtle.

The mass bobbed to the surface the way a swimmer
gasping for breath might. Only she wasn't gasping,
didn't breathe, just rolled over and stared at me out of her
wrong-channel, black-and-white TV eyes.

As I stared at her, she slowly began drifting back down into the water.

My grappling hook had snared her through a piece of her chin.

Bits of lake goo in her hair, Kandy looked even more cervine and lanky than she had this afternoon when I had given her the five dollars.

Naked from the waist up, she had been pummeled severely around the face and eyes. Her cheeks were reddened and puffy, her skull lacerated in several places. Ribs showing plainly, breasts like nibs, she looked hungrier and knobbier than ever. She was so pale she didn't look real.

"Ingrid Darling," I said. "What have you let them do to you?"

She had made good time. In just a few hours she had finished packing, met her sugar daddy, and come up here where somebody beat her to a pulp and then tied her neck to a rock and gave her one last swimming lesson.

The rope had unknotted from around her gangly neck, but you could still see the pinkish-red tracks embedded in her pasty skin.

Threading the hook through a belt loop in her jeans, I wired the other end to a piece of bracing on one of the seats and paddled awkwardly back to shore. The old man and the boy across the expanse of silky water had taken no notice of me and my passenger.

Deanna was more observant. Or perhaps she had been keeping track of the expedition from the start. She leaned against the jamb in the kitchen doorway, staring in disbelief, tears running down her freckled face, flour soiling her hands and forearms.

When she plodded barefoot down the damp grass, I

saw why she had been outside, why she had spotted me and Kandy. In one hand she had a fistful of tiny flowers, buttercups mixed together with delicate flesh-colored pansies. In fact, the pansies were closer to the normal color of human skin than the dead girl was. She had come out to pick a bouquet for the supper table. Everything was going to be perfect for our tête-à-tête.

"Oh God," she said, when she got closer. "Why, she's only a girl. What happened to her?"

Disembarking from the canoe, I stepped into the water up to my ankles. I leaned over and gently slid Kandy's belt loop out of the hook and then steered her lanky cadaver up onto the grass on her back. She was barefoot, clad in the same skin-tight jeans she had worn earlier. The zipper was at half mast. I had the feeling someone had tried to dress her hurriedly. Or that she had tried to dress herself and got caught at it. Her thin, soaking wet hair was pasted to her scalp in strands.

"Thomas?"

"Are you all right, Deanna?"

"Thomas? I feel so lightheaded. Thomas, I don't understand this at all. Where on earth did she come from? Who is she?"

"I interviewed her a few hours ago about Beatrice Hindenburg, the girl your husband was supposed to have killed. She used to work with Beatrice at Trinity. Name is Ingrid Darling."

"A few hours ago?"

"Yeah."

"That means someone was just here!"

"We must have just missed them."

Deanna tiptoed around on the wet stones until the slack, pummeled face was upright in her frame of reference. "I've never seen a dead body before. Except at funerals. And that's different. She's so . . ."

"Unremarkable?"

"Yes. How in the world did you find her?"

"I'm real lucky that way sometimes."

"Have you ever : . . have you ever seen a dead body before?"

Reluctantly, I nodded, bent over and pulled the canoe away from Kandy's legs. "Just about my share."

"Do they always look like this?"

I stepped closer to Deanna Daniels. Her chest was heaving faster and faster. I was afraid she would vomit on the cadaver.

She was slipping into shock. Suddenly her greenish-brown eyes swung up onto mine as if she were drowning and I were her only hope. She rushed into my arms. I kissed her cheek gently. It tasted salty, yeasty.

Pushing her off slowly, I said, "Go in the house and call the county sheriff. Say we pulled a body out of the lake and we think it was murder. Tell them how to get here. Tell them they're going to need divers and lights. Then make a pot of coffee. We're going to have a lot of visitors in a very short while."

"What are you going to do? We can't just leave her here, can we?"

"It doesn't make any difference to her, Deanna. Not anymore. I'm going to paddle across the water and ask that old man if he saw something. I'll be right back."

"Thomas?"

"Take it easy, Deanna. People die every day."

"Not at my house."

"Everything will turn out."

"Mark didn't do this?"

I shook my head. "I spoke to this girl today. A few hours ago. In fact, we probably just missed her murderer, maybe even passed him on the highway."

"You think this is connected to Mark and that girl?"

"I don't know, Deanna. I really don't."

A barn swallow swooped out of the sky at us, chirping and snapping up insects in its beak. Birds seemed to love this sort of weather. I shoved off and twisted around once to watch Deanna flouncing up to the house in the wet grass.

There was something about our discussion that had bothered me. She had made a big production about never having seen a dead body before, yet there had been something in her demeanor, a momentary flash in her eyes, that told me she had been lying. She had seen a body before. Or bodies. Why would she lie about a thing like that?

I stroked across the lake and drifted to within a few feet of the old man and the boy. The moppet looked up at me and grinned, twirled a toy fire engine in his chubby little fingers. "Pretty nice," I said.

The old man smiled a weary smile and turned his sooty eyes onto me.

"You see anything across the way today?" I asked.

The old man shook his head.

"How long have you been out here?"

"Hour. Hour and a half." He held up a string of five perch, their orange fins bright in the dim afternoon, as if he measured time by how many fish he caught. Then he dropped the line gently back into the shallows.

"Do you remember if anyone was over there?"

"They don't usually come up here but once or twice in the summer. Stayed a week once. Since the old woman died, we rarely see a body over there. My stepson, Jason, mows the lawn for them."

"We found a dead girl in the water," I said. "She was put there today. Thought you might have seen something. Or heard some screaming." The boy looked up at me, eyes wide, and I was sorry I had said it.

"Maud did say something as we was comin' down here. Said she thought she seen somebody swimming. Thought she seen somebody splashin' around. But her eyes is bad. A mite nippy for shenanigans like that."

"Thanks. The county sheriff will probably talk to you later."

"I'll be here. Name's McDonell. Willy and Maud. Live right there." He pointed to a shingled house in the trees. A visit from the county sheriff would probably qualify as the excitement of the century.

Gliding back to the Daniels' place I observed the trails in the wet grass. From out on the lake I could see plainly where Deanna had walked down from the kitchen door and then gone back up, using almost the same footprints. I could see my three trails, one with the canoe, one for the paddle, and a third for the wire that I formed into a grappling hook, all overlapping one another. The rest of the dewy, fog-misted lawn seemed untouched. But then, whoever had dumped Ingrid Darling into Lost Lake might have done it before the clouds had settled down and feathered the landscape.

When I scooted the canoe up onto the lawn, a flock of Evening Grosbeaks were perched in a tree over the water, cheeping loudly. Big, yellow-bodied birds, they sounded like chicks chirruping through megaphones.

Ingrid Darling, bedraggled and defiled, hadn't moved. I grabbed her cold shoulders and heaved her up another few feet, so that her toes weren't dangling in the water. She couldn't have weighed more than a hundred pounds ... sopping. She felt like a big lump of damp clay.

The sheriff's deputy who took charge of the investigation was a bombastic man, slovenly dressed in his uniform and sloping Sam Browne belt, who focused his shrewd eyes on Deanna and the purple membrane of her leotard top as often as he could and slurred most of his words. Even with a murder on his hands, she was something he wanted to remember. I didn't blame him. His thinning black hair was wet and combed straight back, the same as the dead girl's. We told him what we knew, what time we had arrived, who the dead girl was, and what we were doing there. Though he didn't voice it, he didn't believe we had come up to search the house. He was certain we were there for a lovers' tryst.

After disgustedly forking the chicken out of the pan into the garbage, Deanna had topped off a brushed-steel carafe with hot coffee.

Deputies burned their tongues on the java, searched the house, confiscated the albums, took fingerprints and discovered a pair of tiny black lace panties tucked down in the sheets of one of the beds. Deanna said she had never seen them before. One deputy upended the garbage can outside and, using his flashlight, sifted through the rubbish.

Two hefty off-shift deputies showed up with scuba tanks and portable lights. After going through the twenty-minute ritual of peeling their suits onto their limbs and testing their regulators, they waded out and plunged into the water. Ten minutes later they brought up a hunk of angle iron with a strip of clothesline tied to it. It was hardly enough to have held down the corpse after it bloated. Whoever had killed Ingrid Darling had been rather inept. Didn't know a lot about death.

They took our statements in the house and abandoned the crime scene. The last person off the property was the county medical examiner. She was a few years younger than me. Flaming red hair, lips painted a shiny dark crimson, cheeks heavily rouged. She wore earrings that looked like tiny silver tambourines.

She didn't even pretend to be glum over the prospect of an autopsy.

I asked her if I could have the results.

Ripping a card out of her wallet, she handed it to me and said, "Call tomorrow sometime after ten. I do 'em first thing in the morning. I should know by then. Ask for Carol Neff."

"Dr. Neff?"

"Yeah, but that doctor stuff is a lot of bull hooey. Just a bunch of overtrained nitwits indulging in God complexes. Call me Carol."

She was the only one of the Snohomish officials who didn't seem disgruntled to be working with a private detective from the big city. In fact, she seemed overjoyed. But then, she seemed overjoyed about everything, especially tomorrow morning's session of slice and dice. Before she drove off she said, "I like the young ones. Most are so old. The young ones . . . it's almost like working on real people. It's good to get them prime like this, too." She grinned and gunned her station wagon out of the driveway.

I didn't know whether or not to say, "You're welcome."

What was the protocol? After all, she had more or less thanked me for handing over a nice, fresh, relatively unscathed corpse. I would send her a card.

 **13** THE DRIVE BACK TO QUEEN
Anne Hill was dark and gloomy.
We got sidetracked in Woodinville and picked over a
dinner at a steak house I had heard good rumors about.
The rumors were wrong. The service was hit-or-miss and
the food was bland and tasteless.

The dead girl had put a pall over us, but now it had
been almost three hours and we both needed relief. As if
by tacit agreement, we spoke of other things, sliding the
afternoon into the distant past.

Midway through the meal I spilled my water glass
onto my shirt, then soaked both my napkin and hers mop-
ping the puddle. I asked her if she had anything else. She
dug a handkerchief out of her purse and handed it to me.
I sponged up the spots on my shirt and shimmed the
heavily perfumed hanky into my pocket.

Deanna, silent in the truck, became loquacious with
food and drink in her system. She hadn't eaten all day
and she wolfed down her meal, then entertained me with
half a dozen hilarious stories from her childhood.
Chutzpah. Pizzazz. She had them both in quantities I
admired.

It dawned on me during the conversation that she was consciously working some sort of voodoo, had set the crosshairs on me and was squeezing the trigger mechanism. I felt like a snowbound deer, helpless, about to be gutshot. I felt as if I were going to like it.

"You know why I like you, Thomas Black?"

I shook my head.

"You're a loner, aren't you? If you see a queue, you go the other way. If there's a crowded bus and an empty bus, you take the empty one. When a salesman tells you his model is the most popular model to ever come down the pike and John Doe and all of his neighbors have already bought one, you turn around on your heel and walk out of the store."

"You're very astute."

"I was a saleswoman for years. I worked in retail sales. I even sold computers at the beginning of the boom. That's where Mark met me, in fact. He was buying a Northstar system for the company. I learned to size up men a long time ago. I had four brothers, two older and two younger, all rascals, and they kept me on my toes. You're good for me, Thomas, because I'm a joiner. Too much of a joiner. I see a line in front of a movie house and I want to go stand in it. You want to run for your life and I want to join it. You detested that party the other night, didn't you?"

"As parties go, it wasn't bad."

"You hated it. I could tell you were uncomfortable. Being around you refreshes my perspective, makes me think twice about what I'm doing. I don't know if I could live with you, but I like being around you. I'll bet you're a detective because it's a job for loners?"

"Or maybe I'm a loner because I'm a detective."

She laughed, a vivacious, rafter-shaking laugh. "It just seems like being a loner would be an advantage in your profession. Is it? Tell me all about it?"

"Not tonight, Deanna."

"But how did you get into it? Were you in the CIA or something horribly sinister like that?"

"I was a Seattle policeman for ten years. That's all."

"Why did you quit?"

"It's a long story. I shot somebody. It kind of broke me up for a while there."

"I bet you don't carry a gun, then."

I shrugged, wondering why she would care, although a lot of people asked me that. She smiled it off.

"Just wondering. I couldn't feel a gun on you."

Maybe Teets was right. Maybe guns turned the dames on.

"Most of the time there's no need."

"Someday will you tell me all about it though? I want to know everything."

I smiled weakly. "Someday."

The conversation tapered off during the drive.

At Harborview we both went upstairs to the intensive care unit and checked on Mark. A Filipino nurse squinted at us out of pretty, unsmiling eyes and said he was the same.

I escorted Deanna downstairs to the public lot where she had parked her Cadillac. Under a streetlight she opened her front door, then turned and looked up at me. Her pinned hair seemed almost red under the streetlight. Her eyes cajoled me, blotting out the rest of the world. "Thomas?"

"Ummm."

"Promise me something?"

"Um hmmm."

"When it's all over? I want to see you."

"Um hmmm."

"Promise?"

"Hmmmm. It's the Bushido of the private eye. We practically never go back on our promises. Never. Practically."

She laughed, kissed the point of my chin, and slithered into the front seat. When she wheeled out of the lot a young intern in a flapping lab coat gave her the once-over, gaping until she was gone. She was more than a beautiful woman in a flashy Cadillac. She was the sort of dreamy vision guys saw on the street and remembered for weeks every time they made love to their wives. I waited until she was safely out of sight before I went to my truck.

I drove home at breakneck speed. I had scrounged a dry shirt and dry socks from Mark Daniels' supply at the lake house and they had been nagging at me to take them off. The socks were too tight and the shoes were still damp. The shirt was enormous, bagged out like a blowzy maternity dress in front of my gut. Mark had an atypical figure, short arms and a huge and long torso. The shirt had been altered accordingly.

Flipping on lights in my dark house, I changed into a sports shirt and a slightly sullied suede jacket I had inherited on a case two years ago. I peeled off the socks and put on a thick cotton pair, along with another pair of shoes and trousers. I rang up my answering machine at the Piscule Building downtown. The recording was blank except for some dirty jokes a giggly, nasal-voiced teenage boy had phoned in. He had been plaguing my machine for months. When I got time, I was going to track him down and wash his mouth out with an entire bar of Lava.

I took a quick leak, then picked up the anonymous letter I had received two weeks ago—the letter that had set me on to Mark Daniels in the first place.

I sniffed the letter. I pulled the handkerchief I had kiped from Deanna out of my pocket and smelled that. I had to repeat the test three times before I was certain.

The fragrance was the same. I didn't know what it was called, but it was the same. Odds were Deanna had been my anonymous employer two weeks ago, and that she had hired me to tail her husband and report on his philanderings. That had been my first guess, of course, but I needed evidence.

For someone with no guilt on her conscience, she was being coy. It made perfect sense for a guilty party. Guilty of what? But I didn't want to believe that. It despoiled a future I was slowly conjuring up, a future with a vivacious strawberry-blonde bubbling around in it.

It was a shade past nine-thirty. With luck, a few night owls would still be prowling about.

I drove to the address that Butch Teets had given me that afternoon, the address Beatrice Hindenburg had used as a mail drop.

Sandwiched between two brick apartment buildings with open balconies, it was a woman's boarding house, shabby, three stories, several blocks from the University of Washington on Ravenna. Even though it was growing late in the rest of the city, the U-District was humming.

Two young women squatted on the unpainted front stoop under a dim light, reading to each other out of a French textbook. They wore coats and slippers and I had the feeling they couldn't find anyplace inside, or else they were waiting for someone.

"Either one of you know a Beatrice Hindenburg?"

A brunette in what looked to be a grown-out mohawk, orange and greenish streaks down the back and one side, turned her face up to me and answered. She spoke English.

"She got killed, mister. It was all over the KOMO news. Somebody shot her in the brain. Her boyfriend. Then he tried to commit suicide."

The other woman, all in black, including jet-black lipstick and charcoal eye shadow, spoke bluntly. "I think it was sick. The whole thing makes me want to puke. The state of this world."

"Well, it could have been romantic, you know. It might have been. We don't know all the details. We don't know what they were thinking. It might have been romantic." The woman in the mohawk looked like someone whose own life lacked romance. Her eyes had a difficult time staying on my face, shifting to my chest and twittering about the street.

I displayed my license. "I understand Beatrice used this as a mail drop."

"She got her letters here, if that's what you mean. Only she didn't get very many. The mail's all stacked on a table in there every morning, and she hardly got anything. Once in a while a letter from California."

"Why did she use this address?"

"Couldn't tell ya. Used to live here. For about three weeks, I think. Mrs. Workman hadda kick her out when she found out how young she was. She's all heart, that woman."

"Mrs. Workman in?"

"Sure."

I rang the bell and spoke to a gaunt woman in horn-rimmed glasses, her graying hair pulled back and knotted into a severe bun. She didn't bother to look at my license when I flipped it out. "Beatrice Hindenburg," I said. "She used to live here?"

"Till I found out about her sneaking ways. She lied about her age and she stole a ring from me and some money from one of the girls. I tried to keep it quiet. Just threw her out was all. Same night I caught her."

"But she gets her mail here?"

"Yeah. I didn't see what harm that would do. Besides, the mail came, she picked it up more often than not from one of the girls while I was out. What could I do? I hate to send letters back to the post office. You know how they are if you get on their wrong side."

"Yeah, I know. They'll dog-ear the corners on your magazines for a month of Sundays."

She nodded in dizzying agreement.

"Did you know she was dead?"

"Who's dead?"

"Bea Hindenburg."

"Bea? Why . . . no. What happened?"

I told her, then advised her to phone the homicide section downtown. She didn't look as though she would take my advice. "Wait a minute," she said, and scuttled away from the doorway into the interior of the house. She scuffed back breathlessly and handed me a letter, a squarish envelope with a child's scribbling on it. It was addressed to "B. Hindenburg." No return address. Postmarked Cupertino, California.

"Give this to the police," I said.

"Forget it." She drawled her syllables out into a long,

assertive whine. "You take it and give it to them. I have enough trouble around here getting mail for people who've moved out without getting mail for dead girls, too." The door clicked shut in my face.

Tramping down the hill to my truck, I hefted the letter. The postmark was four days old. One sheet inside. A child's writing. What could it hurt? I fished a pocket knife out of the glove box and sliced open the envelope. It didn't take me long to wish I hadn't.

Dear Bee,
    Thanx for the gum. I never got gum in a letter befor. It was cool. The train book you sent got here al rite and i am having a grate time with it. I love you. I wish you cood cum bak home. I wish Bill wasnt so meen to you when you been here. Rite me in a letter when you will be coming home. I can wait.
    XXXXXXXXXXXXX
    OOOOOOOOOOOOO
    Yur best brother—Ronny

It rocked me. If I hadn't run across his letter, who knew how long Ronny might have waited for an answer? Last Saturday morning she had been a naked blonde with cornflower blue eyes and a hole in her skull. Now, for the first time, she was a real person. A real person who still received mail from a little brother who obviously didn't know she had already lain, drained and pale, on an eight-foot stainless-steel tray for a week.

If her mother had possessed a letter for her divorced father to pilfer, it was a letter her mother had, in turn, hijacked from Ronny. And Ronny, I guessed, was using the home of an aunt or a friendly neighbor to receive his letters and presents.

Bill must have been the mother's new boyfriend. It wouldn't be too difficult for the cops to track down all the Hindenburgs in the Cupertino area.

I would turn the letter over to Kathy Birchfield in the morning. Giving it and the mail drop to the police might produce some interesting trading material.

On a hunch I drove to the Downtown Service Center. Ingrid Darling had mentioned them briefly because they had been the ones who secured jobs at Trinity for her and Beatrice Hindenburg. I had heard a lot of good things about the Downtown Service Center, a privately funded foundation dedicated to helping young people in trouble. Once a year one of the local TV stations presented a mini-telethon to aid it.

Mostly they helped street kids, kids who had run away from home, kids who were selling their bodies on First Avenue for enough change to buy lollipops and maybe an umbrella to keep Seattle off their backs.

I parked a block away in Pioneer Square, the refurbished section of downtown Seattle, with buildings seventy and eighty years old, redone in their original state. I hiked to the Service Center. Though it was after ten at night, the place was lit up like a Christmas tree.

 **14** THE DOWNTOWN SERVICE
Center was housed in a two-
story brick building, catty-cornered from a computer
store, not far from the Kingdome.

I recalled a blurb about a year earlier in one of the
local slicks about how the neighboring businesses were
trying to coax the Esterly people, the people who had
founded it, to move out, asserting that an endless stream
of vagrants was tarnishing the image of the region.

I plunged into the well-lit main entrance, past a couple
of teenage boys bivouacked on the spic-and-span floor of
the lobby, reading snatches from a science-fiction paperback titled *Vacuum My Skull*. I noted that, although they
were both high-school age, they read using their mouths
and fingers.

A woman in wire-rimmed glasses and a hooplike,
ankle-length dress, sandals protruding from the bottom
hem like broken fence slats, peeped at me.

"May I be of assistance?"

Self-sacrifice was printed all over her.

Flopping out my license, I waited until she was prop-
erly and thoroughly impressed and said, "I'm working on

a murder. About a year ago you people referred two girls to Trinity Dog Food. Remember that?"

"Try another one. Every detective who comes in here tries the murder bit. Even some of the fathers looking for their runaways claim they're working on murders." She showed me a piece of her tongue at the edge of her mouth. "How about white slavery? We don't hear that but once every month or so. Try that one."

I smiled at her but her eyes had been purged of humor.

"Beatrice Hindenburg and Ingrid Darling."

"Never heard of them."

"Somebody here has heard of them."

"Let me take you to John Esterly."

In a businesslike lope, she led me down a pine-walled corridor to a cubicle at the end. Rapping smartly on the door, she pushed it open, the flab on her bare arm jouncing to the movement. She smelled of wildflowers and I could have sworn she had honey on her breath.

"John? There's somebody here to see you." She vanished in a puff of sweet incense.

I put my hand out and introduced myself, explaining briefly why I was there and who I was working for.

A young-looking man, John Esterly was about the same age as me, early thirties. His handshake was clammy and soft. Built like a lodgepole, his face was long and lean, but cheery. His gray eyes twinkled. Several inches shorter and forty pounds lighter than myself, I judged that he was one of those rare individuals who could take a deep breath, relax, and still sink to the bottom of a swimming pool. Not enough fat to float. But he wasn't fit. The turkey-wattle under his chin and his matchstick limbs attested to that. Long hours of soaking up other people's worries had taken its toll.

His desk was a mountain layered with geographical strata. If he wanted something from last week he would look an inch down. From last year, dig another foot.

"Darling and Hindenburg. Let me see. Darling and Hindenburg."

Propelling an old-fashioned tilting office chair around on its chittering casters, John Esterly began scooping slabs of paperwork off his desk and teetering them on a nearby bookcase that was already about to tumble. A wall behind me was door-to-corner and floor-to-ceiling sociology and popular self-help books. If an earthquake hit, the boys with the body bags would never excavate us.

"Those names I know."

"Hindenburg was killed last week. The second one, Ingrid Darling, was just discovered this afternoon at the bottom of a lake. It hasn't hit the papers yet."

"Is that right? Well, you're johnny-on-the-spot, aren't you?"

"Trinity Dog Food," I said, trying to keep him from getting sidetracked. If he insisted on burrowing through the morass on his desk, we might be there all night. "Listen, I'm kind of tired. It's been a long day. Is there . . ."

"I know." John Esterly wheeled his chair backward, swung around and pulled open a drawer in a file cabinet. He riffled some cards. "Sure. Trinity Dog Food. It's owned by Emmett Anderson and Mark Daniels. Right?" I nodded. Esterly looked past my head at something in the doorway. "Speak of the devil. There's the man you want to talk to. Right there."

I pivoted in my seat and met the Reverend Sam Wheeler's gaze. He gave me a fierce, fleeting look, as if to say he had banked on never seeing me again.

When he finally used it, his smile was lopsided, foxy and almost genuine. "Sure thing, Tommy. Be right with you. I have a counseling session going on right now. But I'll be in my office." It took me a few moments to realize Tommy was me.

I got up and closed the door behind him. "He set up the deal with Trinity?"

"Yes, he did, in fact. He's been close personal friends with Mark Daniels since about a year before God was born. The Reverend's got a lot of contacts. It's good to have him working here." Esterly beamed.

"He a partner, or what?"

"The board consists of my father, who founded the Esterly Center, my mother, and myself." John Esterly smiled at me. There was not an ounce of selfishness or ego in him. I was almost ashamed to be in the same room with him. On the way home I would flagellate myself with a scourge, beat my head against the dashboard. "People like the Reverend Wheeler donate their time and services. But I have to admit, they don't come out of it empty-handed. The Reverend gets a lot of mileage out of this in his radio and TV sermons. It's a fair balance."

"Does he spend much time here?"

"Depends on what you mean. He meets troubled kids. Sometimes he works with them here. Sometimes he gets them into a foster home, or back with their parents, or whatever. Maybe a job like he got for Bea and Ingrid. He's streetwise. He knows what these kids will respond to."

"What about Ingrid Darling and Beatrice Hindenburg?"

"They used to hook downtown. You're right. It was about a year ago. Sailors and out-of-towners mostly. Came in here because one of them got beat up. I can't remember which. The Reverend can tell you more. He got them the jobs. I lost track of them myself. We were just getting the overnight center started up out north. It was a hectic summer."

"The Reverend, huh?"

"Mr. Black? I can see by the look on your face you have reservations about the Reverend."

"You're good at reading faces, Esterly. Better than most."

"A talent I picked up on the streets. I'll vouch for him. Sure, he's made some money at it. And he comes on a little cold sometimes. But I've seen him on Pike Street at three in the morning caring when nobody else would. I've seen him take a fifteen-year-old junkie to his own home and keep him there until he could straighten out his life. He may have his quirks, but he's got what we need down here: He cares." I tipped an imaginary hat at John Esterly and moved to leave. "Wheeler's office is up a flight, directly over this one."

"Thanks."

After I climbed the pine stairs, I spotted Wheeler at the other end of the corridor, near the steps that led down to the front lobby. Rocking on his heels, pushing his maternity gut in and out, he was consoling a youth in tight jeans and a pea jacket a size too large. Some might say he was consoling. Some might say he was lecturing. The skinny youth was distraught, bawling.

I couldn't catch all of what he said. Something about things being a big circle. Slipping the kid a bill from his wallet he sent him off with, "Remember, success means getting up one more time than you fall down. That's all. You can do it. I know you can."

I didn't see for sure the denomination of the bill, but it

looked like a single. A dollar bill was going to do him a whole hell of a lot of good.

Wheeler chugged down the hall toward me. His smile was as broad as it was phony. "Tommy. Tommy," he said. "Come into my lair." He laughed artificially.

I trailed him into an office that was a replica of Esterly's pigpen downstairs, except that the Reverend kept his pristine almost to the point of obsession. He sat down behind his desk and took an accounting book out of a drawer, meticulously penned an entry and put it back. Reparations for the bill he had given the boy would be forthcoming.

Wheeler gave me a brittle look and tilted his chair backward. He knew just how far to tip it without sending it over.

"You should have come to me," he said soothingly. "Should have come to me if you had any questions. Want to know about Bea? I can tell you."

He stropped his pudgy hand across his cheek, a sapphire ring on his pinky. It might have been imitation sapphire, but I doubted it. He wore a simple short-sleeved sports shirt. It was the first time I had seen him without his collar.

"So tell me."

"Bea got smashed up by some john last year and decided to cash in her chips for a while. You know, play a safer game. She hitchhiked up from Oregon. One of her rides pulled off the highway and raped her. Real sad story. Had been streetwalking in Portland. Was running away from a small-time Oregon pimp, if I recall. We managed to get her an apartment and a job at Trinity. But she didn't take. Sometimes the rot gets so deep in their souls you can never get it out. It just didn't take. She was on the streets the night she quit Trinity. In fact, I saw her with one of our more influential local citizens, driving off in his car."

"Not Mark Daniels?"

"No. No." He laughed politely at my naiveté. "He must have come later. I've been doing a lot of thinking about it and I think what happened was, Mark must have given her some clue when she worked there. You know, made an offer, or patted her on the fanny, something like that. Then she went back to the streets and when things got rough again, she went to Mark. He must have been seeing her on a semi-regular basis, don't you think?"

I decided the Reverend Wheeler didn't have to know anything about the Galaxie Motor Court Inn.

"What about Ingrid Darling?"

Wheeler's chair snapped forward. "Darling? How does she play in this?"

"I thought you got them jobs together at Trinity. Esterly said they came in here together."

The chair rocked back again, seesawing. "Yeah, I guess maybe they did. We get so many different kids runnin' through here, it's hard to remember all the details sometimes."

"What about Ingrid?"

"Far as I know, she's still working at Trinity."

"Not since last summer."

"Really? I didn't realize that." Wheeler formed his thumb and forefinger into pliers and began worrying a whitehead on his neck just over the collar. "That's really news to me. I'll have to check up on her and see how things are. We generally run follow-up checks, but you know how it is. I talked a kid out of suicide last night.

After losing my good friend, Mark, I don't know if I could stand by and see another suicide."

"You haven't lost him yet."

"No, and I've got my fingers crossed. I pray for him almost hourly."

For which outcome, I wondered, recovery, or rutabaga city? "You think it was a murder-suicide, then?"

The whitehead exploded between thumb and forefinger, and the Reverend winced at the sudden pain. "Maybe. I'll be honest with you, Tommy. I've wanted to see this investigating you're doing quashed."

"Why?"

"You know Deanna and Mark were having troubles? He slapped her around. Boxed her ears. That sort of thing. Did you know she once picked up a pair of scissors and tried to park them in his chest? Did you know that?"

"You're the first to mention it."

"She did. She claimed she was only defending herself, but I don't know. Mark was beginning to think her ladder didn't reach all the way to the attic. Another time she tossed a pot of boiling water at him. Temper, temper. I guess she chased him all over the house with those scissors. When she couldn't catch him, she started hacking up his clothes. Actually, this shirt here was one of them. I don't know why he wanted to throw it out. It only had a little nick. She's a sweet kid, Deanna. She's got an Irish temper, but she doesn't mean it. Whatever happened to Mark, the way he treated his ex-wife and kids and all, I don't like to say this, but maybe it was divine justice. Maybe it was. I'd hate to see Deanna in court, though. That's all."

"Are you saying you think Deanna sneaked out two

weeks ago, caught her husband and the girl and shot them?"

Wheeler shrugged. "Not saying anything. I just think sometimes poking around does more harm than good."

"What about the suicide note?"

"Things like that have been faked before."

"Why would Deanna call attention to it? Why would she say she thought it was a fake if she was the one who shot them?"

"Whoa there, boy. I didn't say she shot anybody. You said that. Don't go putting words into my mouth. If you want to know what I really think . . . I think Mark killed the girl and then himself. That's what the cops say. What makes you smarter than the cops? If you're concocting some weird plot, if your mind works like that, why, I've got some real estate in Nevada I want to sell you. Course, it glows in the dark, but I'll give you a real deal." His laughter was mellow and fabricated, steeped in rancor.

"Know anybody else who knew Beatrice Hindenburg? Besides the Darling girl?"

"Not really. Bea tended to be a loner. So did Ingrid, if you want the truth."

I drove home, jogged three miles on the dark streets, showered and hit the sack. The jogging wasn't enough, but it was all I had time for. A good night's sleep was what I needed. But I didn't sleep well. I had nightmares about fishing and bringing up corpses, all pretty, young, bloodless girls. My last dream before waking was a saga about the big nuclear barbecue. In the morning the pall was still over me. I was standing in front of the bathroom mirror trying to paste my hair down with a wet comb when the phone jangled me out of my stupor.

I answered it in the living room, momentarily blinded

by the strong sunlight beaming through the gauze
curtains.

"Thomas?"

"Kathy?"

"You don't sound so good."

"I feel like I've been thrown by a horse. What's new?"

Kathy hesitated. "Mark Daniels died about half an
hour ago. The hospital just called."

"What about Deanna?"

"They said they called her first. I haven't spoken to her
yet. I'm not sure what this means. I guess we'll still need
you. There obviously won't be a murder trial now, but
there's still the question of it being suicide. Deanna
stands to collect almost $600,000 if it isn't suicide. How
are you doing?"

"Going to be in the office?"

"All day."

"I'll be over sometime this morning to fill you in."

"See you then, Cisco."

I climbed into my truck and drove in the bright sunshine to Queen Anne Hill. A handful of flesh-colored
pansies Deanna had picked yesterday lay wilted on the
dashboard. A five-car non-injury smashup on 45th with
accompanying gaper's block slowed things. People in
this state weren't used to this sunshine. It blinded them.
When it came out they piled into other cars, utility poles,
and even slow-moving houses.

**15** THE BLUE SKY WAS STUN-
ning.

The well-swept narrow streets on Queen Anne Hill
were lined with professionally manicured trees and
expensive new cars, everything crisp and dazzling and
undented in the unexpected sunshine. Record-setting
rains had been dousing the city throughout May, and
everything had stayed green and gray.

Across the street from the Daniels place a Japanese
gardener in a pleated uniform the color of chlorophyll
medicated a row of birches, dosing them from a sprayer.
Deep in my throat I could taste the tang of chemical
toxins.

I shambled up the front steps and ran into Emmett
Anderson erupting out the front door.

If I had been on the ball, I would have recognized the
Mercedes abutting the sidewalk when I drove up. I had
seen it weeks ago at the first murders. But I wasn't on the
ball; I was stumbling around in a purple haze.

The old guy didn't see me until he was a step or two
away, his gray eyes milky with tears.

"Morning."

Anderson stepped aside and swiped at his face,

boosting his glasses up out of the way. When he moved his hand they clunked back down onto his nose. A bandage was pasted to his knuckles. He was the rough-hewn sort who would always need a ready supply of dressings. He stammered, "You heard, I 'spose."

"Yes."

"He was like a goddamned son to me. I couldn't have loved him any more if he was my goddamned son."

I decided not to bring up the squabble they had had two weeks ago, the knock-down-drag-out brawl.

"Too bad," I commiserated.

"I'm closing the plant. Everything. At least for a month. Paid leave for one and all. Can't stand to see it. Fact, it hasn't been running all week. A goddamned shame. Now look at me. If somebody had to get shot, why couldn't it be me? I ain't got that long to go anyway. This may sound like bull hooey to you, but I goddamned wish I could trade places with the bastard. Hell, I ain't doing anything here but hogging space, breathing good air meant for someone better. Mark had a whole lot of good years left in him."

"The girl probably had a few, too."

Tugging on an ear that looked like gum rubber, Anderson said, "Never thought I'd live this long." He gazed out across the rooftops at the sound. "You should have seen the hell I raised when I was a young 'un. Rum-runners. We used to run it in from Canada. We had two big speedboats specially made. Coppers used to chase us for miles, but their boats never was as fast as ours. We used to tease 'em, slow down and keep just out of range. Took a bullet in my thigh once. I still got the scar. We were hellions."

"Sounds like maybe you were."

"And then Mark works honest his whole life. Never cheats a soul. Only problem is he gets het up over a little pussy now and then. Bang! When he's least expecting it, right in the brain pan. What turns a body to do something like that to hisself? And to his family? It don't seem fair." He hobbled down the stairs, pirouetted and looked up at me. "She ain't what I would have expected. I only met her once before—at the wedding. Helen was always my favorite. Now I'm going over there to see if I can do somethin' for the kids. But she . . ." He nodded up at the Daniels house. "She ain't what I expected."

"How's she taking it?"

"See for yourself," he said gruffly. He swiveled and headed toward the ex-wife and the kiddies.

"Emmett?"

"Son?"

"You going to play fair by her?" Emmett didn't even turn around this time. "You going to split things the way Mark would have wanted?"

It took him a lot of groping before he found words, slurring his reply. "People always told us we was crazy to keep everything so informal, that we was askin' for big trouble."

"So?"

"They was right." He plodded down the steps, tramping heavily to his Mercedes.

I yelled at him. "You don't do fair by her, that automatically gives you a motive. You know that, don't you?"

"He did it to hisself!"

"We'll see."

I had to push the bell four times.

Waiting on the stoop, I listened to a starling shriek on a

nearby phone pole. Emmett Anderson drove away slowly, rigid in his bullet-gray luxury car, not deigning to look up at the house. Next door a young man emerged in tennis whites, swinging a racket in a wooden holder, whistling. He smiled my way. He hadn't heard.

When Deanna cracked open the door she was wearing a floor-length silk robe, her hair tucked into a rubber swimming cap that had pink plastic flowers attached like Satan's horns. Her eyes were not teary. Not even fuzzy.

"Come in."

I stepped into the pool room and watched her lock the storm door and then the front door, turning and bouncing her backside against the knob.

"I'm sorry," I said.

Her eyes shot me an intrepid look, tried to hold it and disintegrated. She broke down and sobbed, her face destroying itself and turning ugly—slimy with grief. I reached for her but she put out a hand to fend me off. "No, don't hug me now. Just . . . Thomas. I need you so badly. I'm afraid of what might happen. And it wouldn't be right."

She slipped the robe off her shoulders onto the floor, glissaded two giant steps and dove into the pool, hardly rippling the glassine surface. The robe lay on the floor like the husk of a ghost. Too robust for a bikini, she wore a one-piece bathing suit cut very high on the hips. I watched her swim two laps, her motion easy and fluid. Gliding the last few yards, she winged her arms onto the ledge below me, suddenly full of lassitude. She blinked the chlorinated water out of her eyes.

"Will you stay with me?"

"Deanna, you should be with friends, someone you've known longer than me."

"I haven't known anyone longer than you, Thomas."

"But . . ."

"I've known you a thousand years. And my friends? All these society freaks around here? They all dash away when I say boo. I need somebody to be with me for a few hours. I don't want to talk about Mark or this case or anything. I just want to swim until I'm exhausted, and I need somebody to swim with me."

She gave me a doughty look and I thought of Wheeler's story about her hounding Mark around the house with a pair of scissors, snipping his clothes into bite-size pieces when she couldn't snip him into bite-size pieces—capsizing a pot of boiling water onto him. I wondered if Wheeler had been setting me up with a bunch of blarney.

"I was there," I said. "Where Mark was shot. Just a few minutes later."

"Yes. I know."

"Somebody hired me. It was an anonymous note with five hundred dollars cash in it. The note was hand-printed. Somebody wanted me to follow Mark and report on his philanderings."

Deanna tucked an errant strand of blonde hair back up under the bathing cap, unconcerned. "Did you ever find out who it was?"

"I had my suspicions. I didn't know for certain until last night." Plucking the hanky I had taken in Wood-inville out of my pocket, I waved it at her. She watched it, pursing her lips. "The perfume on this is a perfect match to the perfume on the letter. You hired me two weeks ago to follow your husband, didn't you?"

Deanna shoved off, taking a couple of casual swipes at the water, swimming on her back, studying me. "Thank you for sending the five hundred back. I had to sell jewelry to raise it."

"Why didn't you tell me you were the one?"

"You never asked."

"Would you have admitted it?"

"I was ashamed. For a long time I thought our marriage was made in heaven, that absolutely nothing could go wrong with it. Then he beat me up, broke my teeth, cracked my ribs. He was an animal. It pained me to hire you. In fact, it hurt more to do that than it did this morning when they called and said Mark was gone. Funny how things like that work."

I watched her porpoise around in the water for a few minutes.

"Swim with me, Thomas. Please?"

"I'm not real keen on skinny-dipping."

"There's a selection of suits in the changing room." Her smile was a cross between a tease and a smirk, and I had the feeling she had been dropping it on chagrined males for years and years. Forming a scoop with her hands, Deanna shot a spurt of water at my legs. It came in a heavy stream and drenched my left cuff.

"I didn't come to lollygag around in the pool. I came to see if I could help."

Her voice grew serious and a trifle frosty. "You want to help. Jump in. That'll help. People grieve in their own way. This is my way. Don't send me flowers. Don't say any prayers. Jump in."

The sun's rays angled through the glass roof and crawled down the far wall. The blue, choppy surface of the pool marbled the walls and my body with indirect sunlight.

I walked around the pool and went into the adjoining

room. Deanna, treading water, gyrated around and followed my progress, her sorry smile firmly in place, wet eyes like green stars. I went into the changing room, unlaced my shoes and heeled them off. Then I took off my jacket, tie, shirt and undershirt, folding them neatly over a chair. Peeling the bandage off my chest, I stole a look at myself in one of the ubiquitous floor-to-ceiling mirrors. I was like a pop-eyed cod brought up not on a lure but by sheer hocus-pocus.

Sometimes I had the uneasy feeling Deanna used men like a cripple used crutches: always one within easy reach. I still wasn't certain if I was a temporary haven for her, or something else.

I slipped into the suit, trotted out and into the pool room. I took several running steps and leaped into the choppy water. It was warm, very warm.

And, except for myself, empty.

Rising to the surface amid a billion bubbles, I shook my hair out and said, "Oh tish." I spun around, treading water, inspecting every corner of the room. Before I finished, something big and heavy cannonballed into the water next to my face, rocking the pool. I caught a fleeting glimpse of white thigh, elbow and breast. She surfaced beside me and began swimming laps, pounding at the water.

I swam with her. It took almost an hour in the short pool for her to exhaust herself.

We ended up on the mats beside the pool at the shallow end, the sunshine radiating on our bodies, drying us quickly.

"You take many cases?"

"I take a few cases. I tend to get consumed by them."

"Where do you get your money?"

"I'm on a pension. I don't need much."

Running her fingernails across my shoulder, she spoke in a husky voice, "I thought you would have a lot of scars."

"You like scars?"

"Yeah. Don't they usually have a lot of scars? Detectives?"

"Some do. I met one yesterday who's probably got hundreds."

She laughed. "But you have hardly any."

"They're all inside, sister. On the walls of my heart."

She laughed and bussed my brow. "Here's one." Peering down, she examined the wound on my chest. "But this is new. No fair. I wanted some real old scars. You know, jagged things that look like you got them with whistling swords—fighting a duel in Heidelberg. No fair."

Stretched out side by side, I leaned on one elbow and locked eyes with her. She grew quiet, pulled her bathing cap off and let acres of hair cascade down across her shoulders and back. It was the first time I had ever seen it loose. I reached out and touched it, handling it like a national treasure, totally bewitched.

I leaned over and kissed her lips, tasting the chlorine. She kissed me back. We molded our bodies against each other.

"We shouldn't be doing this," she gasped.

"Really shouldn't."

I was hopelessly hooked. Deanna was a riddle within a riddle. And she was plucky enough that this cockamamie passion didn't seem all that farfetched. If another woman had done this the morning her husband died, it would never come off as anything but illegitimate sex—too pernicious to describe. With Deanna, somehow, it seemed ordained from the moment we met, something that had transpired in that first hot exchange of glances at the party.

We were nearing the delirious point of no return when someone slammed a car door outside and shuffled up the steps to the porch. Half the roof sections over the pool had been mechanically opened to take advantage of the weather, so sounds outside were much louder and closer than they should have been. We froze, both of us heady in the guilt of potential community thought. Deanna sniggered. I couldn't tell if it was hysterics or what.

"Dummy up," she said, though I hadn't spoken. She sniggered harder, jiggling against me.

I had to hold my hand over her mouth to keep her from bursting into gales of laughter.

The chimes rang in the house, then we heard the sound of someone rapping hard on the outer door.

A man's mellow voice said, "Deanna, honey. I know you're in there. Deanna, I've come to be with you." We lay still, children caught counting stolen cookies under the stairs.

When I looked up, I could see the muzzy silhouette of the Reverend Samuel Wheeler standing at the door, nose pressed like a dog against the frosted glass. Surely he had spotted my truck. After a few minutes he went away, his muted footsteps raspy in our aerie.

Outside a car motor turned over and slowly hummed away down the street. An English sparrow chirruped.

I stood up and Deanna followed suit, shaking out her hair. It was the flute and I was the swaying cobra.

"Thomas? What would you say if I asked you to drop the case. Let's go somewhere, okay? Let's go to Reno and play the tables for a week. Doesn't that sound like fun?" She traced a line from my shoulder down my chest and around the ridges of my stomach. "Thomas? For me? Can you do that for me?"

I picked her up and carried her through the house until I found a bedroom, kicking the door open. She was heavy. I laid her on the bed and collapsed on top of her, both of us feeding a hunger that had been with us too long, both finally satiated.

It almost cleared the cobwebs.

We lay in bed and talked about inconsequentials for ten minutes. Then she said, "Thomas?"

"Yeah?"

"I want you to quit the case, okay?"

"That's not the way I'm constituted."

"Just quit. Couldn't you do that for me without asking why?"

"You'll lose 600,000 bucks in insurance."

"Emmett Anderson dropped by just before you got here."

"I spoke to him."

"He's obsessed with this. He thinks there's some sinister plot against Mark. He had a gun with him. He's going to find Mark's killer."

"He intimated to me that he still thought it was a suicide."

She thought that over. "He was all mixed up. But I'm afraid he'll do something crazy."

"Andy won't hurt me."

"For me?"

"What about money?"

"Money doesn't mean anything to me anymore. I was poor when I met Mark, and all this didn't make me happy.

I can be poor again. Besides, if Anderson doesn't give me Mark's share of the business, the insurance money will just go to paying bills anyway. I won't have anything left. I'd get the same result declaring bankruptcy."

"And if Anderson does share?"

"Then the insurance money would only be a drop in the bucket. I'll never have a financial worry again."

She turned and propped her head up on one elbow. I watched her rounded, sweaty contours. "Please give it up for me?"

"Why do you want me to quit it?" I could only think of one reason and it wasn't good.

"I don't know if you'll understand this, but I've had enough. The last weeks have been the sorriest of my life. And it seems to get worse all the time. I can't take the pressure. I'd rather just walk away from it and forget the whole thing. Quit. Please, quit."

I gave her a kiss, which turned into a grappling hug, which turned into something else. Afterward, I showered, borrowed a towel and traced a route back to the changing room to reclaim my clothing. When I had finished dressing, Deanna came out and slipped into her silk robe, carefully backhanding her tresses out of the collar.

"What's the Reverend to you?" I said.

"Nothing. Why? He just came when I needed him. He's been a family friend for a long time. Mark's family."

"Has he said anything about all this?"

"Very little. Mostly he's tried to comfort me. For a man of the cloth, he's really not very good at it, but he's always been a media type. I think he had his last congregation over ten years ago."

"Do you trust him?"

"He's one of the sweetest men in my life."

I wanted to ask if she had slept with him, but I bit my tongue. This was not the time or the place.

Reluctantly, Deanna showed me Mark's things. She must have been thinking I might get it out of my system right there. It took almost an hour to sort through them. When I opened a trunk and took out some mementos of their wedding, she sat heavily in a brocaded chair and shed a few tears.

I leafed through his high school annual and saw that he had been on the baseball team. So had Sam Wheeler. They had gone to high school together. That meant they went a long way back, further than I did with any of my friends.

Deanna said, "Friends in high school. Can you believe that? God, all my friends from high school are still back in North Dakota. We only had seventeen kids in our graduating class. Most of them are still working the farm."

When I was finished, Deanna took me down the hallway to a room where the wall-to-wall carpeting had been taken up. It was a workshop, cluttered with half-finished heads and torsos, sculptures. She was a sculptress, working mostly in clay, which she then cast in bronze or brass.

She looked up from a damp glob of greenish clay she had been kneading earlier that morning. She punched it viciously. A glimmer of her famous Irish temper shone through her motions. Her words were bitter.

"You caught me. This is my conceit. Deanna the artisan. Voilà."

"These are very nice." I reached out and touched a bronze child's head. Actually it looked clumsy and amateurish, but what could you say? "I don't know a lot about art, but I like these." Deanna shrugged. "Would you do me sometime?"

She spoke impassively, spent. "You really want me to?"

"After we get things cleared up. Yes. I'd like that."

"All right."

I hefted a piece of dried clay.

"You're still going to work on this business, aren't you?" Something in her tone warned me.

"Yep."

"I don't want you to."

"I know."

"I could fire you. Leech, Bemis and Ott are my attorneys. I could fire you."

"Sure."

"Why do you say it like that?"

"I've been fired before. Look, Deanna, I'm going to see this through. Somehow I feel responsible for that girl up at the lake. If I hadn't questioned her, I don't think she would be dead now. And besides that, I was attacked Sunday morning. I'm going to find out what that was all about. An explanation has been given, but it doesn't satisfy me. I've got something at stake here myself now."

"But you were doing it for me! It was my case!" She was growing shriller.

"Now, I'm doing it for me."

"You won't be paid!"

"That won't stop me."

"You're a bastard! A goddamned bastard! I asked you as nice as I could. How could you do this to me?"

I pivoted and walked to the door. A heavy gob of clay sailed through the air and whacked the wall next to my head. Either she was used to getting her way or she was taking Mark's death harder than she thought she was—or both. I looked at her over my shoulder. Loose hair awry, eyes blazing, robe half open, she was more beautiful and appealing than ever.

 **16** WHEN I ARRIVED AT THE offices of Leech, Bemis and Ott near University Village I slipped quietly into the men's room and cracked open my shirt. The wound on my chest had been oozing pus since my dunk in the pool and I was afraid it would mat the shirt to me. Carefully, I applied a dressing I had appropriated from the glove box of my truck.

Kathy Birchfield was seated at her desk, a sheaf of papers in hands. Behind the papers she was holding a library copy of *A Distant Mirror: The Calamitous 14th Century* by Barbara Tuchman.

"Good book," I said.

"Have you read it?"

"I told you about it. Remember?"

She stared up at my damp hair. "Just get up?"

"Not really."

"Your hair is wet." Her tone was both suspicious and sardonic.

"I, uh, worked out before I came down here."

"Must have been quite a workout. You look like you've been through the ringer. You jog to the top of Mount Rainier carrying barbells, or what?" The corners of her mouth curled limply in mild amusement. I had the feeling she somehow knew about Deanna and was toying with me the way an expert angler who had already bagged his limit toyed with a trout.

"It wasn't much."

"Maybe you're just upset about this case. You get strung out sometimes."

"Me? I never get strung out."

"Deanna just called."

"Did she?"

"Wants you off the case. She wants us to stop investigating altogether. What happened?"

"Nothing."

I was breaking a custom between us. We generally told each other about our love affairs. It had been a tradition since the time we had met and I was still in the SPD and going hooly-gooly over the boy I had shot.

A sixteen-year-old delinquent had been driving a stolen Volvo at me, trying to mow me down. I shot him through the windshield—in the eye. After I agonized several hours in the hospital corridor with his distraught and condemning family, he died. It broke me, plain and simple.

It broke me.

But nothing in our rules said I couldn't hold off telling her about Deanna. At least until my body temperature dropped back down to 105 or so.

"Maybe we should go over and speak to Mrs. Daniels together, thrash this out? I'm not quite certain where we all stand now that Mark has passed away."

I sat on the edge of her enormous desk. "We might wait a day or two."

"We might?"

"Deanna and I had a minor falling out."

"A tiff? Is that why she sounded so upset on the phone?"

"Could be."

"What happened?"

"Nothing."

"You still think she has the hots for you?"

I shrugged.

"Oh, Thomas. I just got a horrible idea. You didn't make a pass at her, did you?"

I said nothing, just gritted my teeth and cursed her gift of ESP.

"You're so bullheaded about things like that. You still think she . . . Thomas Black! Did you go over there the morning her husband died and make a pass at her? You did, didn't you?" I winced. "You're unbelievable. You really did, didn't you?"

I closed the office door so the rest of Seattle wouldn't eavesdrop on her unsavory accusations. "It was not what you think."

"I'll just bet."

"Life is a bitch, okay? Mark died this morning. Yesterday I found a friend of the dead girl. Her name was Ingrid Darling. She wanted me to call her Kandy with a K. I went up to her place on Capitol Hill and interviewed her. Then Deanna took me out to their summer place on Lost Lake to check it out—you know, in case Mark had been using it for trysts."

"Sure, Thomas."

"I thought there might be something lying around to help. There was. Ingrid Darling. She was floating in the lake."

"Sure, Thomas." She fixed her eyes on me. They were

the sort of violet you could wallow in. "What do you mean in the lake? Dead?"

"Somebody beat her up and tied a clothesline to her neck; snagged the other end to a piece of angle iron."

"Oh, God. Do you know who?"

"Somebody who isn't a sailor. The knot came undone and she floated to the surface."

"You always seem to find bodies. It's like you have your own divining rod to . . ."

"Don't say it."

"To death."

I chucked the letter from Beatrice Hindenburg's little brother, Ronny, onto her desk. She plucked it up, opened it and read it. A unique combination of angst, wet eye shadow and sparkling tears began polluting her face. "Oh, Thomas. You're going to have to call these people. You're going to have to explain it all."

"I can't explain any of it."

"But you have to call."

"I've already made my share of phone calls. Why don't we give it to homicide? They're getting paid to phone relatives and listen to all that weeping. And maybe you can milk some more information out of Ralph Crum. Trade him. Stuff like this is always good for trafficking with the cops. You can swap the address of Beatrice Hindenburg's mail drop, too. In fact, I have the name of a detective who followed her around for a couple of days. Give it to him in small doses and see what he coughs up in return." I jotted down names and addresses on a blank pad on her desk.

"But we're not on the case anymore."

"Just give it a whirl. See what pops up."

When she left the room to freshen up and contact Crum, I asked if I could make a long distance call.

"You're not phoning another woman?"

"I'm ringing up a Hollywood agent to see if I can break into the movies." She made a face.

The jaunty voice of Dr. Carol Neff, the medical examiner for Snohomish County, answered on the first ring.

"Yes?" She turned it into a three-syllable musical extravaganza.

"Thomas Black here. The one who found the girl in the lake yesterday?"

"I'm glad you called. You might be able to fill in some missing pieces. She was prime, all right. I figured in her late teens. Her parents told the sheriff out here she was sixteen. She had sex maybe an hour before she died. Her appendix had been removed over a year ago by some quack with jittery hands. And she'd borne at least one child. Poor thing."

"What did she die of?"

"Hypoxia. We thought it might be drowning at first. You see, most drowning victims actually suffocate. Lack of oxygen. But she didn't drown. There was no water in her lungs, but then that's not startling. You pulled her out not too long after her heart stopped. A lot of the time there's no water in the lungs. They have what we call a laryngeal spasm and they actually choke. No water— they choke. But she didn't die like that. She had subcutaneous emphysema in the soft tissues of the neck. Her trachea was pretty well crushed. The reason water didn't enter her lungs was because she was already dead when she went into the lake."

"Somebody strangled her?"

"Maybe. But I think it was more like somebody

slugged her in the windpipe, crushed it that way. Not a pleasant way to go. Probably lingered several minutes or longer before she died. Possibly with the perpetrator standing by watching."

"Hell of a way to go."

"There was something else, too. I couldn't figure it out for the longest time. Her body temperature just didn't correlate. If you saw her alive just hours before, she should have been much warmer. She should have been several degrees warmer, according to all my charts. Then I found something interesting on the back of one hand, on her thigh and on one cheek and ear. All on one side of her body. I couldn't figure it out for the longest time, follow me? A lot of what you find in this game depends upon what you're looking for. And I wasn't looking for anything like this. Had she been up in the mountains?"

"Why?"

"She was frostbitten. Not bad, but she was frostbitten. I thought perhaps she had been lying in the snow, or on ice. It's just about the only thing that would fit. My guess was that's why her body temperature was off. She shouldn't have cooled off so quickly, not even in the lake."

When Kathy came back into the room she was almost as gloomy as I was perplexed. "Ralph Crum didn't have anything to barter with. He really didn't. In fact, they're going to close the case. It's going to be officially classed a murder-suicide. That means Deanna won't get that insurance money. And he said he would call the girl's parents in California."

I stood up and began meandering toward the doorway.

"Thomas? Where are you going?"

"Ingrid Darling was frostbitten. Isn't that strange? Frostbitten. It gives me an idea."

"What?"

"At Trinity Dog Food there's a freezer."

"You don't think somebody at Trinity . . . ?"

"It's a big one, as big as a house. Maybe bigger. When I was in there the other day with Emmett Anderson it was forty below. He told me that's what they keep it at."

"But Thomas? With all the people around? I mean, nobody's going to hide a girl in a freezer in a dog food plant. Are they?"

"The plant's been closed all week. Anderson told me that this morning."

Before I could stop her, she grabbed her purse out of a drawer. "Can I come with you? I know you like to do things alone, but can I come? Just this once?"

"Don't you have clients to talk to?"

"This is for a client."

"Your client fired us."

"She fired you. I'm still her attorney."

We took my truck, Kathy refusing to wear her jacket. The sun was warming up to its task now and it was promising to be the hottest day in May.

"If we take your truck," said Kathy, "how am I going to get back?" She was resentful that I didn't want to ride in her new sports car.

"I'll drive you. Or you can use your broomstick." She laughed. Kathy did a shtick as a clown in her off hours, and several weeks ago at the Seattle Center a tot had asked her if she weren't a witch. He was too young to know the difference between a clown and a witch. It had become an oft-repeated gag between us, especially since her remedial ESP was so often witchlike.

When we got to Harbor Island the traffic was mostly loaded gasoline tankers from the tank farms on the island and other heavy trucks. True to his word, Emmett Anderson had given his plant workers the week off. There were only two vehicles in the lot, and one of them was parked off in a corner.

The other was a small, foreign pickup topped with a canopy. Maybe one of the janitors. A bumper sticker read, "Don't be a knockin' if this crate's a rockin'."

"Thomas, if it's all locked up, how are you going to get in?"

I grinned evilly.

"You're not going to pick the lock? Thomas?" Kathy had irrational fears of being arrested with me. The legal system meant everything to her and she would never have been able to live down a record. Certainly not as long as my memory remained intact.

I flexed my mouth and made my grin as vile as possible. She almost didn't come to the office door with me. At the last moment she relented, springing out of the truck and trotting after me.

"This better be legit," she said. But I had already opened it and dropped the keys back into my coat pocket.

"Was that legit, Thomas? How did you do that?"

"Keep up. You're missing things."

A sign on the door said: "Due to the misfortune that has befallen one of the senior partners, Mr. M. Daniels, this plant will be shut down until further notice. Those applying for work, summer replacements or otherwise, may phone Emmett Anderson at his home. 737-4567."

"Can you believe that?" I strode into the musty office and headed toward the door to the warehouse. "All this trouble and Andy takes a stance like that. Those applying for work may phone him at home. That eggsucker never has forgotten the little guy. What a deal."

"Thomas? How did you get that door open?"

"Keep up with me and you'll know how these things are happening."

"Thomas? Are we in here illegally? If we're in here illegally, I'm going to have to leave."

A man who looked like he belonged to the foreign pickup outside met us in the hallway next to the warehouse. He didn't bother to ask who we were. It was evident from his cart of brooms, detergents and fox tails he was a janitor.

We zipped through the plant without turning on any lights, through the warehouse, across the vast expanse of the Trinity Dog Food plant to the indoor loading docks. On the other side of the docks, past a yellow forklift, stood the ten-foot-high door to the freezer.

"You weren't kidding," said Kathy.

"Inside it's even larger than it looks."

I popped the door open and a blast of arctic air rushed out and almost smothered us.

"Do you have your gun?"

"It's only a freezer, Kathy. What can happen in a freezer?"

"What if we get locked in?"

"There's no lock on this door. Even if there was, you couldn't shoot it off. If the handle doesn't push, you can beef the door open with your shoulder. It's not any tighter than your Amana at home." I stepped into the freezer, found the lights, shut myself in, then opened it from the inside. Satisfied, she tiptoed in with me, hugging her arms across her breasts, across the light poplin material of her blouse.

The first section of the freezer was stacked with twenty-pound bags of chicken parts, the stacks four, six, and eight feet high. They had enough reserves to feed a small city. The rest of that first room was hung with steer quarters, two racks high. I couldn't see how they retrieved them from the higher rack, but I was sure they had some slick system. Anderson had everything in the plant figured out. Kathy gaped at the twenty-foot-high ceiling and its stalactites of ice.

"They won't fall on us, will they?"

"You see anybody around here with a big hunk of ice stuck in him?"

"Not yet."

"Trust me."

"How long are we going to be?"

"Keep up. You won't miss a thing."

"I didn't think a person could get cold this fast. This is just like stepping into a Minnesota winter. If someone had told me, I would have thought they were being foolish. But I'm about ready to die. My ears hurt. Brrr."

"Just a few minutes. You can wait outside, if you like."

"No, I have to keep up."

"You're a peach."

"Yeah, a frozen cobbler."

The second half of the freezer was stacked high with brown sacks. Frozen beef parts. Frozen sacks of fish. In the far corner the piles went almost to the ceiling. Against one wall I spotted three cases of candy bars, one half broken. Whoever supplied the machines in the plant kept their stores in here. Why not? I picked up a Butterfinger and tapped the tin-lined wall with it. It felt like a steel pipe.

I was looking for someplace where a body might have

been stashed, someplace relatively safe from prying eyes. In the second section of the enormous room there seemed to be a gap between the stacks and the far wall, an aisle. I jammed my benumbed hands into my trousers pockets and walked around to the far wall and the gap.

The area between the stacks and the wall was cluttered with old machinery, machinery I assumed had been used in the freezer at one time for various processes. Making ice. Or whatnot.

I sidled among the obsolete parts and found several long trays once used for producing bulk ice. Someone would run a hose in, fill the trays and leave them overnight. In the morning the huge cakes could be wheeled out on skids or on forklifts, then chipped, chopped, or delivered as is.

At the end of the row, at the very corner of the freezer, and also the very corner of the building, a tarp was stretched across several more boxy appliances. They appeared to be more bulk ice-makers.

There was something funny about the tarp. It didn't carry the patina of frost on it everything else in the cavern did.

"Thomas? I'm freezing."

"In a minute." I edged through the junk and picked up a corner of the tarp. I flipped it off in one clean movement, a magician clearing the tablecloth without disturbing the dishes.

"Oh God," said Kathy, peering over my shoulder. "What is it?"

It was a block of ice in a tin-lined wooden frame about seven feet long, three feet wide and two feet deep.

Lying in the center of the block of ice was a man. On his back.

He stared up at us as if in repose. The man was stiff as a frozen halibut and just as dead.

"You keeping up?"

"Oh God. I wish I'd stayed at the office."

"That's what you call a stiff."

"Don't make jokes. Who is it, Thomas? Do you know him?"

"His name is Seymore Teets."

 **"GET SERIOUS, THOMAS. IS IT real? A dummy? Do you know him?"**

"You mean, is it real, or is it Memorex?"

"Don't be funny. I'm getting frightened."

"He's the detective I told you about. He followed Beatrice Hindenburg around for a couple of days. Died like a comic book hero, eh?"

"When did you speak to him?"

"Yesterday. He was all right then."

"Things are happening so fast. This is scary."

I knelt on the crumpled tarp and fingered the glazed surface of the ice. It was solid and glossy to my touch, smooth as polished marble. My fingertips began to adhere and I jerked them away. Virgin ice.

"Thomas, I'm frightened. I feel something. There's something wrong in here."

"We just found a dead man."

"No, worse than that. Something else."

"Seymore Teets, the great flycatcher. He won't catch any flies in there."

"Don't be flip. I mean this is serious. I'm having one

162

of my premonitions. We're in big trouble. We've got to get out of here."

"You serious, Kathy?" I looked up at her. I didn't believe in ESP or any of that hokum. Just the sixth sense Kathy had. That I believed in. I had seen her miraculous prognostications come true too often. She had prophesied accidents ahead of us on the freeway, even to the color of clothing the victims would be wearing; had accurately predicted I would find bones in a cave in the mountains on one of my cases. When her powers were oiled and working, they were uncanny.

"There's . . . I think we're going to die. You and me. Together."

"When?"

"Soon."

"You are serious."

"Let's get out of here."

Teets still wore his gun. Peering through the magnifying ice, I could see the serrated hammer in the holster where his coat had fallen back, probably when they had hosed water onto him. His hat was crushed under his head. Whoever had done him violence had concealed it well. There weren't any marks visible. Only a bluish tinge to his face. Halfway between his nose and the surface of the ice a tiny off-white card was frozen, one of his calling cards, as if he hadn't been able to present it fast enough.

I lifted the heavy tarp which rustled like thunder in another city and draped it back over the ice casket.

Stiff-limbed, hugging herself, Kathy was already stumping to the big door. She lambasted me with a look when I got there. Kathy was good at leveling people with one hard look.

"Very funny. How did you do it?"

"What?"

She cocked her head at the door. I tried it and found it unyielding. I tried it again, throwing my shoulder into it this time. Still immovable. I kicked it, then jammed both palms against the tin and shoved until my shoes skidded on the floor, a growing panic infusing my motions. Somebody was playing a very macabre practical joke. It didn't budge. I might as well have been pushing against the Great Wall of China.

"It's locked, Thomas."

I looked up at Kathy, grinned and said, "If you wanted to cozy up to me, all you had to do was ask."

"Okay, now show me where the other door is."

"This is it. *Uno.* The only one."

Staggering toward me, she burst into tears, her frame shuddering at the shock of our plight. I squeezed her shoulders and pulled her to me, cuddling her slender chattering physique against the wool of my jacket. She was freezing. I could feel the numbing cold in her flesh under the blouse. I doffed my sport coat and drew it over her shoulders, cinching it tight at her neck.

She snorted an unladylike snort, wiped her nose on both sides of my tie and said, "Thanks, Thomas. We locked ourselves in, didn't we?"

"There's no way to lock it, Kathy. My guess is somebody drove that forklift over and wedged it against the freezer door."

"We're being killed, aren't we?"

"That's one way of looking at it."

"I've never been killed before."

"I have."

She peered up at me, sniveling. "How was it?"

"Tons of fun. If you survive you get a merit badge."

Wiping an eye, she said, "What's the best part?"

"The best part is when your next birthday rolls around and you're still counting gray hairs."

Her voice got very tiny. "I don't have any gray hairs."

"You will."

I reared back and pushed on the door again. Kathy hollered, but we both knew her tones wouldn't penetrate that thick, insulated freezer door. I gestured for her to help me push, and she did, with no visible effect. I scanned the perimeter of the door to see if there was a warning bell or some way to dismantle the door. There wasn't.

"What are we going to do?" Effortlessly she dropped into a heavy Mexican drawl. "Thees is my dream, Cisco. Don't you know? I dream we stiff like frozen herrings. Hey, Cisco?"

I rubbed my hands together briskly. It didn't warm them, only pumped cold air up my shirtsleeves. "At least we won't attract any flies."

She started bawling again. I cupped her face and brought it close to mine and tried to think of something very wise to say. When I wanted to be, I was a regular cheerleader. "Kathy, we're not going to die in a dog freezer. All right?" She nodded feebly. "Some pussball out there is trying to get us and he's not going to."

"Pussball," Kathy repeated, teeth sounding out a rat-a-tat-tat. My icy hands on her face had chilled and unnerved her even more.

A fiberglass-handled fire ax was slung on the wall ten feet from the door, a permanent fixture in the place. By the look of it, it had never been used. I hefted it, knocking a ridge of ice off the haft. If I was careful and didn't smack the handle too often, it might hold up to a pounding. If it didn't, we were both going to end up in a bag of party cubes.

"What are we going to do?" said Kathy.

"We could wait him out? Write notes in case we don't make it. That way the cops would find out, eventually." She shook her head soberly.

"We could sabotage the freezer. Find the coils and break them. But even then, it would probably take a week or more for this place to thaw out. I'm not sure how long we would last. Maybe ten, eleven hours." Kathy shook her head.

"We could go back and thaw out Seymore. He had a gun on him. It might even be loaded." Kathy shook her head.

"I might chop through this door, but there's probably someone out there waiting with a six-pack of Coors and a loaded Mauser." Kathy shook her head.

"I could go in the back and chop a hole in the wall and sneak around and break the bastard's neck. What do you think?"

Kathy nodded vigorously.

"Break the bastard's neck?"

"Chop our way out the back," she stuttered.

While Kathy scrounged around for some gloves, I began hacking at the wall behind the hanging beef quarters. Pacing myself, I swung in a rhythm, trying to preserve the ax. It was a genuine fire ax, a blade on one side, a pick on the other. It was easy enough to bash a hole through the tin and through six or eight inches of insulating material, fragments of which orbited around my work space like billions of microscopic planets. I breathed through my nose as much as possible and finally ripped the seam on my tie and knotted it around my face, using it for a face mask. One end had snot frozen to it. My hands were so cold I could barely fasten the granny knot.

When Kathy couldn't find a pair of gloves, I had her begin tunneling into one of the piles of bagged beef from the top, carving out a niche for us to hide in when and if our assailant decided to burst through the door and finish us off.

"Do you think whoever killed Teets is outside?" Kathy asked.

"Who else?"

"Maybe it was that janitor. Maybe he got uppity because we didn't introduce ourselves?"

"He's number two on my list of suspects."

"Oh boy. Suspects. I like this." I could see that the shock of our predicament was beginning to wear thin.

"When I was here at the first of the week a gang of Asians attacked me. The leader was a guy named Hung Doan. He's the foreman here at Trinity. Seems to take an abnormal interest in what's going on around the plant."

"You think he's outside?"

"Number one on my list."

"Did somebody follow us?"

"Maybe. Maybe they were just waiting for somebody to run across Seymore."

"You think it was this Hung Doan guy?"

"Or one of his henchmen." As I chopped, I detailed the scuffle with Doan and my first meeting with Emmett Anderson.

It didn't take her very long to scoop out a hidey-hole on the second tier of beef sacks. Kathy, whose cheeks were turning purple, kept her eye on the large freezer door. I shivered and swung the ax. I took a few breaks, striding back over to the freezer door and testing it. It remained unyielding. I was getting colder and colder. At this rate, even working as hard as I was, my blood would freeze through in another three hours.

Kathy rummaged around for something to keep us warm. She found that the tarp covering on Teets' ice casket was pinned down on one side by the cake of ice. Neither of us had anything sharp enough on our person to sever the heavy material. Finally she ferreted out a scrap of burlap and handed it to me.

"What's this?"

"Tie it over your head. Most of your body heat escapes through the top of your head." I did as she advised. "The Easter bonnets are nice this year," she cooed.

"I thought you wanted to play this serious? We're going to die, remember?"

"I now have implicit faith in your ability to get us out of this. You're *my* comic book hero."

"I'm going to write that in my diary tonight before I say my prayers."

I struck the wall with the ax. I wasn't so sure anymore. If we were still in here tomorrow at this time we would both be dead. Kathy first. She had fewer clothes on and her body mass wasn't as great as mine.

The inner wall, the wall that ran between the inside loading dock and the freezer, we didn't dare breach, as whoever had sealed us in was probably out there waiting. Besides, as I recalled, it was over three feet thick. Maybe a solid three feet. Maybe not. And now this wall was proving much thicker than I had imagined.

Kathy took turns chopping and acquitted herself well, her breath wafting out in curlicues, tendrils of perspiration rising off her back. It gave her a chance to build up some body heat and it gave me a breather. Blisters were burgeoning on both hands. A woodsman, I was not.

Peeling strips of burlap off my makeshift babushka, which actually seemed to be helping me keep warm, I wrapped them around the fiberglass handle of the ax. It gave me an improved, if somewhat slippery, grip and cushioned the chafing somewhat. The blisters continued to puff up, swelling and throbbing in cadence to my pulse.

We peeled the wall away, leaving shards of tin and ragged hunks of insulation materials at our feet, then hit a layer of timber. I couldn't believe it. Actual timber. It turned out to be about four inches thick and a little on the rotten side. It took twenty-five minutes to get through it, to clear a hole three feet by three feet. On my right hand a blister had popped and was bleeding.

Excavating the final shreds of broken timber out of the hole, we discovered a layer of old brick.

"Oh, tish," said Kathy when she saw the mortar and brick. She was really getting numb; I could tell by the way her mouth wrapped itself clumsily around her words.

"No, this is good," I said. "This must be the outer wall. I just hope there's nobody standing out there with a gun."

"Do you think they can hear the chopping?"

I hadn't thought of that.

I chopped away at the bricks, using the pick end of the ax, which was pretty well dulled now. The crumbling bricks made a new sound, a plinking sound, one we weren't used to. After I dismantled two rows, I was able to hook the head of the ax over individual bricks and loosen them. Behind the bricks was a space about three inches wide and then more bricks—another complete wall of them.

Kathy slumped down and began sobbing. I sat down beside her and took a breather, quick serpents of vapor huffing out of my mouth. The fiberglass floor was unbelievably cold on my buttocks. "Somehow," I said, "I'm getting the feeling I'm somebody's cat's-paw."

"What's a cat's-paw?"

"A dupe. A sucker. The nerd in college who shows up nude at the formal party at the sorority and gets arrested because somebody told him they were having a nude dance."

"Cisco?"

"Pancho."

"How long does it take to freeze to death?"

I stood up, reached down, grabbed one of her hands and pulled her to her feet. "Not real long if our butts are stuck to the floor."

"No, how long? Really?"

"We're getting out."

She nodded weakly. We had been in there for over an hour, and at this rate, surviving until supper would be a miracle. I let Kathy wield the ax again, until she heated up and some of the purple leached out of her complexion. She was much clumsier now. When she was finished she handed it back and said, "You know, Thomas, I love you."

"Sure, sister."

I began hacking. She hadn't done any damage to the second row of bricks, had only enlarged the first opening. I chipped out most of the first brick in the second thickness, then held up the ax and felt the head. It was wobbling. "Thomas, I mean it. I love you."

"I love you too, sister."

"Will we always be friends?"

"We always have been."

She rushed me, clasping me hard around the waist, pressing her head against the wound on my chest until, even in the cold, it ached. "Kathy, Kathy, it ain't that bad. Once my mother told me not to touch my tongue to the walls of our home freezer." She looked up at me, an odd mixture of amusement and grief on her face. "I was about ten. 'Don't put your tongue on that freezer wall,' she said. I was home alone. I couldn't resist it. I licked the freezer wall and there I was, alone in the house, my head in the freezer box, my tongue glued to the wall of the freezer."

She laughed, a nervous laugh that reminded me suddenly of the way Deanna Daniels always laughed. "How did you get out of it?"

"I didn't. I stood there with my head in the freezer until my mother got home and poured water over my tongue."

"How long was she gone?"

"I dunno. About two days."

Kathy snickered again and then broke out into downright guffaws. "Okay," she said. "You win. We're getting out of this."

"Good girl."

I swung the ax and the head flew off, spinning down into the slot between the two brick walls.

Kathy and I looked at each other.

One brick in the second wall had cracked with the blow and was almost destroyed. I rammed it with the fiberglass handle. It seemed to move. I rammed it again. Again. The fiberglass handle sent jolts through the bones in my arms.

The brick stirred, moved again and then popped out. From where I was standing I could see a strata of sunlight blazing onto the street outside. I glanced over at Kathy. "Oh, tish."

Dejected, she said, "Another wall?"

"Look, as my one last civilized act, I'm going to make your life complete."

"What?"

"You can have my body. Take me, I'm yours."

"Thomas, you ass." She bumped me aside and bounced up and down, peeping out the hole in the wall at the sunlight. "We did it. We did it."

I poked another brick out of the second wall, and another. Soon we had a two-foot-square hole through tin, insulation, one-inch boards, plaster and lathe, timber, and two walls of brick. It had cost us an hour and forty-five minutes, some tears, several blisters and one fire ax. The hole had started off four feet by four feet and had narrowed down at each successive level until now it looked like a giant ragged funnel.

Checking the freezer door one more time, I jogtrotted back, whirled the burlap off my head and laid it across the scalloped ridges of tin and splintered timber. I vaulted into the hole and scrambled headfirst through the opening.

The tunnel turned out to be five feet above the ground. I was halfway out into the sunshine when a parcel delivery truck slammed its brakes on in the street and the driver stopped to gape at me. I wormed out, and dropped to the ground in a flower bed of wilting tulips. I was too numb with cold to feel any pain, though the fall tweaked my back.

I clambered unsteadily to my feet, saluted the driver in the street, grinned maniacally and turned to receive Kathy from the bowels of the Trinity Dog Food plant freezer.

It was only when I realized how dotty my grin was that I knew I had escaped that icy dungeon. I took a deep breath and suddenly felt the warm air permeating my lungs. From forty below to seventy above. We could easily have laid there all night: frozen chicken parts, frozen beef parts, frozen detective parts and frozen lady lawyer parts. Two hours in the meat locker had seemed like two days.

Kathy Birchfield squirmed out feet first, looking very unladylike from my angle. The delivery driver got a big kick out of that, catcalls and hoots of glee echoing in his closed cab. She fell into my arms, spotted the cheering truck driver and gave him a salute virtually identical to the one I had presented him. He laughed and drove on.

Cheeks still purple, body trembling, mouth quivering, Kathy said, "I thought we were dead."

"I don't think I'll ever be too hot again."

"If I'd been in there alone I would still be in there. I owe you, Thomas."

"Don't be silly. You never would have gone in there alone."

"No. You saved my life."

"You know I hate mawkish women."

We walked across the street like sailors just off a schooner, trying to get our land legs. I scouted a weather-beaten building of corrugated aluminum and steel, and we went in. It was a junk salvage company. An old man in muttonchop whiskers whose face was all grime and soot said we could use his telephone. I rang the police and told them we had found a body and gave the address.

Staunch and pleased with ourselves, Kathy and I went out and stood in the sun for a few moments, surveying the damage we had done across the street. From here it looked as if someone had fired a cannonball into the brick wall. The hole looked clean and precise, except for the bricks and mortar littering the tulip bed.

"Stay here until you see cops," I said.

"Where are you going?" She reached out with a quivering hand and picked flecks of burlap out of my hair.

"To find out who's waiting outside that freezer."

"But the police will be here."

"Yeah, and they just might frighten our pigeon away."

The fiberglass ax handle was still in my hands. On the way across the street I flipped it end to end in one hand, trying to bring the dexterity and quickness back into my limbs. I walked briskly, then broke into a jog, warming my blood up. I might have gone round the back to the loading dock—I had a suspicion that's how our boy had gained entry—but I couldn't be certain the loading dock door wouldn't be locked, and it was a long walk back around to the front. I headed directly for the front.

The foreign pickup was gone. In its place stood another vehicle, one I regrettably recognized on first sight.

Unlocking the office door, I blocked it open for the cops, sneaked in, listened, then went through the warehouse. I crept across the shadowed floor of the empty factory and found the pigeon in the loading dock.

I had figured it right. The forklift had been driven up against the freezer door, pinning it tight by running the forks up and punching them into the center of the freezer door, making big dimples in the tin.

His back was to me, a pistol in his right fist, a squarish amber liquor bottle in his left.

Slipping off my shoes, I stalked toward him, tiptoeing, then shuffling and finally running silently. I was only five feet away when he swung around and pointed the pistol at my heart.

I swatted at the pistol with a tennis swing and batted it out of his fist. Thunking the floor, it spun away and skidded out of sight. It sang on the smooth concrete floor.

"Nice job, Andy. It almost worked."

Emmett Anderson looked at me as if I were a slobbering cretin and had just climbed over the fence at Western State Hospital. "What the hell you talking about?"

"Don't fool with me, Andy. I'm ticked."

"I can see that." He took a swig from the bottle. "You damn near broke my hand with that ax handle."

 "SOME BIRDBRAIN LOCKED ME in with your doggie biscuits."

"If you were locked in, how come you're out here and the door's still jammed?"

"I broke out the far wall. With this." I shook the ax handle in his face.

"You busted our fire ax."

"Life is a bitch, eh?"

"Don't look at me. I didn't lock you in no freezer. Why the hell would I do that? You think I'd punch a couple of big holes in my own door?" Emmett Anderson sauntered in his bowlegged slouch to the forklift, where he squatted on a fender and guzzled his alcohol. He hoisted the amber bottle in offering to me.

"We assumed whoever did it would be out here waiting with a gun. You know, in case we figured some way to nibble through the door."

"Fetched that gun out when I seen the forklift. Went back to my car and got it. The whole thing looked fishy. I seen your truck out in the lot and I smelled trouble. But then I got in here and seen the forklift. That door was open too." He nodded at the huge loading door behind me. "Hell, I just now got here."

I twisted around and saw that the loading dock door was still partially open, a sliver of snowy sunlight dazzling the billiard-smooth concrete inside.

"Shit, boy, I was just now having a little refreshment and lookin' things over. You stayed back in there I woulda had that forklift moved in another sixty seconds."

"Maybe."

"Fuck you and the horse you rode in on. I don't give a shit. How long were you in there, anyway?"

"Coupla hours."

"Where'd you get out?"

"The outside wall." He gave me a querulous look. "It's going to need a little patching."

"Damn fool. That's the thickest wall in the whole city, maybe the whole state. I'll get Doan down here to brick it up." He sipped from the bottle. "I knew you had all your shit in one sock the day I met you."

"Thanks, I think."

I walked over and picked his gun up. He didn't budge from the forklift. When I came back, the pistol in one hand, the ax handle in the other, he said, "I suppose you'll want to know just exactly who had access to this place."

"You're awful sure you'll be cleared, old man."

"Mosey outside and lay your hands on the engine block of my rig. If I been in here two hours waiting for your head to pop up like the ground hog, that engine block will be colder than a witch's tit."

"You're saying it's not?"

"Don't burn yourself."

"Okay, I'll bite. Who has access to this joint?"

"I do." He grinned and peered at me through the lower portion of his bifocals, tipping his head backward.

"Deanna Daniels does. Mark's ex, Helen does. She used to work in accounting when we got swamped. I should think Helen's new husband has a key, though I never seen him around. My foreman, Doan, does. Two managers under Doan have keys. The janitorial staff. There's two of them with keys. And most of the office staff has keys to the office. It's just a walk into here from the office. Hell, we haven't changed the lock configuration in fifteen years. No telling who else kept their key."

"Maybe we should get the phone book out and make a list of who *can't* waltz in here?"

" 'Spose we should change the locks."

"Does Deanna Daniels ever come?"

"Been in from time to time. I seen her in here a couple of weeks ago."

I stumped over to the loading dock, wedged myself into the crack with my back against the wall and bench-pressed the huge sliding door open. Thirty yards away another peach-colored structure lay parallel to the Trinity Building, the two forming a long corridor in the grass. Rusted railroad tracks nestled between them. It looked as if someone had parked a vehicle in the weeds not long ago, but then I was no forensic specialist. My hunch was that the police wouldn't pursue the crushed grass, there being entirely too many avenues of approach to the freezer. To them, the likelihood that Teets' killer had come in this way would appear remote.

The cops trooped in with Kathy in tow. Emmett Anderson gaped at the uniforms and said, "What the hell's going on here?"

"There's a frozen gumshoe in your freezer. These fine gentlemen want to take a look."

After shaking his head in consternation, the old man

hopped up into the driver's seat, fired up the forklift, reversed it, lowered the blades and backed it off into a corner. None of the police officers dawdled in the freezer. We told them where to find Teets, and they wandered in and hustled out shivering a few minutes later, rubbing their hands together. A balding detective asked Anderson if there wasn't some way to turn the freezer off while they poked and probed the crime scene.

"Sure, boy," he said, alienating the cop with his conceit. "You want to lay out a hundred forty thousand bucks for thawed meat, be my guest."

I sneaked out to the parking lot and rubbed my hand across the hood of Emmett Anderson's Mercedes. The wax job was thick and slick. He was right. The engine block was hotter than a two-dollar pistol after a Saturday night hoot. But it didn't mean anything. He could have locked us in, gone, and come back.

Ralph Crum showed up, looking haggard and ruddy in the warm weather, his jetstream blue eyes watery, gazing at Kathy when he thought nobody else was looking. I followed him into the mammoth freezer and watched him stand over the frozen detective.

"Looks weirder than hell," I said.

"Yeah, kind of like something from a Superman movie, huh?"

"Maybe from a comic book."

"Looks almost like a gangland thing, doesn't it?"

It wasn't until he uttered the words that I recalled Emmett Anderson's rumrunning days. I didn't mention it. I wanted Crum to send his evidence specialists out into the space between the two buildings to try to get a fix on whatever vehicle had been there. I calculated that if his thoughts got too cluttered, he wouldn't do it.

I had underestimated him. He deployed someone to secure the name of the janitor who had been servicing the building earlier, and began compiling a list of possibles who might have been in the building yesterday or last night. One man was assigned to comb the grassy lot between the buildings. I told him to look into Anderson's criminal past.

"I don't want you dabbling in this, Black," he said, leveling his blue eyes on me.

"You're going to have to reopen the Daniels-Hindenburg case."

"Maybe."

"How can you say maybe? Teets had followed Hindenburg. Somebody murdered him. I was working on the Daniels-Hindenburg thing. Somebody tried to make a six-foot icicle out of me. How can you say maybe?"

"Easy. Maybe." His words were soft and understated as he watched a host of cops loping in and out of the freezer. He took my statement, took Kathy's statement, and grilled the old man.

Before I left, Crum marched over to me and held up a fistful of candy bars. "What's this?"

"Candy."

"We found a little hideaway up in the stacks of frozen beef bags. Found these in it. It was a camp like kids might make."

I laughed. "Don't worry about it. We did it."

Crum said, "There are a lot of unanswerables in cases like this, Black. Don't get yourself killed looking for an unanswerable. 'Kay?"

When we left, Emmett Anderson was slouched against one wall, iron-willed and isolated from the hustle and bustle, thumbs hooked in his belt loops. He looked like a cowboy long past his prime, a cowboy who had forgotten to die.

I drove Kathy back to her office in the University District. "So who locked us in?" she asked.

"You're the one with ESP."

"Thomas, you know it only works once in a while. Never when I want."

Swinging around in a large circle in the parking lot outside the offices of Leech, Bemis and Ott, I waited for Kathy to get out of the Ford. She turned to me and said, "Be careful."

"Me?"

"Yeah, you, bozo breath." She smiled a timorous smile. "Okay. Promise me you'll be careful."

"Sure."

"And . . . Hey, uh, I would have succumbed in there if it hadn't been for you. I really would have. I would have gone to pieces and just plain shivered to death. Thanks."

"Don't even think about it."

She reached across and tweaked my cheek, hard. "And thanks for the date, too. You really know how to show a girl a good time."

The door clicked shut on me before I could think of a reply.

"Smartass." I wheeled out of the lot.

Kandy Darling had died from a blow to the windpipe, possibly a karate blow. Mark and Beatrice had been shot in the Trinity offices. Teets had been quick-frozen in the Trinity freezer. My guess was someone had only been storing him, the way they had probably stored Kandy before taking her up to the lake.

Kathy and I had been attacked in the Trinity plant.

Trinity was one line. Karate was another. At the point

where they intersected a man was waiting for me. I couldn't help thinking his name was Hung Doan. Who would know karate better than a colonel in the South Vietnamese army? And he had access to the plant. He knew all the dead people except maybe Teets, and for all I knew, he had known Teets, too.

While the cops had been cantering through the plant looking for clues, I had gone to the glass-walled office in the dog food plant and secured the address and phone number of the head honcho, Hung Doan.

Crum didn't know anything about him yet.

Doan resided in a huge complex of apartments in the Rainier Valley, affectionately branded the Ho Chi Minh Condos by some of the cops in the area. They also called it the boat village and gook city, depending upon their mood or temperament or who spit on their windshield last.

Ten years ago the complexes had been built, financed and sold as condominiums to mostly white clientele. When the osmosis of the central area began spreading south, the whites fled and sold out to blacks. After the collapse of South Vietnam, Washington State became one of the three primary receiving stations for refugees. Asians began settling the area and pushed the blacks out.

There had been a scandal in the papers a couple of years before. Several Asian gentlemen had cultivated opium poppies on the dirt terraces they had carved out on the hillside behind the condominiums. In some of the hill tribes opium had been raised, not with the intent to trade drugs, but as a part of the family medicine plot. When they were uprooted by war and famine and plopped down in Seattle, it was only natural to plant a garden. Bok choy. Onions. Garlic. Poppies. A genuine clash of cultures.

I kept thinking about the man who had come to Trinity looking for work and who had gotten so nervous and overwrought when he spotted Doan. If the man had been correct, Doan had been a genuine despot in the old country, a journeyman torturer who delighted in his craftsmanship.

By the time I got there, wispy clouds were strung across the sky, ruining our sole peek at spring this month.

The building was in better shape than I expected. Three stories, it was constructed in a long half-moon shape. Outside hallway balconies ran alongside the doors to each apartment, balconies that were roofed and enclosed in wire fencing, painted a faded plum color. It let the air circulate but kept the kids from falling overboard.

Doan lived on the top floor center.

I abandoned my truck next to a tricked-out AMC Gremlin with slicks and lots of tacky artwork on the sides, and worked my way up the interior of the complex to Doan's apartment. A smiling Asian boy let me through the locked gate at the base of the stairs without question.

Foreign dialects assailed my ears, quick and chittering, as I passed several open-doored apartments. It was three in the afternoon and most of the men were off sweating somewhere for the sahib.

The woman who answered my rapping was not what I expected.

Tiny, hard-eyed, she looked almost Spanish, her black hair teased into a stiff bouffant. She spoke meticulous English, with only a few mispronunciations. If her speech patterns hadn't been so cultured and precise, I would have thought she might be a reformed madam. Or maybe a not-so-reformed madam. The most noticeable thing about her was her tight skirt and unbelievably pointed breasts, housed in what could only have been an extremely old-fashioned, stiff brassiere. It had probably come from Vietnam with her.

She eyed me. "Yes?"

"Does Hung Doan live here?" Two small children played with daichis on the rug in the apartment behind her, flinging them to the floor with glee.

"He's out right now. He'll be back in a little while. He went down to his work to repair a hole somebody make."

We must have crossed paths about the time I was escorting Kathy back to work. I glanced at my watch. It wasn't likely they would complete the job on the wall, just jury-rig something to tide it over for the night.

"I'll wait out in my truck."

"No, no." She had been sizing me up carefully. "You come in and wait. My husband be home soon. You come in. Are you friends with my husband?"

"Not exactly."

"I know he wouldn't want you to stay out in the truck."

"You never know."

"No, you come in. Come in." She motioned to me, waving her arm like an oar, a flashy turquoise ring swallowing most of her dinky hand. I ventured in. The moppets on the floor stared up at me with delicate eyes, and the woman said, "This is a friend of your uncle's. He's going to wait here."

In silent unison they stood and lined up beside their aunt, brown eyes glued to me. I suddenly started to feel a little queasy, like I had eaten too much fatty meat and was waking up in the middle of the night, sweaty and sick and looking for someplace to empty my guts. It was a nice little family and I was here to put a great big hole in it. I stayed nauseated until I went around the table to the sole couch in the room where she was motioning for me to sit. As I did so, I happened to look through a partially open bedroom door and saw an AK47 assault rifle leaning in a corner next to a mattress on the floor. The rifle sent a spurt of adrenaline through my system and the queasiness evaporated.

"Hung is expecting you?"

I shook my head. Not only was he not expecting me, now, with his wife and the children here, I didn't know what the hell I was going to say when he arrived. How many people did you kill this week? Who showed you how to make detective-Popsicles? How would you like a trip to a nice big American prison?

"Has your husband been home all day?"

She smiled. Her teeth were crooked in a jumbled way I wasn't used to seeing, but the smile was as cheery and inviting as any that had ever greeted me. "I think so. He got a vacation. I teach at the school so I only got home, oh, about an hour ago."

"You're a teacher?"

"I teach English. I taught high school in Vietnam."

One child, a boy of about five, sidled over, politely folded both hands on my knee and set his chin on top of his hands, gazing up at me. The woman reprimanded him in another tongue, a sharp, grunting, guttural language.

"It's okay," I said. "I like it." I ruffled his hair and wondered if his uncle was going to try to kill me when he got home. The freezer in this place would hardly hold a pussy-cat, much less a big old detective. Maybe he would trick me into sticking my tongue on it.

The four of us sat there for a minute or two, studying each other. I said, "How long have you lived in this country?"

It was like pulling a rip cord on a parachute. She had a canned spiel and I had pulled the trip wire. At first I resented it, was bored and slightly vexed, but she was unimpeachably sincere. She had witnessed horrors I could only imagine, was from a culture I couldn't even guess at—a culture that had flourished when the Puget Sound harbored only sea lions and salmon. As she spoke, I began to have more respect for her, for her courage, her strength and her ability to cope. I began to hope I was wrong about her mate.

"In Vietnam my husband keep asking during the last week if he can send his family away. We have five children and his father. The communists will surely . . . you know. So we need permission to get on one of the planes. We lived in the compound in Saigon and the communists were closing in. Everybody is very scared. People commit suicide. Many people we know kill themselves.

"My husband's best friend filled a bathtub with gasoline and sat in it and lit himself. It was a very terrible time. But no permission and no permission. We can hear the fighting outside the city. Then my husband, he gets permission. In ten minutes, we can go. I have time to pack only clothes for the kids. And some pictures. Just a few pictures. We lose everything. And two of the children are in diapers so it is mostly clothing for them that I take. And his father is very old, almost ninety. So he cannot walk without me to lean on. My hands were full.

"But the most trouble, the most trouble for me is getting permission from my parents to leave. They did not want me to leave the country. They will never see me again. Never see their grandchildren again. It is very sad for them and they do not understand. It took me a long time to convince them to let me leave. I had to beg them many times."

"You had to ask your parents?"

"Oh, yes. I cannot go without their permission." I stared at her. She didn't know how incomprehensible such a thing was in this country, a country where Lizzie Borden and others had been taking parental liberties for years.

"So then your husband came with you?"

"Hung was a colonel in the army. He couldn't come. He stayed. I went to Air Force base in Philippines. I was there four months before I know if Hung is alive or dead. And his father is sick. He is sick all this time. And I am in the hotel with these little children and his sick father. And every night I cannot sleep because I worry. It was a bad time."

She kept talking, telling me how lucky they were.

If her husband really had been guilty of atrocities in Nam, chances are she knew nothing about them, nothing at all. She came from a people who obeyed implicitly. Obeyed their parents. Obeyed their husbands. She probably knew even less of his affairs here.

She was explaining about the system of sponsor families in the U.S. and how much trouble they had had with their sponsor family when we heard somebody at the front door.

Two men chitchatting in Vietnamese walked down the corridor and emerged into the living room.

It was Hung Doan and another Asian man, a man I had never seen before. He looked like an executioner, small, compact, with mean, sunken eyes and a glinting gold tooth in the front of his mouth. He was taller and larger than Hung Doan, and I noticed immediately that he made a habit of keeping one hand buried deep in the pocket of his leather jacket. I had known gunmen who did the same thing.

Without a second thought Hung Doan turned around, raced down the hallway and out of the apartment, hollering over his shoulder in Vietnamese. His wife bestowed a horrified look on me and fell back against one wall, cradling one of the children in her arms. The boy on my knee looked appalled at first. Then grinned.

"I just want to talk," I said, rising slowly. But the apartment door slammed shut on my plea.

Locking eyes with me, the executioner backed up into the shadowed entranceway, blocking my exit, crouched, hands outstretched. His long-nailed fingers were curled into serpentine shapes, as if he might be required to gouge out an eyeball and some brains in the near future.

I looked at Hung's wife. "What did he say?"

"Maybe you wait awhile and then you go?"

"What did he say?" I yelled.

"He said you are here to arrest him for drugs."

"What'd he tell this guy?" I nodded at the man in the corridor.

"He said to stop you. He had to get away and hide things. He said to stop you."

I started down the hallway toward the hunched executioner. "Is your husband dealing drugs?"

"Maybe. Sometimes. I don't know."

I marched down the hall, feinted once and put my fist into the face of the man barring my path. The blow knocked him back against the door, where he bounced onto the carpet like a child's sand-filled balloon punching bag.

The little scamp behind me said, "Hot diggety, dog diggety. Wowee. Did you see that, Auntie Sue?" Over my shoulder I saw him perform the same stunt, a perfect mimicry.

On my way out I noticed the back of the man's head had punched a melon-shaped crater into the door.

**OUTSIDE DOAN'S APARTMENT**
I stopped and listened for the
sound of running footsteps. There was nothing but traffic
hissing a few blocks away on Rainier and a stinky city
breeze humming through the plum-colored mesh.

Below I recognized the squeaking as the gate to the
half-moon complex opened and Hung Doan clumped
across the concrete bridge, prowling the parking lot.

Automatically centering his eyesight on his own apartment door, he twisted around and spotted me first thing.

He drew something small and dark out of his jacket
pocket and extended his hand toward me, pointing the
black object.

A popping sound. A ta-whirr on the plum-colored
wire mesh. Pop. Pop. Small white puffs of smoke wafted
from the object in his fist. Ta-whirr. Chunk. Something
sounding like a very heavy bug slammed into the wall
behind me.

He was shooting. The black item impaled on his fist
was a Saturday night special. And that wasn't a discount
at the local cathouse. What a deal. I was getting slower
every day. Five years ago I would have hit the deck
before he got off the first shot.

Dropping into one very quick reverse push-up on the cement floor, I dilly-dallied an appropriate interval and then peeked through the gap at the bottom hem of the plum mesh.

Doan was disappearing into an ink-black Dodge van with one of those open vents cut into the roof. It was hard to be sure at this distance but I scratched what I thought was the license number into my notebook and started to climb to my feet.

I got almost into a half-crouch when Doan's compatriot came blasting out of Doan's apartment and bowled me over.

Startled, he backed away and clawed in his pocket. The blow from his knee into my ribs had knocked me into the mesh. When I had righted myself, I could see that he had a very ugly-looking knife in his right hand. A switchblade. The business section was long enough to pierce my chest clean through to my back and still have something left over to trim dental floss.

"Your friend is gone," I said, cocking a thumb at the van which was racing out of the parking lot, its tires shrieking like tortured cats. "No need for this."

I edged away, praying that I could backpedal out of this predicament. He trailed me, looking all the more like an executioner. No chopping block or heavy-bladed hatchet for this man. No sirree. This knight of the inner city could cheerfully lop off your head with a toad stabber.

We moved a step at a time, a rhumba student and his teacher picking across the painted footprints.

Behind the executioner an Asian woman who had been industriously stirring up small dust clouds on the concrete walk in front of her apartment caught a glimpse of his knife, of my sour-pickle face, and rushed into her apartment. The door boomed shut behind her. I could still hear her burbling a hundred words a minute in a language from the other side of the earth.

"Take it easy, fella," I said. "I'll remember your birthday next year. Okay? No wonder nobody comes to your parties."

A squiggle of blood had coursed out his nostrils and met another, wider swathe of crimson at the edge of his mouth. When he opened wide and flashed his pearlies, it looked as if he were sucking a mouthful of ketchup. The executioner's smile. His language was clipped, economical and right to the point.

"You be wearing your guts for a bow tie, mister," he said.

"Nice sentiments. But my spring wardrobe is just about complete. How about next season?"

As I finished my sentence he lunged forward, jabbing with the knife, nicking my belly. He was fast. As fast as anyone I had seen recently. Faster and trickier than Teets and his fly-catching burlesque.

I nodded at him.

"I already had this jacket tailored. Thanks anyway."

He sprang forward when I spoke, again hoping the distraction of my words would give him the edge. He swiped once, twice, three times, thrusting each time, keeping his body positioned well back of the knife.

Beside me was a small room. Inside was the mechanical ker-chunk ker-chunk noise of a washing machine. The laundry room. I heard voices advancing up the walk, the chittering of women and children. I feinted at the executioner, a right hook that I pulled before he could cut me, and used his cautionary counterfeint to snap my head to the side and check out the laundry room. It was a mere cubicle, eight feet wide and twelve feet deep holding two washers and one coin-operated dryer.

The voices behind were converging on us. The man in front of me would have no qualms about maiming third parties and I had visions of wide-eyed hostages, screaming mothers and other scenes from a foreign war.

I backed into the laundry room, quickly glancing from side to side for any domestic article I might turn into a weapon. You know the type—a chain saw somebody had already warmed up, maybe a bulldozer, a Thompson sub-machine gun with a full clip.

As soon as his small body blotted the light in the doorway, I hurled a glass ashtray at his face. He ducked his head to the side in a lightning-quick move. This sucker was fast.

I gripped the metal handle of a garbage can lid, jerked the singing lid off the can and shielded my left side with it.

A gaggle of women and children appeared in the doorway behind my tormentor, peeping over and around to see what he was butchering. When they saw the big Christmas turkey they murmured among themselves.

I grinned. I was like that. Detectives had to be cool under pressure.

None of them gave any signs of understanding English when I said, "Would you ladies mind calling the police?"

He cocked his head at the doorway and I made a move at him. I was going to pulp his brains with the garbage can lid. Instead, I skated on some damp soap flakes and went down hard, thumping my knee on the floor and pulling a muscle in my groin.

He strutted closer, a look of utter contempt contorting his bloody face. I had never seen a man who could sneer with as much heartfelt ecstasy as this man.

He was thinking to himself, how the hell did he let a gumball like me punch him out back in Doan's apartment. I was beginning to wonder the same thing.

Twice he slashed, both times making tinny cymbal sounds against the lid. I fell into the corner on my rump and scooted myself up the wall the way a rock climber might in a natural chimney, until I was on my feet again. At least for now. I gave him a ga-ga look. His expression had not changed once.

He slashed. I fended.

The people behind him in the doorway had evaporated. I guessed from their tepid expressions they had no inclination whatsoever to advise the police about the skirmish in their laundry room.

He slit the air in front of my nose. Another inch and my nose would have been flapping like the tongue of a baby's shoe.

Bracing the lid in my left hand, I threw a hook, lid and all. I managed to smash it against his knife and fist, making a muted bonging noise. He backed up, favoring that wrist. Then he switched hands with the knife. Great. A switch-hitter.

I didn't even see him move. I was watching his eyes.

Weren't the eyes supposed to telegraph the blow? They didn't. His face didn't alter one iota. Nor did the rest of his body even twitch. It didn't even shiver.

The knife just flicked out and bit me in the right shoulder.

A jolt of pain shot through to the bone.

"Mommy," I wailed. "Geez, that hurts. Why did you

do that? Oh, man, I need an ambulance. I'm going to bleed to death. You hurt me." I began crying, letting my right arm hang limp and useless. What an artiste. Surely, I would be nominated for the Maltese Falcon at this year's detectives' banquet.

The only clue I had that he was buying it was that he stood a little straighter, his eyes got a little sleepier, and the knife hand drooped a fraction of an inch. Just a fraction.

He stepped in close enough to knot up that bow tie he had promised me.

Using the wall for an anchor, I swung a right hook, aiming for the center of his face. I put all my heart into it.

If this wasn't good, my heart would end up on the floor in a puddle anyway. He caught my move, feinted, and began jabbing upward with the switchblade.

Too late.

Smack.

I hit him in the middle of his nose and mouth and just kept on driving right through him, as if I might send his head sprawling all the way to Tacoma. It was like striking a water balloon filled with blood. The little executioner flew backward, leaving his feet and landing hard—flat on his back.

Dazed, bloody, eyes watering, nose spurting, he still had a grip on the knife. I stepped in and booted his arm.

The knife flew out of his hand and he curled up like a worm some sadistic kid had plopped onto a hot plate. I peered down my nose at the tear in my jacket on my right shoulder. It stung like hell and I had almost screamed at the pain of it when I scrunched up my muscles to punch him. But there was no blood. At least not on the jacket.

He was crawling in the direction he thought the knife

had flown. He wasn't moving gracefully, or even very quickly, but he was going after the weapon. I hit him in the spine with the edge of the garbage can lid. Then the shoulder. The neck.

I frisked him. I found nothing except a packet of Marlboros and a wallet with $700 in it. I put it all back, picked him up by the scruff of his neck and his belt and packed him into a side-loading Maytag dryer. He went in as limp and compliant as a jellyfish washed up on the beach. I slammed the door behind him. Inside, he twitched once.

I placed the lid back on the can as well as it would go, found his switchblade, folded it and plopped it into my pocket. Then I located a clean cotton cloth diaper in a plastic laundry basket. I sopped up some of the bleeding on my shoulder with it, wedging it under my jacket.

Maybe I could have quizzed him, but I figured he was at least fifty percent tougher than I was, and I knew I wouldn't have said a word, so I let it go.

On the way out I flicked off the lights.

I felt woozy. I wondered whether I was going to be depressed over this one. I wasn't a killer. I knew it. Whether it was compassion or a moral sense or what—I really couldn't say—I had not been bothered enough to dissect it. I had slain only one person in my life and I was determined to keep it that way. Maybe I had been around when a few others died, but I only counted the one. But every once in a while I got crazy and mauled or got mauled by some goon. Usually we deserved what we dished out to each other, or worse. But that didn't alleviate the personal misery I felt afterward.

On the winning end of the stick or not, I felt filthy. Afterward for a time, my life seemed to flatten out. Life was supposed to be an upward journey, always finer, more beautiful, wiser, more loving, calmer, more peaceful. Onward and upward. The flattening effect was worse than depressing. And I knew it was coming again.

When I looked back down the corridor, Doan's little moppet nephew was peekabooing out the doorway of the apartment, doting on me, a broad smile insinuating itself on his face. I waved two fingers at him and was gone.

It wasn't until I was ensconced in my truck that I pulled my shirt out and found the gash across my belly. It wasn't deep. A quarter-inch line running horizontally across my gut. I took a few minutes, pulled a dressing out of the glove box and taped it on. I had a torn chest, a knife wound to the shoulder and a lacerated stomach. But I was winning all my fights. At this rate I only had to win a few more before I'd be underground.

I drove home. I limped out of the truck under my neighbor Horace's steady gaze and cloaked my bloody shirt with the flaps of my jacket. After a case a year ago when I had gotten beaten up pretty bad, Horace—retired, bored and snoopy—had snidely accused me of being a masochist, of belonging to some sick club of perverts where I hung myself on a nail and let people poke and prod and flail with sharp instruments. He didn't take my detective business seriously, was always looking for another excuse for my activities: dope dealing, burglary, selling white women to the Arabs. Horace's retirement was kept lively by my comings and goings.

"You been out huntin' wild boars?" he asked, glee ringing in his tones. "They'll gore ya like that, you let 'em get in close."

He had seen the blood tracking up my shirt and hands.

"I've been down at the pet store twisting heads off

canaries. Manny's was overstocked. How about your place? You got too many?"

Horace cleared his throat and spat across the fence into my rose bed. His home was a madhouse of squawking aviators from far-off jungles. I had been in there once, years ago, and counted eight cages. I think he had more now. One of the birds had been wearing a tiny sweater.

Stripping out of my bloodied shirt, rumpled slacks and sweaty undershirt, I eased a dressing onto the slit in my shoulder and awkwardly taped it in place. It was beginning to stiffen. I had punched the executioner pretty good after he'd jabbed me, but it was getting more and more tender. I knew that in a few hours a mere tap would make me retch. A blow to the shoulder would put me down for the count. I would get it attended to. But not now. Now, before the cops got the same notion, I had to go see what the flycatcher had left for me.

Outside, Horace was galloping around his yard behind a new power lawn mower that needed a governor on the engine.

Although it wasn't yet four o'clock, the gentle heat of the day was beginning to dissipate. An opaque layer of grayish clouds was scudding in from the north just as a special treat for me. It looked like volcanic steam.

On the drive I tried to take stock, but little came of it. Hung Doan would slither into the woodwork, at least for a while. He wouldn't have to report to work again for a month, so it was going to be hard to nab him. I still didn't know what I wanted to ask him, even if he had certain ideas of what he didn't want to say. Except that it was beginning to look more and more like he was implicated in this.

Could it be that Mark Daniels had caught Hung Doan

peddling drugs? That he had threatened to turn him over to the police? That Doan had assassinated Mark and the girl? But how did Kandy Darling figure in the imbroglio? And Teets? That poor old sagging detective with booze on his breath and bullets in his pocket. What had Teets seen that had gotten him dunked into that icy coffin?

His agency opposite the ship canal was only a minute away now. I might find out there, if the cops hadn't already ransacked it.

 SQUATTING SMACK IN THE
gut of a sleepy residential
neighborhood, the Teets Detective Agency was on the
second floor of a run-down triangular structure. The tan,
gritty siding material on the outside of the building was
split and peeling. It resembled a big hunk of chocolate
cream pie that had been forgotten at a picnic and had
hardened in the sun. A cracked upper window was
stitched with clear tape, snakeskins on the window. He
had probably ruptured the glass swatting flies. To the
locals, it had to be an eyesore.

I parked in the prickly shade of a blue spruce two
blocks away.

Finagling a warrant to search this place would eat up a
couple of hours and my guess was the cops wouldn't feel
it was worth dithering over this late in the day. They
would have to find a judge and then buck the get-home-
and-grab-a-beer traffic. I would have the hero's office all
to my lonesome.

In the musty interior stairwell I stretched up and
walked my fingers along the dust-coated sill above the
door. I flipped the mat over and sneezed at the storm it
sent up. No key. Under a ledge farther back in the

hallway I launched myself upward and did one long and laborious chin-up. Dust devils chased at my hard-breathing face. I finally unearthed his hideout key eight stairs down, cleverly secreted behind a knot in the wood.

I unlocked the door and cached the key away again, jigsawing the knot back in.

The lazy buzzing of a gaggle of fat bluebottle flies harmonized with the noises of my intrusion.

Butch Teets had left a window partially open, but the joint still reeked heavily of the man: the tang of tobacco, of booze, the stale, sun-dried paper smell of comic books and newspapers, and the musk of very idle and very lecherous thoughts.

The yellowed pine desk was chipped and scarred. Its drawers were littered with food wrappers, paper clips, bullets, packages of condoms with the cellophane seals still intact, several Washington county maps, a tattered map of L.A. and two half-full bottles of gin.

The file cabinet had four rickety drawers. The top two were crammed with comic books, most of them dog-eared from endless readings. The third drawer contained his sparse case material in file folders.

I quickly jerked open the bottom drawer before pawing through the case material. It was empty except for a worn shoulder holster with a broken buckle, two blackjacks with fish scales on them, a stiletto and some rusted wiring that looked like it was meant to be part of a bomb. His junk drawer.

None of the file folders in the third drawer down were marked, so I began at the back and worked my way forward. Gauging by the dates on the receipts, Teets had been working in Seattle for only two years. Either he hadn't kept complex notes on his cases, or he hadn't had very many cases. He must have been near starvation. No wonder the first thing on his mind when I showed up was skullduggery.

A little graft, some scam, a pinch of extortion was probably all that kept him in bullets and booze and the Classic Comics version of Charles Dickens.

Midway through the folders I stumbled upon one teeming with pornography.

None of it was commercial. Just seamy stuff he—or other detectives—had amassed on cases. From the time span indicated by the styles in the photos and the dates on the letters, he must have swapped some of this trash with other investigators who had subsisted on messy divorce cases back in the Forties and Fifties when adultery was a common stipulation for divorce—back in the good old days when door-busting and flashbulb-popping were popular rites.

Nowadays, the more common use of detectives in divorce was to track down hubbies—poor-pays. Or to locate stolen children in custody squabbles.

These photographs were more comical than lurid.

Comical or not, it took me two run-throughs to lose interest in the bundle.

Included were glossy snapshots of several minor Hollywood actors and one actress who had made it to the big leagues a few years back and then had retrogressed to TV. She had held down a bit part in a series until a year or two ago. The guy putting it to her looked twenty years her junior. Gigolo-city. My guess was that more than one of these snapshots had been the cornerstone for blackmail in L.A. County.

The folder on the Hindenburg case was almost empty, consisting of scraps of notebook paper with assorted scribbled snippets of information on them. Everything was tossed in helter-skelter as if an angry child had done his filing.

I took the folder over to the desk and plopped down with it, laying out each piece separately until I had a rectangular mosaic.

Teets had been a disorganized slob. No wonder he didn't work more than a couple of days a week. Skip tracing and runaways should have kept him solvent, even if he never took on anything else. If this was all he had on Hindenburg, I was astounded that he had even been able to scrawl a report. Maybe he hadn't. I could find no carbons.

I saw the address of the mail drop Beatrice Hindenburg had been using in the U-district. The name of the motel. Mark Daniels' name. Hindenburg's father's address in California, along with a phone number. And another name I had never seen before scratched on a corner ripped out of a glossy magazine.

Roy Earlywine.

His address and phone number were printed beneath. He lived in West Seattle, only a few minutes from the Trinity Building on Harbor Island. It was a strange piece of geography called Pigeon Point.

Riffling through the remaining file folders in Teets' battered cabinet, I didn't find anything else of interest.

I copied the address of Hindenburg's father in California and Roy Earlywine's address at Pigeon Point. Then I left.

I drove through the congealing mush of rush-hour traffic, trying to hold my temper. I got all the way across the Spokane Street Bridge without junking my truck or tooting my horn.

It took me a few minutes to unriddle the maze of detours on the other side of the bridge.

Traffic had been a snake pit in this area ever since a freighter rammed the old drawbridge in 1978. It was said that this traffic corridor saw more cars a day than any other stretch in the state except I-5. Now they had almost completed the new high span, a huge concrete arch erected to the god of commerce, the evening rush hour.

I steamed up a bitch of a hill and coursed around a sleepy little neighborhood at the top.

It was a relatively flat bluff; only the residences on the rim had a view.

Pigeon Point overlooked the bridge and the industrial tideflats. In fact, using a telescope and given a clear day, Trinity and the Daniels' house across the bay could both be seen from here.

Just up the hill from the steel mill, these had all been mill houses originally. A few of the homes were cared for, well-tended gardens being cultivated in the cruddy May afternoon, but most of them were Middle-American Junky. The Earlywine residence was an exception.

It was plopped on a tiny spur street that stretched right out to the northern edge of the bluff. In fact, it was difficult to imagine—in this slide-prone area—that in a few years the structure wouldn't suddenly vanish. Some windy December in the midst of a rainstorm it would go whoopee all the way to the bottom of the hill and skate into the river.

Earlywine greeted me at the door with a batty grin that I was certain never removed itself from his face. He was a peculiar man, elfin, balding, toothy, his mouth a mere doodle until he opened it and blinded you with all that gold bridgework. Though he was undoubtedly retired, he wore a generic green work shirt, matching work pants and muddy-brown brogans. From the first, he looked upon me as an ally.

"Hey there," he said, overflowing with ebullience. "Afternoon, afternoon. What can I do you for?" He chuckled.

"You ever talk to a detective named Seymore Teets?"

"Who? Is this a joke? Got Prince Albert in a can? Yeah, I've heard that one before. Seymore Teets. That's good."

"He called himself Butch."

"Butch?" His eyes traveled up and down my frame. "Butch? Of course. You a friend of his'n? Come on in. Sure, I remember Butch. It was kind of a strange transaction 'cause I seen him through my scope there and then 'bout half an hour later he comes knockin' at my door. Ain't never seen anybody do that before. Said he caught a glint off my scope. The man has good eyes. You imagine that, from all the way down beyond West Marginal, clean up to here?"

He ushered me into his house and to a sitting room off a balcony. The wooden balcony had nothing below it but rustling treetops and below that, traffic: cars and boats, and a policeman racing across the waterway, blue and red lights winking at us.

What magnetized me, though, was the mammoth telescope mounted on a tripod. It was set next to the balcony door so that in foul weather one could gaze through the glass.

It was a marine telescope of some sort, only went up to a 120 power. It had a huge eyepiece. Earlywine giggled when he saw me gaping at it. He was the kind of guy who spent a half hour telling a grocery clerk he had never seen before all about the tumor on his colon. Gas station attendants he saw regularly were considered best friends. His barber was in his will.

"You must be a detective, too. That's the same damn thing Teets headed for. Just like a homing pigeon. Zoom. Right for that scope."

I introduced myself. "Roy Earlywine," he said, extending a dry hand.

"I'm interested in what you discussed with Teets."

"Wasn't much. 'Bout two months ago. Must have been the first of March or the tail end of February. See, I seen him down there. I keep a mighty keen watch below the bridge." He rubbed his hands together.

"It's a spoonin' spot. Don't you know? I seen more . . ." He gave me a conspiratorial wink and peered around the house for the old woman. "I seen more fuckin' and suckin' down there in the last thirty years than you could shake a stick at. You look through this scope here, you'll see what I mean. Hell, I don't need no television when I got this. Fact is, I hardly never go out. The old lady can't figure it. She thinks I watch boat traffic on the Duwamish."

He gestured for me to peek through the scope. I walked over, bent, and placed my face up to it, half expecting my eye to get blackened.

Earlywine was just the type to pull that tired gag. It was blurry until I screwed down the adjustment knob. He had it fine tuned to one of the crews working on the new bridge.

"Let me get it right for you," he said, shouldering me away. He smelled of weeds and trees and throat medication.

When he freed the scope it was centered on a female

worker on the bridge, wearing tight jeans and a flapping tool belt.

"Ain't them steel workers something?" He gulped.

"What about Teets? Where did you see him?" Using an expert facility borne of years of patient self-tutelage, Earlywine swung the scope down, zeroed in on his target and surrendered the instrument to me.

At this range and low power the distortions from heat waves were almost nonexistent. The scope had sucked a piece of land underneath the old Spokane Street Bridge up to my eyes, making it look close enough to be just across the room. The packed earth had that parched-flesh color to it.

"Nobody there right now," said Earlywine. "But that's where they park. Come down to spoon where they think nobody can see 'em." He tittered. "You won't believe some of the hijinks I seen down there. I mean, it'd keep you entertained for a month of Sundays. Right in broad daylight, too, if you can believe that. There's one couple, must be skipping out at lunch hour. They show up every Monday and Thursday, just like clockwork. Sit in his camper and spoon. Pretty soon they slide up through the rear window of the cab into the back. Usually they park so I can see it all through the windshield. Now, last week the light struck it wrong and I couldn't see so well. It gets a little bad in May and then again for a week or so in September."

"What was Teets doing down there?"

"Seen a pair of kids down there once. A pair in the front seat, a pair in the back. They went at it and about every five minutes the kid in the front would hop over the seat and trade rides with the kid in the back. If that don't beat all." Earlywine's smile was frozen, his gold-laced

teeth slightly bucktoothed. His deep-throated chortles
sounded like something from after midnight at the zoo.

"You said you saw the detective down there. What was
he doing? Did he have a woman with him?"

"Woman? Hell, no. He was just poking around.
Turned out he was followin' this lady in a Caddy. They
was a couple of my regulars until just recently. For some
damned reason they used to show up early in the
morning. I guess people have to be naughty when they
got the time. Threw my schedule all out of whack. I like
to work out in the yard in the mornings. Havin' to sit here
and wait for them threw a real crimp in my day."

"A Cadillac?"

"Brand-new. Leastways, I think it was a Cadillac.
Them new cars is so danged hard to tell apart anymore.
That detective fella was the one—I guess—told me it
was a Caddy. He was down there poking around. Had a
fellow once used to go down there almost every morning
and pick up used conundrums. Know what I mean?
Picked 'em up with a stick and dropped 'em into a little
paper bag. Never could figure out what his game was."

"So Teets saw you up here?"

"Mother McCree, he did. First time that ever happened, too. He had a pair of bitsy field glasses hanging
around his neck and he went down to where they parked
and just started a-swinging around the territory. Pretty
soon he fixed on me. Dangdest thing you ever saw.
About a half hour later he shows up at the door. He
wanted to see the whole setup. Just like you."

"What'd he ask you about?"

"Just that Caddy. Wanted to know how many times a
week it showed up. That sort of thing."

"Think you might recognize the driver?"

He shrugged, smirked and spoke softly. "Maybe not with all his clothes on. Course, he liked to strip the girl naked and leave most of his things on. Kept that cowboy hat on most of the times I seen him."

"Cowboy hat?"

"Big. You know. Ten-gallon jobbie. With one of those brims that bites down in front, like that there supersonic airplane the French made."

"The Concorde?"

"Yeah. The brim bites down just like that."

"Same girl every time?"

"Not him. Had all sorts. Young though. Always young. Why are you after him? He some sort of criminal?"

I unfolded my newspaper clippings of Hindenburg and Mark Daniels. "Recognize either of these?"

"Her?" He shook his head. "Him? I suppose that might be him. Sure, that's him. The beard."

"Did Butch show you any pictures?"

"Nope. He sat there and gawked through that scope for a good three hours though. Didn't see nothin'. You almost have to live with it to make it pay off. You know, take a peek every half hour or so when you're passing through the room. I ain't been living on this point for thirty years for nothin'."

"You ever see this same fellow driving another car?"

"Don't think so."

"How about a Volkswagen Rabbit? You ever see him in one of those?"

He shook his head. "Them Rabbits has got a lot of glass. Somebody gets a-humpin' and a-sweatin' in one of them and you see it all. Lots of glass. Love 'em. I would have remembered if I'd seen him in one of those."

Odd. According to his friends, Mark Daniels drove the Rabbit exclusively. The Cadillac was Deanna's car. The way I understood it, he only drove it when they were going somewhere together. It seemed more than unlikely that he would drive his wife below the bridge to make out in the car. Only a nut would do a thing like that. Maybe he was borrowing his wife's car to impress his dates.

So if Teets had tailed Hindenburg to the bridge, Teets had either made a mistake—had tailed someone else with Hindenburg—or Daniels was routinely borrowing somebody else's car. Several of his friends had Cadillacs. But that didn't make any sense. Why under the bridge? He had the office he could go to at night. He had the love nest up at the lake. He even had the Galaxie Motor Court Inn.

What was wrong with him that he would be penny-pinching underneath a bridge with the trolls on the hill scoping out every move he made and following along in their paperback copy of the *Kama Sutra*? Penny-pinching? Nothing that I had found out about Mark had indicated he was cheap. Just the reverse. Daniels had always been generous to a fault, except for the Galaxie Motor Court Inn, and I attributed that to his desire for secrecy.

I was staring at the sawtooth tutti-frutti cityscape when the old man interrupted my reveries. "You care to sit here a spell?"

"No, thanks. This fella always wore the beard?"

Earlywine scratched his scalp and then rammed an index finger into his ear and screwed it around until he had enough wax to roll up into a ball between his fingers. He rolled and thought and then dug into the mine again for more raw material.

"Now that you mention it, I don't think he did. Come to think of it. When he first started coming down there he never had the beard. Then he had it for a while and then . . . I don't know, but I would swear he come once or twice without it. Them whiskers a-his must grow awful danged fast."

"Probably some sort of tonic," I said, moving through the living room to the front door. "By the way. What color was that Cadillac?"

"Gray? Steel gray."

"Think it might have been something else? A Chrysler, maybe?"

"Sure, coulda been. I didn't watch the car that much."

I got into my truck and jumped back into the stream of rush-hour commuters, bucking the tide this time, heading back into town.

Gray. Steel gray. Deanna's Cadillac was steel gray. For that matter, with her hair done up differently each time, Deanna could easily have passed for a succession of different girls. Trouble was, Wheeler's Chrysler was steel gray, too.

 **THE REVEREND SAM WHEELER**
lived in Renton, a burgeoning
community off the southern tip of Lake Washington. I
had never visited the Reverend in his digs. Maybe this
evening would be a good time, if he wasn't entertaining
too many insurance salesmen, or converting too many
tearful runaways.

All I had propelling me was a description of a car that
may or may not have been his—I figured a Chrysler was
easy enough to confuse with a Caddy (and his car was
gray)—along with my complete and unreasoned dislike
for the man.

With my tender right shoulder, it was growing difficult
to steer, and I was doing most of my driving now with
my left hand. The pain had blossomed into something
I wouldn't forget soon. I winced when I worked the
gearshift on the column, even moaned to myself when I
thought nobody in another car would see me. Some
people got caught singing to themselves in the car, some
picking their noses. I didn't want to get caught moaning.

It would be a long night.

It was a new house in a look-alike development. Some
harebrained genius with an itch in his wallet had chopped

down all the trees and, skimping by using only one set of plans, had nailed up sixty look-alike ranchero-style houses in drab pastel hues. In front of Wheeler's dream box were two skinny ornamental cherry trees in circular flower beds along with a slab of putting turf trucked in from Portland. You could tell how old these projects were by the age of the trees in the yards. This one was about six years. Behind the house was a narrow strip of woods awaiting the next sharp-eyed developer and his bulldozers.

Wheeler's Chrysler was in the drive, looking more like a Caddy than ever. Beside it sat a sporty new Mazda.

Cruising past, I caught sight of a heavyset woman in the kitchen window, her hair clipped so short they wouldn't bother to crop the stubble when she enlisted. Her age made her a stronger prospect for Sam's wife than his mother, though she looked more like the latter, her expression lusterless and weary, features sagging in the twilight.

I didn't see Sam. Deanna had told me they had no children.

Two miles beyond their house I hit a shopping center and tanked up on hamburgers and soft ice cream cones. I slipped into a convenience store and selected a cheap pair of sunglasses, a dippy plaid golfing cap, and to assist in speeding the night along, a couple of magazines and the evening paper.

Then I went to a phone booth, thumbed a quarter in and dialed my business number. The whiny kid had left another session of smut on my recorder. "Hey, mister detective. Did you hear the one about the four high school boys who hitchhiked to Tijuana to catch the donkey act? They took a dog, a cat, a rat and a mouse."

The finish of the joke didn't impress me. Each joke he put on my tape was more gross than the preceding one. I would nab him. When I got time I would track down and apprehend the little bastard. I phoned Leech, Bemis and Ott and asked for Kathy. The nasal-sounding switchboard operator told me she had gone home for the day.

I drove back past the Wheeler house. Nothing had changed. Making certain the snout of the truck was hidden, I reversed into a gravel road six blocks south, slumped down until my wounded shoulder was in a comfortable posture and munched from a can of unsalted party nuts.

From here I could only cover half of their possible exits, but it seemed the more likely direction of travel. The major highways and the shopping center were both this way. When I finally logged the time into my notebook, it was a shade past six o'clock.

I slouched in my plaid hat and cheesy sunglasses and watched the tail end of the world race home to gobble dinner and de-flea the dog. The sunlight might last another hour, maybe less.

When the sporadic traffic abated, I paged through the paper. Butch Teets had made the last column of the first section, directly over a sexy ad for women's lingerie. He would have liked that. The article didn't mention that he had been found frozen in a block of ice, just that his corpse had been discovered at the Trinity Dog Food plant. There was no mention of the two other bodies that had been discovered there a week earlier.

Shortly after 8:30, Wheeler sped past in his Chrysler. I recognized his profile in the diaphanous dusk. He was alone in the car, driving like a volunteer fireman on his way to a conflagration, except that he was wearing a ten-gallon cowboy hat, the brim turned down in front, like a Concorde superliner.

I turned over my engine, but before I could head for his house to reconnoiter, another vehicle passed in front of me, traveling the same direction Wheeler had. It was a dark gray Mercedes 380SL—Emmett Anderson's car. And Anderson was behind the wheel, sitting forward, nose up almost against the windshield, a hound after the fox. Interesting. I let them flitter away.

I drove past Wheeler's house. The Mazda was still slotted in the drive. The curtains were pulled, the living room lights low.

A couple of hours of electronic diversion and she'd hit the sack. If I didn't poke fate in the keister, I might be there until dawn waiting for my chance to slip a lock and paw through Wheeler's Bible clippings. The area was too open for a daylight burglary. And if I kept the place staked out from my truck for that length of time, somebody was bound to spot me and grow suspicious. Then, too, my arm was growing steadily more painful, throbbing with a heavy, dull ache that had struck up a cadence to the tune of my heartbeat. Later I might not have the mobility. Besides, things were breaking fast. If my assumptions were correct, a lot of interesting artifacts might be obliterated before the sun popped up.

A foray into another person's house was something an ethical detective had to think twice about. And I did. I always thought about it—*twice*. My problem was, I had performed the abomination so frequently it no longer seemed abnormal. Sometimes I even felt a pang of guilt, but it rarely slowed me. And it never dampened my enthusiasm. Poking through somebody else's life was one of the prime thrills of the job. If the police were allowed to toss the home of everyone they suspected, their success rate would rocket twenty-fold. More often than not they had a gut feeling about who they were after, but just couldn't hatch any evidence.

I trekked all the way back to the shopping center. Looking up Wheeler's number in the Renton white pages, I dialed and cooked up a spiel while I listened to the buzzing.

"Mrs. Wheeler?"

"Yes." Her voice was husky and smoky, as if she did a lot of screaming or sucking on cigarettes. Or both.

"This is Officer Raphael from the State Patrol. I don't want to alarm you, but a man has been in a minor traffic accident. We've got him here at Valley General and he's taken a little bump on the noggin. He doesn't quite remember who he is at the moment."

"Sammy? Sammy's been in an accident? Is the car all right?"

"Mrs. Wheeler, we found your phone number in his things. But he doesn't seem to have any ID on him. At least we couldn't find it. Do you think you might know this man?"

"That's my husband. He always drives like a maniac. He's not . . ."

"Just a bump on the head, Mrs. Wheeler. He will need someone to fill out the forms and take him home. He's in no condition to drive."

"He always speeds. I told him. Is the car all right?"

"I couldn't say. Trooper Hanford is handling that end of it. When can you be down here?"

"Twenty minutes. I'll be there in twenty minutes. Damn. He let the insurance lapse. I knew he shouldn't have done that."

On the drive out I passed Mrs. Wheeler who was looking grim-faced and distraught and bending the steering wheel of her sporty little Mazda. She had decamped in such a mad scramble she had forgotten to flip her headlights on. I blinked her and peeked in the mirror to see if it took. No dice.

Twenty minutes out to the hospital. Five minutes to discover it had been a fraud. Maybe longer if she were inept and began phoning other hospitals instead of calling the State Patrol direct. She didn't look inept. So, twenty minutes out. Five minutes of screwing around and twenty minutes back. Forty-five minutes. I set the stop watch on my digital. I would vacate the premises in twenty-five.

The biggest problem would be if she got really cute and dialed the Renton cops from the hospital to warn them a burglary was in progress at her place. Or if Sam returned.

It took eight minutes to locate the road behind the development. I parked under cover of some twelve-foot-tall Scotch broom.

Taking a small flashlight from the glove box, along with my all-purpose sawed-off crowbar on a loop, I navigated through the thinning woods until I could see the line of lights on the other side. Not bad. I was only three houses too far south.

A dog on a chain next door yapped. I hurled a piece of cold hamburger from my dinner at him. He gobbled it, woofed once, and stood wagging his tail, silent, waiting for me to pitch another morsel. Like a lot of us, he could be bought.

She had left the lights burning. Blistering my

fingertips, I unscrewed the back porch bug bulb until it winked out. I tried the door. Bolted.

It took only a second to locate a sliding window she had neglected to secure. I popped the screen off. It was a small window, chest height, the room behind it pitch-black. Probably a utility room. No need for my flashlight yet. I would crawl in and land on the washing machine. A cinch. When you'd been at something as long as I had, you learned things.

I wormed through the window feet-first, one-armed and awkward because of the soreness and growing stiffness in my shoulder. Immediately I sank up to my hips in what felt like a hot mineral spring.

It smelled as if I had been dipped in a huge bucket of lukewarm piss.

I took a step to the east and sank deeper.

Stifling an almost overpowering urge to yelp, I pulled my flashlight out and evaluated the situation.

"Oh, tish."

I was up to my belt buckle in a hot tub. They had dumped some chemicals into it, thus the peculiar, unnerving odor.

Wading to the wooden edge and gripping the rim, I hoisted myself out and dropped onto the floor, my shoes sounding like a cow chewing her cud each time I took a step. I grappled with a towel in the dark and dried myself off as well as I could.

Ever try toweling your pants off when you're still wearing them?

Eleven minutes had elapsed. It had only taken me three to bamboozle a dog, break into a house and plunge into their hot tub. In another ten maybe I could take advantage of the cat and plop into the septic tank.

I sloshed to the back door, cracked it open and set it so it would lock after I went out, readying my getaway. Then I replaced the window screen and straightened up the mess I had made in the hot tub room.

My footsteps were loud and watery as I tiptoed around the house, watchful for a guard dog. I knew they didn't have any children, but I wasn't sure about bloodthirsty canines. A year ago a pit bull had snapped at my buttocks from behind a couch when I was prowling somewhere I wasn't supposed to be prowling. I whapped him with my sawed-off crow bar and accidentally broke his neck, killing him. I had been forced to carry him out in a gunnysack and bury him. I don't know what his owner made of it. Lock your dog in the house; go to the store and come home to find he has vanished.

Usually I could smell a dog on the premises, or a smoker, even a doper; but tonight all I could smell was the humid and salty chemical bath I had just immersed myself in. My sloshing, sodden clothes reeked.

Everything on the main level of the house was her territory. It all had her stamp. The elegant and spindly gold-colored furniture. The kitchen, so jammed with convenience items she had no counter space. But most of all, the living room with its organ—a simplified musical arrangement of "Raindrops Keep Falling on My Head" splayed open on the music holder—and rows of softball trophies lined up on the granite mantel. There were photos of Mrs. Wheeler with three different women's softball teams. Photos of her as a child, alongside her mother, and one of her graduating from college. Her entire life was chronicled in the room, with nary a hint that Sam Wheeler existed. Strange.

Moving quickly, I frisked the bedrooms. Skulking

from room to room, I looked for his lair. His hangout. It turned out to be a nook over the garage up a set of stairs off the living room. Sam Wheeler was using it for a den. One entire wall was lined up with packaged gifts of the type promoters gave away at weekend-condominium sales meetings. Coffeemakers. Ice-cream makers. Inexpensive power tools. Some of them even had the promotional trappings still taped on. Ponderosa Pines Lodge and Condos. Fir Trails Living.

Miserly to the last, Sam had wrapped some in Christmas wrapping paper and stowed them in the closet. Only seven months early. The Reverend Wheeler braved all the promotional hype, accepted the free two-day vacation with a sincere look on his mug and collected his booty. If they were giving, he was taking. I sorted through the name tags, but couldn't find mine.

The rolltop desk was not locked. I went through it quickly. On top sat an eight-by-ten of Deanna Daniels. It was signed "With love, DeeDee." It could have meant nothing. Or everything. Her face gazed out at me while I burglarized Wheeler's den. I glanced back at it from time to time, wondering about this morning's frolic.

The desk didn't have anything in it that I thought I needed.

On the stereo in the back of the room a record album had been abandoned. The Oak Ridge Boys. He listened to country and western. That meant something. Three pairs of hand-tooled cowboy boots were lined up along the wall. On the top shelf of the closet, along with prewrapped Christmas presents, were several cowboy hats and, hanging on a hook, three or four gaudy bolo ties.

I looked at my watch. Sixteen minutes had elapsed. Nine left.

It irked me that I wasn't making progress. I didn't like anything about Sam Wheeler and now I didn't like anything about his house. It was too neat and it was segregated into male and female sections in such a rigid manner I knew something had to be drastically wrong with their marriage. But so far I hadn't found the incriminating items I had hoped for.

His papers were either published copies of sermons other ministers had given, highlighted in yellow grease pen—the portions he was going to purloin—or various financial documents. He had over $18,000 in a money market fund. In one mutual fund he owned over 30,000 shares. I didn't know what the market value of the shares was, but it had to be substantial. Over $100,000 worth, easily. There were several other share certificates from mutual funds. And a Keogh account worth over $150,000. The man had raked in his spoils.

Everything was tidy and in its place. Even the book of carefully clipped and filed coupons. Fifteen cents off on asparagus soup. Twenty-five cents off on single-ply toilet tissue. If there was a penny to be saved, Wheeler saved it.

I glanced at my watch. If I was going to get out of the house within the safety margin, I only had three minutes.

A small, flat metal box next to the telephone contained a notepad. I held it up to the light and saw the impressions from the last message he had scribbled. Ripping the page off, I tucked it into my shirt pocket.

Behind the desk on the wall was a cork board. Most of the notes were telephone numbers and business cards, but one scrap of paper said: Deanna Ascue—Purdy Correctional Center, spring of 1978 to January of 1979. Deanna Ascue? That couldn't be the maiden name of a woman I was growing attached to?

The steamer trunk in the bottom of his closet had a bulletproof padlock on it. I had seen them shooting steel-jacketed bullets at one on TV, so it had to be bulletproof. I tugged the trunk out into the light and levered the hasp off with the crow bar, prying until I had torn an ugly hole in the lid where the rivets had been. Any hope of keeping my break-in covert was gone now.

I had broken the lock, and it was probably filled with Bibles.

Inside I found three pairs of handcuffs, some old sweaters and a mashed spot in the clothing where it looked like a large book had lain until recently. The imprint in the sweaters was very clear.

Below the cuffs was a photo album, aged, the binding cracked. The Wheeler family album. The front page was devoted to yellowed newspaper articles about a husband-wife murder-suicide that had occurred forty years ago in Ravensdale, Washington. Wheeler had been raised by stepparents. When he was a child, his real mother had been murdered by her jealous husband—Sam's father—who, in turn, sent a bullet through his own gums and into his brain pan. A toddler at the time, after the murder-suicide Sam had been found asleep in another room by curious neighbors.

Fleeced by fate, Sam had lived his life under a cloud. The scenario two weeks ago at the Trinity Building had been a rerun of the Reverend Sam Michael Wheeler's own private nightmare.

I shifted my weight and I looked at my watch. Twenty-seven minutes. The cops might be here any second. I was cutting it close. Far too close.

Chinking open the blinds at the window, I glanced up and down the street.

It was just bald-ass luck that I looked out when I did.

Blue lights flashing a quarter of a mile away. The Renton police were on to me. Without sirens, they were racing up the street to apprehend the intruder. Perhaps gun him down. I had maybe fifteen seconds to escape.

Mrs. Wheeler was an alert hombre. She must have phoned the police as soon as she got to the hospital. Or maybe one of the neighbors had seen something suspicious. I had switched on a light or two. Damn, I was getting sloppy and careless in my old age. Kathy, who thought everyone over thirty was senile, had been warning me for five years about Alzheimer's. Breaking and entering. Tish, I could get a year in jail for this, maybe two.

Two at a time, I descended the stairs to the living room. I missed the last step, stumbled, twisted an ankle, and smashed into the wall. I hobbled to the back door, clicked it shut behind myself and sprinted in an ungainly gait to the woods.

I didn't slow down when I heard the deep-chested barking behind me.

A German shepherd. A police tracking dog.

22 I SLAMMED THE DOOR OF the pickup shut a split second before an indignant German shepherd galloped out of the brush and performed a little fox trot on his hind legs. His plump front paws chiselled curlicues of red paint off the side panel of my Ford.

"That's a new wax job, buddy."

Tongue lolling out the side of his ragged, yellowing molars, drool yo-yoing off his toothy jaw, he woofed in my face while I hastily cranked up the window.

After I had a sheet of safety glass between the Alsatian and myself, I woofed back, turned the engine over and eased the clutch in, trying not to churn up too much dust with my exit. The dog vacillated next to the Scotch broom and blackberry thickets, barking.

No shamus steaks tonight.

The officers had to be a good ways behind and if I was lucky they wouldn't figure out I was scramming in a vehicle until it was too late to pursue. They were probably still back at the house inspecting locks and cupping their hands against the windows. Years ago when I was wearing a uniform, that's what I would have done.

Not that they could trace me; I had worn rubber gloves during the burglary.

It wasn't until I was driving under the dirty, shadowy air of Seattle again that I began to relax. My right shoulder was killing me from slamming into the wall. Until now the pain had been blotted out by massive doses of uncalled-for adrenaline.

On Beacon Hill I parked in front of a Chinese restaurant. I went in to see how greasy the earpiece on the public phone was. My pants were still damp and sticking uncomfortably to my legs, but the people in the dark restaurant didn't seem to notice.

I pushed some coins into the black box and dialed.

"Kathy?"

"Thomas? Where are you? I've been calling madly all over town trying to find you. I've had a real bad feeling all afternoon. You all right?"

"Who rode a horse named Tarzan?"

She thought a minute. "Ken Maynard."

"You just won a free plane trip around Wayne Cody."

I told her where I was and asked her to meet me there.

"Are you in trouble?"

"I'm a little bruised, but no trouble. I ran into a minor snafu, but I'm out of it now."

"I never should have let you roam off on your own after we found that dead detective today. Your stupid machismo—code of the West and all that. You're out to avenge him, aren't you?"

"Listen, Mark Daniels didn't commit suicide. Somebody murdered him—and murdered the girl, too. I think I know who."

"Who? Can you prove it?"

"There's so much involved I don't even know where

to start. I need you to kick this around with me. I always get ideas when I'm talking to you."

"Thomas, you're not still trying to pin some of this on Reverend Wheeler?"

"Whoever."

The line was silent for a few moments. "Thomas, you didn't like him from the moment you laid eyes on him. Some sort of male territorial dispute is my guess. Over Deanna Daniels. Don't quibble when you know I'm right. I took psychology in college. We're not that far removed from the apes. You know what the odor under your arms is for, don't you?"

"A signal to change my shirt?"

"The sweat glands are what apes use to stake out their territory, just like cats when they go around spraying. Apes rub their underarms on leaves and things.

"You males are all alike. You think I didn't see what was going on? Reverend Wheeler had her. You wanted her. He had staked out his territory. You wanted it. Well, it wasn't going to work out. You should have seen that from the first."

"You read me like a book, Kathy. Just come on over and see me."

"What . . . are you wearing a raincoat?"

"You *wish*. I'll order you a fortune cookie. If you leave now, you can make it in fifteen minutes. My head's spinning and what I need is for somebody I trust to talk this through with me. I'm right on the verge of busting this whole thing wide open."

"The detective and the girl at the lake? I spoke to Ralph Crum. The detective died the same way the girl did. A blow to the windpipe. They're connected to Mark and the Hindenburg girl?"

"Hop to it."

I slumped down in a booth under an ornate fire-breathing dragon stippled into the wall.

When the lady in the red silk sheath minced to my table I ordered tea. The dinner hour was long gone and most of the hired hands were in the back chewing the fat.

After the tea came, I absent-mindedly inquired of the waitress if I could borrow the pencil stub tucked over her ear. She gave me a queer look and lined up the stub beside my teapot. After I scalded my tongue on the tea, I took out the slip of paper I had taken from the pad in Wheeler's study.

Selecting a steak knife from the silver setting the waitress had left, I chipped away at the pencil lead until I had enough pulverized graphite. Then I dabbed my index finger in it and rubbed it across the paper.

The etchings were pale, barely readable. I darkened them with the edge of the pencil. It said Trinity. There was a number: 9:30. And a name. I X-rayed it at the light, scanning the faint scrawls.

Then I bolted from the restaurant.

The wide-eyed waitress rushed after me and caught me at the door. I pushed a five-dollar bill into her hands and said, "A pretty brunette is going to show up in about five minutes. Tell her I had an emergency. Tell her not to worry."

As if English were a second language for both of us, the waitress nodded dumbly.

The Trinity plant was a place with a hex on it and I almost couldn't believe what I had read on the note paper. The name was barely distinguishable so there was a good chance I was in error. It had to be a mix-up. Sure, it was all a misunderstanding.

Spokane Street whisked me to Harbor Island quicker than I thought possible. It was 9:25 when I bolted out of the restaurant and 9:33 when I parked in the Trinity lot. Leaving my truck door ajar so as not to make any unnecessary racket, I switched off my headlights and trundled across the lot.

I could see that the lights were on in the warehouse, and farther back the lamps in the dog food plant were blazing, too. Inside the office building, only the lamps over the reception area were lit. The offices off the open balcony were all dark and shadowy except for one. It had belonged to Mark Daniels.

Quietly I ascended the carpeted steps and tiptoed down the hallway. The door was half open and the only sound coming out of the office was a radio tuned to some broken-voiced, sad sack crooner moaning about his cheatin' woman—a country-western station.

Crouched behind the desk, she was going through Mark's drawers, stuffing items in a series of cardboard boxes, her hair floating down past her waist, brushing the floor. She was dressed in khaki pants and a bright, short-sleeved blouse.

As soon as I saw her, the morning's clinches blurred through my mind at twice the speed of light. I remembered legs and kisses and hugs and stupid whisperings that had seemed momentous at the time, but rang with insincerity in my already-fuzzy memory. Rings around her eyes, she looked weary and saddened. I wanted to walk over and take her in my arms. I didn't budge.

When Deanna looked up at me she gave a start, traced her tongue around the outline of her fuchsia lips. "Thomas? How did you know I was here?"

As she spoke, she glanced behind the door. I followed her eyes.

The man said, "Howdy."

Grinning, Sam Wheeler stood behind me in cowboy boots, faded jeans, a rustic-looking shirt with a bolo tie knotted at his neck, topped off with a fancy, chalk-colored cowboy hat. Spiffy. He was duded up for a square dance. He imbued the manner of a TV newscaster who was shooting for the top of the heap—Network. He was genial, charming and a bit opaque. He folded his arms across his chest and continued grinning, a twisted mixture of frenzy, gloating and bald discomfort.

"Fancy meeting you here," he said, enunciating out the side of one cheek. Suddenly he was all apple pie, and wet and bruised as I was, I felt like the grease monkey who had stumbled into the wedding.

Gracefully, Deanna stood and, using the flats of both palms, smoothed the wrinkles across the front of her slacks. She took a wide swing with her head and flipped her hair behind her shoulder.

"What brings you here?" she asked, a hitch in her voice.

"I could ask you both the same thing."

"We're just . . ." Her mouth and throat went dry. "We're just cleaning up a few . . . a few things."

"I bet you've got a lot of things in your life you want to clean up."

Deanna shot me a hurt look and then glanced at Sam Wheeler.

Wheeler spoke, his words confident and brash. "Don't get uppity, Black. You don't have any business in this place or with this woman. You've overstepped your bounds one too many times."

He moved toward me.

"I'm going to find out the truth about Deanna's husband."

"Everybody knows what happened. It's an open book."

"It will be very shortly."

"What does that mean?" Wheeler stepped closer. He was one of those rare scalawags who didn't seem to know when he was violating somebody else's personal space. Without fail, every time we met he blundered into mine. He stepped into it now, and it was all I could do to keep from putting my fist into his face.

"Thomas, I asked you not to pursue this. I begged you." A tear squeezed out of Deanna's eye and starred her blouse. She looked like a woman standing over a fresh grave.

"Hear that?" said Wheeler, tersely. "You've just been decommissioned. Buzz off."

"Sam." She shook her head and repeated herself, speaking much more softly. "Sam."

He looked at her and sneered. I wanted more than ever to plant a handful of knuckles into that smarmy face.

"Please leave, Sam. Remember what we said? Please leave."

"You don't want me to go away, DeeDee. Things are going to be tough for a while. You don't want me to go away."

"Get out, Sam!"

He pivoted and ran his pale blue eyes over my face, sizing up the opposition. "I could say some things."

"You wouldn't, Sam . . ."

"Sure, I would. I'll bet Tommy here doesn't have an inkling, does he?"

"Sam, don't do it."

"Why not? Some big secret? I could tell him a whole heck of a lot of things that might open his eyes."

"You mean you might tell Thomas we had an affair? I was just about to do that myself." Deanna swerved her eyes frantically between Sam Wheeler and me, trying to gauge the voltage and meter of the electrical current in the air. She needed to know where she stood with *one* of us. I couldn't tell which one concerned her more, but her eyes seemed to be spending most of their time on me.

Sam didn't move. He didn't have to. I had been on the verge of lambasting him since I had walked into the room.

What set me off was the mere cant of that goofy, thick-lipped smirk.

"Sure thing," he said glibly. "DeeDee's been my little sweetheart for quite some time now."

Swinging from my belt, I caught him under the chin with a steely left. It was just as much of a stunner to me as it was to him. I didn't even realize I was doing it until it was over.

He staggered back two or three steps, wiped his mouth, a look of fear on his mug. Blood wormed down his chin from a split in his lower lip. I almost laughed. What was an out-of-shape fat man going to do to me?

He turned his back on me, and too late, I realized it was a karate move, a very advanced karate move. You've seen it—the one where the man turns his back on his opponent only to pick up speed and swipe his head off with a high sweep of his leg.

Two walls and the ceiling lunged at me simultaneously.

As it happened I thought it must have been a freak

earthquake mixed with some sort of extraterrestrial experience.

Then the floor reached up and snatched me hard, banging me with about a ton of force. When I tried to get up, I found that I was lying partially under Mark Daniels' desk.

Woozy, eyes unfocused, I cocked my head up and thumped my forehead on the sharp corner of the desk. Sam Wheeler was standing over me, blood dripping from his chin, crouched in a battle posture, both arms winged out for combat.

"Get out, Sam," Deanna said between clenched teeth. "You are no longer welcome here. Now, get the hell out."

By the time I cleared the cobwebs and sat myself on the stainless steel and leather couch, the door was closed and I was alone in the room with Deanna Daniels. All I could smell was perfume and blood and maybe a little fear. My own. It seemed like I was losing all my recent skirmishes.

 SHE SAT ON THE COUCH
beside me—so close her
weight sank me against her until I could feel the pleasant
warmth of her thighs through my still-damp pants.

Ministering gently, she walked her fingertips across a
part of my head that—from the inside—felt like a truck
tire some ignoramus had chewed up on a curb.

"That awful boot of his made a nasty mark," she said,
making me feel like a baby. It was a feeling I could grow
used to. "Are you all right, Thomas? You had a faraway
look in your eyes."

By degrees I screwed up my face and brought her into
focus, forcing my roiling thoughts down to a mere
simmer. In a minute I would get up and start a minor war
with a small country. In a minute.

"I thought you were twins," I quipped. She laughed a
quick, chittering laugh.

"Sam's a surprise a minute, isn't he? Somebody who
knew how to fight taught him everything."

"So I see." I was lucky he hadn't gone bonkers and
gouged out my eyeballs. Years ago I had seen a man in a
back-alley brawl tap dance on a pair of eyeballs. It
wasn't pretty. Right now I felt like those gritty eyeballs.

233

Deanna had fetched a washrag and dampened it at the sink during the interlude when my brain was barnstorming the hinterlands. As she sponged off my feverish brow, I realized my neck was shot through with excruciating pinprick pains. My right eye, swelling like the rupture in an inner tube, was taking in less every moment.

"Don't feel bad," she said. "You got in a good one."

"A good what?"

"A good lick. You gave him a real smart rap on the chin. It almost knocked him out. For a minute there I thought he was going down for the count."

"He seemed to have plenty of spunk left when *I* last saw him."

"You did fine."

"Did somebody kick me or was that a beer truck?"

Though I had initiated the joust, she was on my side all the way. Unhorsed and thoroughly thrashed as I was, here the fair maiden sat patiently at my side, comforting and consoling, patting me, soothing. Somehow it didn't vitiate the pain and humiliation.

"My arm was hurt earlier, see. And I haven't really been feeling all that hot. I've been running around all day . . . off my feed. A guy stabbed me this afternoon . . ."

"You don't have to make up excuses. I don't think any less of you because of what just happened."

The fat little pig, I thought. Where on earth had he learned something like that? Punctured ego. She was right. She was looking at me as if I were a prideful little boy who had taken a spill off his first two-wheeler, and what made it even more agonizing was that she was right.

"The little porker creamed me."

"Sam told me all about it. He was a fat kid and it

seemed no one ever liked him. He used to get beat up about once a week. When he was a teenager he took every self-defense course there was. He still practices an hour a day, kicking and punching. That's where he met his wife—in a self-defense course."

I decided to make things better.

"How could you sleep with a jerk like that?"

Her vivid face went blank, and for a moment I thought I had lost her for all time. Strangely, the thought panicked me. I stammered.

"What I meant was . . ." Smooth as silk; that was Thomas Black. Maybe I should write a book: *How To Win Any Woman With Nine Simple Words*. You silver-tongued devil of a detective, you. "By the way. Where did he go?"

"Don't worry," Deanna said, flopping the washrag onto the desk. "I sent him packing." She gave me a look, a forgiving look; the old Deanna. She giggled. "And I doubt if his wife will show up."

"He'd never be able to do that move again. He just caught me off-guard was all. And I have this injury, see . . ."

"Sure, sure, sure," she said, stroking my brow with each word.

I stared at her. I was thinking a lot of thoughts, most of them not very generous, and they must have shown through the bruises on my face.

She looked away. She fluffed her blouse. She fiddled with her hair. She did everything but greet my eyes. I was angry with her because I was the big strong he-man and she had just saved my butt. If she hadn't been there, Sam might have done a lot of ugly trajectory experiments on my bones. It angered and frightened me to have been at the mercy of a pineapple like Wheeler. And the fact that a woman had rescued me was not encouraging. It made me angriest of all that she had slept with him. I had had my suspicions earlier and now my brain was rife with unwanted visions. She was athletic in her sex and it painted horrid pictures in my mind.

Staring at her hands while she fidgeted with the hunk of diamond on her ring finger, she said, "I believe I know what you're thinking. It didn't have anything to do with us. In fact, it was over before I met you."

"You spent a hell of a lot of time with him."

"It was just that Sam didn't know it was over. And after Mark's *incident* . . . I didn't know what was going on for a while there. You see, I went to him weeks ago when I thought Mark was stepping out on me. Mark beat me up and I thought he was seeing other women and I went to Sam for counseling."

"Sure, and he took advantage of you?"

"Yes, he did. He did! I was all mixed up. I didn't know where to turn. I was scared. You bet he took advantage of me."

"That's very hard for me to believe, Deanna."

"Why?"

"Because you're a big girl now. You know who you are and what you want. A guy like Sam doesn't come out of nowhere and cow somebody like you, not unless you're a willing participant."

"You *should* believe me. It's true. I've been reading about it. It happens to all sorts of women. It's a regular cliché in the counseling literature. The counselor who talks his patient into bed. 'We can work better together if we're closer as human beings.' "

"Is that what he said?"

"Something like that."

"And you fell for it?"

"That's right! I fell for it. Don't be so damned self-righteous."

"What made you think Mark was playing around in the first place?"

"I don't even know if Mark was playing around. That dead girl is the only real evidence I have."

"You just suddenly got suspicious?"

"Something like that."

"And you hired me anonymously?"

"I heard your name mentioned years ago when I went out on a blind date with a cop. Then I heard you mentioned again at Mark's attorney's."

"Somebody told me you had a temper yourself. Said something about you chasing Mark around the house with a pair of scissors."

She shrugged. "When somebody outweighs you by eighty pounds and they start knocking you around, you tend to want to fight back."

"Your maiden name wouldn't be Deanna Ascue, would it?"

"Where did you hear that?"

"A birdy."

"It was all a mistake, okay? I suppose you know it all?"

"Just about you doing time in Purdy."

"I was young and stupid, okay. Having an affair with my boss. He was twenty years older than I was. His wife went nutso and came after us with a gun one night in my apartment. She shot him. Killed him. Then she and I struggled and she got shot, too. I got the credit for the whole thing. I served time for manslaughter."

"But you were innocent?"

Deanna swung her greenish-browns around to give me a steely look. "If you loved me, you wouldn't ask a question like that."

"Don't expect miracles. I've only known you a few days, Deanna."

"Now, I suppose you think I sneaked out here, came in the back door and gunned down Mark and the girl?"

"The thought has crossed my mind."

She pouted, her cheeks drooping as if wires were attached to them, little gremlins tugging the wires at their whim.

"You don't know what was involved. I was so alone. I was so mixed up. And Mark was always off somewhere either at work or out to a ball game with his buddies. I was like a fifth wheel. He made me quit my job. He wanted me to sell my Volkswagen. It was almost like I was a prisoner or something. In fact, I guess I was ready for something to happen when I got involved with Sam."

"Wait a minute. He knocked on the door this morning, didn't he? And the way he called out to you, it was almost as if he were expected. You had it all set up this morning to do your laps with him, didn't you? And then I came in and you decided I was more the thing for brunch. Cancel the ham and eggs. Think I'll have blackberry jam on rye toast this morning." Like a landlubber aboard ship, I carefully navigated toward the door.

Things were even more convoluted than I had imagined. Now I knew why she had been so adamant about getting me off the case. She hadn't wanted me, among other things, to find out about her and Sam. Had she been so involved with the Reverend that she killed Mark so they could carry on? Or had *he* killed Mark so they could continue? Had she been involved in the shooting?

At the door I took the knob in my hand and warmed it for a long while.

She was at Mark's desk and began mechanically sorting through the items she had laid out, pretending that I wasn't in her universe. I watched her for a long while.

"Deanna?"

She tidied up the articles she was stacking in the cardboard box, sniffed and pointedly ignored me.

"Deanna? I'm sorry."

Turning her back on me, she opened the drawer in a small cabinet. She pulled out a photograph album and casually split it open. "Oh my God!"

"I've had a bad day, Deanna. I know that's no excuse but I'm a little dragged out. I broke into Sam's house about an hour ago."

Pivoting, she turned to me, her eyes puffy with crying. "Oh my God!"

I went to her and looked at the album, taking it out of her grief-stricken hands. She plunked down in the executive swivel chair and stared at the seventeenth planet in somebody else's solar system.

It was an album of Polaroid nudes. All teenage girls. Seven in all. The only ones I recognized were Beatrice Hindenburg and Kandy Darling. I quickly flipped the album over and scanned it for identification. Printed in block letters across the front of the cover with a blue ink pen was the name: M. Daniels.

I held it up for Deanna to inspect. "Is this your husband's album?"

"I dunno."

"How about this printing? Do you recognize it?"

It took her a long while to break off her conference with the gods. When she did she squinted at the name on the cover and said, "I dunno. It might be Mark's. He printed like that sometimes, I guess."

There were seven different sections to the book, a concoction almost like some oversexed adolescent pervert might glue together. The girls had been made to pose in the backseat of an automobile I didn't recognize, in a funky motel room which might have been the Galaxie Motor Court Inn or anywhere, and in this very office. All of them were young, too young for this sort of boondoggle.

"Have you been in here before, Deanna?"

"Not since it happened."

"I have. I didn't see this."

"What does that mean?"

"It means somebody put it here. And recently."

"The police might have taken it during the original investigation and brought it back."

"Yeah, they might have. But they didn't."

"Who did?"

"Somebody who wanted you to find it. Somebody who wanted you convinced that Mark was playing around, that he actually did kill himself. Maybe it was the somebody who pulled the trigger on your husband."

Deanna looked at me, searching my eyes. Then she stood up, packed the belongings she had gathered together, dumped the album into the carton and walked to the door with it.

"Deanna?" She opened the door. "I'm sorry about

what I said to you. I shouldn't have snapped. I was way out of line."

"Sure, Thomas."

I watched her toss her luxuriant tresses across the shoulder of her blouse.

"Why was Sam here with you?"

"He's been . . ."

"What? What has he been doing?"

"He's been pestering me. He wants to go to bed with me again. He says he can counsel me better if we're on an intimate basis."

"He's got his technique down pat, doesn't he?"

"Please don't make fun of me."

"So what was he doing here?"

"This was neutral ground. I called him up and told him we weren't going to be seeing each other again. He began arguing. I told him to meet me over here so I could say my final goodbye to him. I didn't want him at the house again."

"You told him? Then what?"

"He stood there like a zombie. He didn't move and he didn't speak. Then you came. You goaded him. Then you hit him. He was already in a sour mood."

"Taught him a lesson, eh? Don't tangle with Thomas Black unless you want face wax all over your boots."

Deanna didn't smile. She twisted the knob, opened the door and went out, leaving only a dazzling whiff of her perfume to linger, dazing me with the keen memories it resurrected.

It took me a long time to get up the gumption to move.

I had made a mess of things.

Deanna was down on me.

Sam Wheeler was off in the dark beyond somewhere

waiting for another chance to avenge his lost love and kick my head across the parking lot.

Things were getting muddled and I was too tired to sort them out.

Switching off the lights, I trudged downstairs and walked to the door. Deanna's Cadillac was gone. But Sam's look-alike Chrysler was still there. I turned and peered around the darkened office and atrium area. Nothing.

But there was something else, farther out in the parking lot, behind some alders: a Mercedes. I hadn't noticed it when I came in. Emmett Anderson's Mercedes. I could have sworn it hadn't been there when I arrived. It was empty.

He spoke from behind me, from inside the office complex.

"Okay, mister tough guy. Let's see what you're made of."

He pranced through the doorway from the ware-house, a fat and sassy cat stalking a mole. I was the bedraggled mole.

 I WAS WET AND WEAK
and weary, and my body
was beginning to fester. I didn't need this. I didn't need a
nighttime confrontation with *The Omnipotent Master of
Kung Fu.*

Certain prissy and self-serving men could swagger
with their bellies. A few pregnant women and some cops
who swilled a lot of suds were good at it.

Sam Wheeler was better than most.

He dogtrotted toward me, his swollen watermelon gut
held out pompously in front of himself like athletes held
out their chests. Flushed and ruddy-looking under the
haze of artificial light from the receptionist's desk, his
face took on the aura of a glazed plastic mask. The weird
mask of a boy's face that an old man might wear for a
grisly joke.

The lights in the warehouse behind him were blazing.
No doubt he had been prowling through the factory . . .
maybe prepping the freezer . . . getting it ready for
another frozen dick.

"Got a little shiner there, huh pal?" he said, smugness
seeping out of every pore.

"It was a nice dance step. Well-executed with a good landing. The Polish judge gave you a nine point six."

"Quite the wise guy, aren't you, Black?"

I could have made a dash for my waiting truck, but he would have caught me when I slowed to open the building door. He was poised for flight on my part. It was funny how angry a smack in the kisser could make some people.

Though I had been cradling my sore right arm for the past few minutes, I let it dangle, then shook it gently to get some blood in it. The pain was sharper than I imagined it would be.

Anderson was in the plant somewhere. I wondered if Sam knew it.

"Is this what they teach in the seminary? How to brutalize people?"

He snorted. "What are you worried about? Big strong piece of macho meat like you."

"Bible study has done wonders for your personality, TV star."

"I can quote a verse from every chapter in the Bible. Go ahead. Quiz me."

"I'll leave that to the little old ladies you gull and who send in money out of their social security along with a batch of brownies. I thought Deanna told you to leave."

"I never got any brownies."

"What were you doing in the factory?"

"Heard a noise. Just checking it out."

"The same way you were checking it out that Saturday morning with Beatrice Hindenburg?"

"What are you talking about?"

"You know damn well what I'm talking about. You were in this plant the day Mark and the girl were shot."

"Profanity doesn't impress me, Mr. Black. In fact, you won't impress me no matter what you do. And what is this fiddle-faddle about me being in the plant? An allegation like that is as stupid as it is ridiculous. It was a suicide."

"And so was Kandy Darling's death? And Butch Teets'? All suicides? A rash of suicides? Must be something Big Brother sprinkled into the food dyes, huh? Very convenient."

"You don't hit me in the mouth and get away with it, Black."

"This is all about a slap in the kisser. Sure. It doesn't have anything to do with the way your parents died."

That jibe stopped him in his tracks. I had been slowly backing up and he had been slowly pursuing, but my wisecrack halted him in his tracks. "What do you know about my parents?"

"Your dad got a little funny in the head and shot your mother, didn't he? Then shot himself. A thing like that lurks in your subconscious. Maybe someday when the opportunity presents itself, you might reproduce it, eh? A scenario like that sticks with a guy and someday he might see something close . . . and reproduce it. Like maybe with Mark and the girl."

"Nobody knows how my parents died."

"*I* know, Samuel. I know."

"My wife has never even been told. Where did you . . . ? You didn't . . . There's only one place you could have found that out." His baby-blue eyes widened as he stared at my insolent grin. I had to make it good. The way he handled himself in a bout, it might be my last chance to be sassy. "Why, you bastard! You broke into my place."

I winked and tugged at the hem of my trousers. "You pee into that hot tub to get it to stink like that or what? You and your wife play golden showers?"

He was sputtering with anger. "You s-s-sneaking, lying bastard. You're so anxious to tie this business up . . . to confirm your silly little paranoid theories, that you broke into my place. Black . . . you're worse than a sorry excuse for a human being. You're despicable cow dung."

"Ow," I said, wincing at an imaginary prick of pain. "I'm going to need a psychiatrist to get this out of my system, Sam."

"Bastard."

"You counsel those little runaways and then when they're ripe for the plucking you sleep with them, don't you? Nice job. Good hours. Free sex?"

"If you want to play mind games, why don't you go play them with the little girly you had at the party. The goddamn lawyer with the twitchy butt."

"Profanity does not impress me, Mr. Wheeler."

Seeing that he was about to launch an attack, I made a hasty move for the doorway but the chubby man scurried forward and cut me off, his hands cocked like the dangerous weapons I knew they were. I backed into the atrium, into the gigantic waiting area with the long low couches and glass magazine tables. Now that he had cut off my retreat, Sam slowed down, relishing our sport of cat and mouse. It's always fun to be the cat.

"The album. That was your album, wasn't it? I saw a mark in your trunk where a book about that size had been hidden. Deanna told you to meet her here and you rushed over and slipped it into Mark's things. A neat trick. Very convincing too. If I hadn't already searched Mark's office once, I might have fallen for it."

A tic made both his long-lashed eyes squint and release, but not quite in synchronization. "Album?"

"You know what I'm talking about."

"This is just between you and me, buddy," he said, stalking me, moving in a waddle.

How could a man that clumsy-looking fight so proficiently? All he had to figure out was where he wanted to stick me and how hard he wanted to do it. I wasn't a fighter. I won most of my scraps, but that was because I was careful in my selections, because I fought dirtier than I looked like I would, and because I had a rouser of a sucker punch and used it without waiting for my conscience to give the high sign.

Backing up, I reached into my jacket pocket and discovered the switchblade I had confiscated from Hung Doan's partner. I clutched the closed knife in my left fist, a talisman, an ally, a lump of surprise that I would try out as a sap and use for more vicious enterprises if that didn't work.

"You seduced Deanna when you were counseling her. You seduced the runaways, too, didn't you? The good Christian preacher. This isn't going to look good on the evening news."

"It ain't gonna be on the evening news, buddy boy."

"And then to cap things off, when Deanna told you to meet her, you rushed over and hid that album upstairs as if it belonged to Mark."

"What album?"

"The nudes. You don't have to play dumb, Sam. All you have to do now is kill me and you'll be scot-free. Pretty good deal, huh?" I grinned.

"Don't be absurd. I'm not going to kill anybody. I'm going to teach you a lesson, is all. A gentleman's lesson in manners. And as far as that album is concerned, you're right, I did put it up there. I wanted DeeDee to find it, but I didn't want to be the one to give it to her. Mark handed it to me weeks ago. Mark came to me for help. His whole life was jammed up. He had troubles with girls . . . young girls. He couldn't keep his hands off them. It was Mark, not me, you boob. He came to me for help, don't you see?"

"*You* were hitting on the teenaged girls you were supposed to be counseling. Beatrice Hindenburg. Kandy Darling. The four or five others that you had strip down so you could immortalize them in smeared Polaroid. You must have been using Mark's office. Years ago you hauled ice out of here. You had a key. You knew the routine. On a Saturday you thought you were safe. Nobody would be coming to work. Just sneak up for an hour or two of the old in-and-out on Mark's couch. Then Mark walked in and ruined it. He was shocked. Maybe he even threatened to expose you to the world. Mark was going to ruin you. So you ruined Mark."

"You . . . actually think I assassinated Mark?"

Plunging recklessly ahead, I said, "You counsel young women. Some of them are ripe for the plucking. You are tempted. So you succumbed to your temptations, you play bouncy-bounce one evening. You have a girl. And another. Pretty soon you're on a steady diet. But you're a cheapskate. You park under the Spokane Bridge and do gyrations in the backseat, but then they start building a new bridge and the place loses its sheen. Too many people. Too much dust. So, cheap as you are, you borrow your friend's office. Simple. One morning he catches you at it. You know that if the world at large ever heard about your secret life, your career would be ruined. So you take the easy way out and shoot Mark. Then you shoot the girl."

Wheeler snorted a snort of contempt, of indescribable and unutterable disdain for me, for my theory, and for the fact that I was still squandering valuable oxygen meant for him. He contemplated my face carefully before replying, a half-smile of inexplicable contentment warping his thick, buttery lips.

"You detectives," he said. "You really take the cake. This is good. This is really good. I'm going to have to use this in next week's sermon. You think I . . ." He broke off and began giggling hysterically. He laughed long and hard, bobbling his rigid gut in one movement.

I let him finish the performance, if it was a performance. I didn't know anymore.

"Mark was having all sorts of troubles. He was bickering with his partner, Anderson. He had found out somebody in the plant was smuggling drugs. He didn't know what to do about any of these things. So he came to me. I tried my best, but I guess I failed him. *Mark* entrusted me with the album. He gave it to me out of shame."

I shook my head. "This just isn't hanging right, Sam. You were the one sleeping with the young girls. I know you were. You were Kandy Darling's sugar daddy. You took her up to the lake and you killed her, didn't you? Did she guess about you and her friend Beatrice? Did she get too close to the truth?"

"You're deluding yourself, Black. How do you account for the dead detective?"

"Easy. He was trailing Beatrice. He got your license number when he was tailing her, but he thought the car belonged to Mark Daniels. He just never bothered to

check. Then after he met me and began to think there
might be some hard cash in it, he backtracked and ran
your plate. Knowing him, he probably tried to blackmail
you."

"Don't you think if I had really done all those things
that I would admit it right now? I mean, after all, I
could take your head off at the shoulders anytime I
wanted."

"You don't look like a confessor to me, Sam. You'll
go right into your casket swearing you never played with
yourself."

"I never did." He wriggled his nose nervously like a
rabbit. He would never admit anything. Not playing with
himself, and certainly not murder. But he was beginning
to lose some of his composure.

"Ever since the day I graduated from high school I
have desired nothing out of life other than to guide my
fellow man to the Lord Jesus Christ. And you stand there
and have the gall to accuse me . . . Do you want to know
where that album came from? Mark Daniels gave it to me
a week before he died. He told me he thought the old
man, Anderson, was mixed up in this drug deal. He said
some of the Orientals in his plant were selling heroin and
he thought Anderson had something to do with it. He
knew Anderson was sick and Anderson was taking the
stuff for the pain."

Wheeler was beginning to make some sense. The way
he was explaining it could easily have been the way it
happened. Maybe he didn't seduce young girls. Maybe
he had only seduced Deanna. And maybe Mark had
come to him and had given him the album. I was beginning to see there was more than one way to put this
jigsaw together.

And, of course, the morning of the first murders, who had been the first person on the scene? Anderson! I had watched him drive up behind Mark Daniels myself, had watched him go into the building and then summon the police. He had admitted himself that in his earlier years he had been a cutthroat. Daniels and Anderson had quarreled the week before the deaths. Maybe they had quarreled about the drug dealing.

The slow realization crept over me that what I had been uttering might just be totally preposterous, that I might be sucking on my own shoe leather in a moment.

There was a persistent ring of sincerity to Sam Wheeler tonight.

I hadn't noticed this particular strain in the man before, but then Kathy had been right, I had been nursing a grudge ever since I laid eyes on him.

Beatrice had been sleeping with Mark Daniels. She just happened to get in the way. Kandy Darling must have been sleeping with the old man. He had killed her when she started cogitating too hard about her friend Beatrice's death. Or maybe he just panicked and slugged her in the throat. And Seymore Teets had cottoned to the drug dealing somehow and had wanted somebody to divvy up his share of the booty.

Teets had gone to Anderson and Anderson had iced him, so to speak. That accounted for why Anderson had been outside the freezer when Kathy and I broke out. The lying old booger had locked us in. Then he had gone somewhere in his car and come back to check. That's why the engine had been warm.

Sam Wheeler had moved very close now, watching my eyes complacently. I had the unopened switchblade in my left fist, had been planning to use it like a roll of quarters, to toughen my fist and harden my blows.

There was just one last nagging loose end. Where had the old man learned to kill with a blow to the windpipe? That seemed like something a martial arts expert would know, not an old man, even if he had been a hooligan in his youth. And the country-western album? They pointed to Sam, not Andy.

As I mulled it over, Wheeler's eyes enlarged and the gray pupils shriveled to pinpricks.

Was it my imagination, or did he have the cold and simultaneously frenzied stare of a snake about to strike? The well-modulated voice burst forth. "The Lord is my shepherd."

If I hadn't been so sore and tired and unguarded I might have escaped the blow entirely. I saw it in the nick of time. Not in time to escape, but in time to keep from being killed.

Wheeler hardly moved his body at all. Nor did his eyes flinch.

When he flicked his right hand at my throat, his fingers were bent at the second joints into a deadly slicing ax of a weapon.

His intention was to shatter my trachea.

Kandy Darling's trachea had been smashed. Teets had died the same way.

Twisting, wrenching around, I belly-flopped onto the floor, grasped my neck with my bad hand, and bellowed like a strangling calf.

Collapse that rigid tube and you strangled to death. While a crowd gathered and some well-meaning soul who had seen too much phony emergency work on the tube said, "Give him air," you just plopped down on the spot and slowly asphyxiated. Two minutes. Three minutes. Four. Flopping and gasping, clawing and scratching to open a pipe that was squashed flat. It was a hell of a way to go. Bluer than blue.

The gargling desperation in my snores sounded bad even to me. Though he hadn't crushed my trachea, any blow to the neck is painful, is bound to rupture vital targets. I was hurting, seeing stars, worried about what was next on the agenda. Maybe he didn't realize he had missed. Maybe I could pretend to turn blue.

He booted me in the kidneys. The toes of his cowboy boots felt like needles. He kicked me in the spine and shoulders and hip and anywhere he could get a good shot in. The bastard was going to put the boots to me until I was dead. Turning blue wasn't fooling anyone.

"The Lord is my shepherd," he said, and then proceeded to repeat himself over and over, a litany of pain and destruction and obfuscation.

I could clearly hear Sam's stepfather decades earlier invoking the scriptures when he dragged the young whimpering Sam out to the woodshed and whaled the tar out of him.

That was the last thing Mark Daniels had said in the hospital. It hadn't been an invocation. It had been a clue. It had been the last phrase Mark Daniels had heard on this planet.

"The Lord is my shepherd."

 HE HAD ALMOST CONNED
me out of it, but not quite.

When he punched me it was because he knew I would
have jigsawed the pieces back together—later—after I
had time to reflect. So he simply moved first.

The famous Thomas Black Sucker Punch had been
delivered to the originator. That was like Alfred Nobel
getting blown up by TNT. Ben Franklin getting electro-
cuted. Henry Ford getting run down in four o'clock
traffic.

I rolled across the carpet like a fallen tree that hadn't
been debranched yet, my movements bumpy and uneven.
He followed clumsily, kicking and missing and swiping
at the air. Finally, I screwed myself behind a steel and
leather sofa placed out in the open, bumped my head as I
squeezed around it and pushed up to my feet, free. I
could barely breathe, but I grasped my neck using both
hands and pretended that it was even worse than it was. I
was a pretty doggone good thespian when I needed to be.
This stunt would give me a breather. I might even buy
enough time to think up a plan.

He soared over the back of the sofa, feet poised to
strike, screeching at the top of his lungs. He wasn't

giving me time for diddly-squat. I dodged, wheeling to the side. A slashing foot brushed the hairs on my temple.

Before he could get his bearings and rise, I kicked at his kidneys. But in my haste and furor I missed, striking him squarely in the spine. He flopped forward and did a fancy tumbling move and finished up on his feet, weight balanced, facing me.

"The trouble with these Oriental fighting arts," Wheeler said, "is a guy never really gets a chance to use them. You won't believe how many times I've waited for somebody to jump me. But nobody's ever been stupid enough to do it."

"Until Kandy Darling and Teets," I said, grinning so hard my gums hurt.

"Until *you*, buddy boy. You just bought yourself a ticket to a low spot in hell."

"You killed them all, didn't you?"

Whooping and springing up into the air with a grimace on his face, he snapped off a kick at my testicles. A miss. I did a couple of basketball moves and eluded him. Then again. He began to wise up and alternate his blows, slashing with his hands, then kicking, then slashing, putting the combinations together the way his conscienceless master had taught him.

He riddled me with slaps and punches. He popped me in the thigh once and laid a good one across my nose. Blood began dropping out of my nostrils and flowing across my lips. It tasted like a particularly dirty and bitter brand of sweat.

I threw a lamp at him, then a small chair, then a table, each movement electrifying my right shoulder in an excruciating series of prickling pains, as if I were tearing stitches out with my teeth. The tiny table swiped across his back and cartwheeled beyond him. He ducked, stumbled, held his back with one hand, swore and came at me quicker and clumsier than ever, the nimbleness abandoning his limbs.

Scuttling over to a large conference table in a corner, I managed to get it between Sam and myself. I grabbed it with both hands and sledded the six-by-twelve table at Sam's legs. He wasn't expecting an attack, and it caught him by surprise, slamming into his thighs and almost knocking him down.

Before he could sidle around it, I went through a door that led into a copier room and then through that into the warehouse. The lights were all on. I scrambled through the stacks of cartons and past steel wire baskets of shiny unlabeled cans, passing various spots where I might have stopped and drygulched him.

I was scared. Sam was good.

The pop to my nose hurt as much as anything had in a long while. I would be one very lucky buckaroo if it wasn't broken.

A door banged behind me. The lights blinked off and then came back on. Sam was so panicky he didn't even know if he could see, had flipped the lights off by mistake. That was good. He was almost as jittery as I was.

I grabbed three cans out of a bin and lobbed them in Sam's general direction. I doubted if I would connect, but I might slow him down. I heard all three clip the concrete in a syncopated stutter. All misses.

Making my way to the other end of the warehouse, skipping across rows of stacked merchandise so he couldn't track me, I found the door where Hung Doan and his cronies had been waiting Sunday morning. I heaved it open and slogged into the dog food factory.

The lights were on in there too. I saw no trace of Emmett Anderson. I only hoped that when we barged in on him he would have a gun.

Then I saw the wooden stairway along the wall. I had never noticed it before. My guess was it led up into an old office complex, something that was probably vacant or reserved exclusively for storage now.

I scrambled up the steps, breathing hard, my throat aching. I mopped a gob of blood off on my sleeve, stunned at how badly I was bleeding. The reddish torrents were pattering down my shirt front and my pants as well. In fact, I was leaving a trail of dribbles like an errant painter with a hole in his paint can.

It was a dead end.

I was in a high, dusty, unused room overlooking the factory. It had been the boss's office once. Now it was stacked with cartons of files, thirty years of files. I had broken one of my own maxims and forged into the unknown at a time when I needed all the hole cards. It only showed how weary I was. A cartoon belonging to one of the former occupants hung on one wall. It read: "It's nice to be important, but it's more important to be nice."

Sam was at the top of the stairs behind me before I knew it. He had moved silently and efficiently, holding his breath on the climb. He was paying for it now, standing in the doorway in a half-squat, arms cocked for action, his lungs pumping overtime.

I moved toward him, feigned a left hook and kicked at him. He sidestepped, breathed harder, and kept his beady eyes on me.

He was good at not telegraphing what he was about to do. Very good.

He launched a kick at my face. I stepped back and felt the wind from his foot on the wetness on my face. When he landed he slipped. I laughed until I saw what he was slipping on. It was *my* blood. Good strategy. Bleed him to death. Another pint or two and he might fall down and kill himself.

Coming in fast, he struck at my face, missed, connected hard with my ribs and then did some sort of flying pirouette and knocked me down with his leg. My knee felt like a glass jar somebody had just shattered with a ball-peen hammer.

I rolled. It didn't take me far. Sam knew he had me now. He wasn't even concerned about getting it over with. It was all finished but the goodbyes.

He came close, bent over me, made a fist and held it up next to his grinning teeth. My south end began to pucker.

As he rammed his fist at my solar plexus with all the force he could muster, he heard the click—but he heard it too late. He completed the blow.

We stared at each other, our faces inches apart. He had dosed himself from a mouth spray before meeting Deanna. It was wearing off now. It took him a moment to figure out what had happened. I had flicked open the switchblade and he had crashed his fist straight into it.

He gaped in disbelief. He had punched straight down on the pointed knife blade. It was buried to the hilt between the middle two knuckles of his right fist.

Hissing, he flew back, propping up his right arm at the elbow, gaping at the horror. After the blade had entered between his knuckles, it had kept right on going, had shimmed under the palm of his hand and continued into his wrist, piercing right up under the tendons. I could see the welt it made under his skin, as ugly a thing as I ever viewed.

"You have to be careful around knives, Sam."

Unbelieving, he sucked air through his teeth and carefully held the wicked apparition a foot in front of his eyes. He winced, whimpered and finally wailed.

I crawled away, picked my broken body up and braced it in the doorway.

He knelt. I thought at first it was to pray, but he used his good hand to hoist up his jeans past one stitched white cowboy boot inlaid with designs in turquoise. Then he dug into the boot. I wasn't thinking. It felt like I hadn't been thinking for a year. Everything had gone wrong. And my mind was as dull and dumb as a medical resident after a 48-hour shift.

Laying a porcine look on me, he withdrew a small, lumpy, ugly revolver from his boot, reached across his pudgy body, pointed it at me and jerked the trigger. A splinter of wood exploded off the doorway and whirred past my face.

I dove for the stairs.

He squeezed off more rounds, but I didn't bother to keep track of how many. A crazy vertigo ripped my consciousness from its roots. I was falling. Tumbling. Twisting. Spinning down the stairs. Some giant brat had picked up the dog food factory and was rolling it down a hill and I was inside whirling like a pebble in a tire. Twirling and spinning until I was a broken mess. Until I was asleep, dreaming a fantasy about Deanna and her swimming pool and her luscious bare swimmer's shoulders. It seemed like we swam together almost forever.

 I REGAINED CONSCIOUS-
ness the way a lazy bubble
rises to the surface of an oil tank, with a slow, fluid and
inexorably wavy motion.

An emergency paper blanket, its plastic wrapper crinkling, was propped under my head like a rolled cigar, and an old scratchy wool army blanket was tucked tidily around my outstretched legs. My ribs sang at me when I inhaled and exhaled.

Listening to them was so much fun I kept right on inhaling and exhaling.

Half my face was swollen and tight. My right shoulder felt as if it had been torn out of its socket and hastily reinserted by a giant ghoul, but my mind was amazingly limpid.

Lying in what must have been the exact spot where I had crashed and burned, I looked across the aisleway at a long flat conveyor system lined with metal rollers. The thunderous machine that ran the conveyor was on, though the conveyor itself was motionless, thousands of gleaming tin cans queued up. Several other motors in the empty plant were humming, clanking or whinnying. The humid smells of cooked grain assailed my senses.

Exploring the back of my skull with my fingers, I discovered a lump just over and encroaching upon my left ear. It felt like a rotten pomegranate. It took awhile before I recalled what had happened.

I had lunged for the stairs, lost my footing and knocked myself silly on the tumbling descent.

According to my watch, which had slid around the wrong way on my wrist, over three hours had passed. It was after midnight.

It wasn't until I shifted my weight that I realized how bruised and shattered I was. By rights, I should waste the rest of the night in a hospital bed. Maybe the rest of the week.

Moaning, I rolled onto my face and folded upward until I was on my hands and knees. Using my left arm, I gripped a piece of the apparatus above me and hoisted myself up. I stood alone in a factory full of buzzing machines, feeling the heat blasts from the large cylindrical baking ovens I knew were around the corner.

It took more than a minute before my blood pressure was constant enough so I could move without fear of listing and fainting.

Woozy and disoriented, I looked around for signs of Sam Wheeler. I tottered across the way to where one of the machines had what I would have sworn were bullet pocks stippling its green paint. On the glassy smooth concrete floor I spotted a drop or two of blackish blood and five empty .44 shell casings. Bending laboriously, I picked them up one by one and clicked them together in my fist. I sniffed them. Freshly fired. Sam had not shot at me with a .44. His gun had been a smaller caliber, possibly a .38. These shell casings were from another weapon, somebody else's.

"There you are," he shouted.

The old man strode toward me in his studied bow-legged gait, grim and somber, and more mellow than I had seen him in a while. He picked the brass casings out of my hands, bobbled them like popcorn seeds in a cooker and slid them into the pocket of his long white lab coat. They clinked like a handful of broken teeth. "Forgot about these."

"Where's Wheeler?"

Emmett Anderson did not reply, only grasped me gently by the chin and the top of my head, tilting my skull and inspecting the damage. "You took a pasting, there. Big guy like you? Seems like you should have been able to take a little smartass fat boy."

"I might have taken him, but I had a bum horoscope for today. Where is he?"

"Don't fret. Ain't no big boogyman gonna jump out and snatch you. You mosey back to the office with me, I'll get another chemical ice pack for that face. I had one on you, but it give out after a spell. Can you walk?"

Mildly insulted at the inquiry, I said, "I can walk. I can't jog, but I can walk."

Tall, dignified and a bit sad-looking tonight, Emmett Anderson strode in front of me, picked up the trappings with which he had been caring for me and led me to the glass-walled office in the center of the plant.

During the trek I noted that almost every machine used in the canning process was either turned on or looked as if it had been run recently. Behind the modern labeler sat an old-fashioned wooden-slatted hand truck. On it were four huge steel mesh crates of chrome cans waiting to be labeled. Probably three or four hundred pounds of cans.

In the glass-walled office Anderson cleaned me up

with alcohol wipes, working to the brassy sound of a female country-western singer on the radio. Then he peeled my shirt away and swabbed out the knife wound on my shoulder. To keep from screaming, I clenched my teeth until old fillings squeaked and pinged in my mouth.

"How'd you get this?"

"Hung Doan and his friends. I went up to see them this afternoon. Seems like they were dealing drugs. Doan took a couple of pot shots at me. His colleague decided I was full of hot air."

"So he stuck you?"

"Just a scratch."

"Another quarter inch and he would have pinned you to a wall. Your little tussle with Wheeler probably didn't help this incision any."

"Somebody made a big mistake and taught him how to fight."

"I noticed that when I spoke to him. That's why I pulled out this." Anderson lifted the lab coat and, using two fingers, patted the ornate walnut handle of a Ruger .44 caliber pistol tucked into his belt. "Trouble was, the little shit had one of his own."

"He nick you?"

Anderson touched a finger to a dark lumpy spot on his scalp. It was already scabbing over pretty good. "It ain't nuthin'. What brought you down here?"

"I'd ask you the same thing, Andy."

"Me? I knew Mark didn't do himself in. And it hurt that he died up there in ICU. It hurt real bad. I spent most of last week up there in the hospital room waitin' for him to wake up. That little fart Reverend came in and gave me a couple of lectures on the power of prayer. Even then I wanted to put a corkscrew in his eye. At one time

Mark . . . he was like a son to me. We been bickering of late, but I was hoping we would be pals again, know what I mean?" He squinted his gray eyes at me.

"I think so."

"I thought on it and I thought on it, but it wasn't until you found that bugger in our freezer that it hit home. You know that box you found him in? That was an old ice-making contraption Sammy Wheeler used right back there in that same corner of the freezer years ago when he delivered ice blocks out to his folks' store. Hell, that box has been kickin' around here for ages and I don't think but three of us here knew what it was used for."

"And Sam was one of the three?"

"Yep. He used to throw a tarp over the box just the way it was done today. I drove out to his place this evening. Figured to do a little sleuthing myself. Followed him here to the plant. That really piqued my curiosity. Then I seen Deanna come in. Then you. I went around back and slipped in that way."

"So you were here all along? How much did you hear?"

"Not a damn thing. I was too far away. I figured you two was in a ruckus, but I couldn't quite get a bead on it until he fired."

"So where is Sam?"

"I was like you. I thought I could beat him to death. Little fat boy. Surprised the hell out of me. I saw you boogy down the stairs. Then he tried to put one into your eyeball. Took aim and tried to slide one right into your occipital bone. I called out to him before he could fire. He saw me and the party commenced. Guess I took a stray across my scalp. After he emptied his pistol, I had the goods on him. I figured to punch out his lights. But he got close and jumped up in the air and did some sort of whirly thing. Almost took my head off with his boot. I think if he hadn't had them tight jeans and cowboy boots and a knife buried in his hand he would have decapitated me."

I was surprised he hadn't. A karate expert pitted against an old man. And the old man was standing here chatting; the karate expert was missing. Anderson obviously could take care of himself. Back in his prime, he would have been a man not to run up against.

"What happened to Wheeler?"

The old man didn't reply, merely went about his work—shutting the ovens down, turning off the machinery, flicking switches a machine at a time. I traipsed behind him, tagging along through the whole factory area. There was absolutely no sign of Sam Wheeler. Not a gun, not a cowboy boot, not a Bible in sight.

When everything was shut down and he had cut most of the lights, Anderson grabbed the wobbly handle of a dolly that was loaded with baskets of jumbled, unlabeled dog food cans. He towed it into the warehouse section.

"You been in here working or what, old man?"

"Takes my mind off things. I come down here and do things once in a while."

He shut the main breaker off in the warehouse, led me through the office complex and outside to the parking lot. It was dark and Harbor Island was deserted. Three vehicles were in the lot. My truck. Anderson's Mercedes. And the Chrysler that belonged to Sam Michael Wheeler. Until this moment I still cherished the notion that the old man had driven Sam Wheeler off, that he had left of his own volition, was scampering off to find a lawyer.

After the old man accompanied me to my truck, I said, "Where is he?"

He had been wheezing, so it took him awhile to answer me. When he did it wasn't with words. He turned around and stared at the Trinity Building. I did the same.

"In the ice?" I asked.

The old man squinted in the darkness, an expression partially of satisfaction, partially of angst.

"You wouldn't do a thing like that?"

He grunted.

"What? Did you shoot him?"

Anderson wheezed as he spoke. "Didn't have any shells left. But he didn't know that. I made it as slow as a day in perdition. He knew it was coming and he whimpered like a puppy been boot-stomped. You would have enjoyed it."

"Don't count on that. Did he tell you anything?"

"Couldn't talk fast enough. Fact was, he didn't even get it all out in time. Didn't bother me none. I ain't writin' none of this in my diary. I save that for important things like when the milkman run over the cat."

"He told you he killed Mark?"

"Admitted he did that. Killed that detective and the girl up at the lake too. Admitted it all. No one else involved, just him. Started going into some hogwash about being an almost perfect double for Mark. Something about being mistaken for him a couple of times, especially when he was wearing clothes Mark gave him. I didn't catch it all. A false beard? You know anything about that? He wanted to stand in the bottom of that goddamned grinder and talk all night but I told him I had business to attend."

"The police are going to want to know where he is."

"Tell 'em to use this," said Anderson, handing me a small, chrome-plated implement. Breathing hard, he hobbled to his car, fired up the engine and drove out of the lot.

I watched the Mercedes sail down the midnight-dark street until it disappeared. The old man said Sam Wheeler had been standing in the bottom of the grinder. Not the enormous cast-iron meat grinder that chunked beef quarters into bite-size tidbits so the rest of the machinery could handle it and grind it into dog meal? Those steel mesh baskets had been stuffed full of freshly packed dog food cans. Cans that had been packed to-night. Fish flavor? Chicken flavor? Baptist flavor?

I looked down at the instrument in my hands. A can opener.

Good Lord.

**27** Two weeks later my face had pretty much knitted up, and so had most of the other knots, bumps and contusions that had been inflicted on me.

My only souvenirs of the case were a purplish, puckered indentation on my right shoulder and a tiny dark echo that kept ricocheting inside my head like the refrain to an exasperating song I couldn't rid myself of. The echo was a woman's laughter—nervous laughter, like water boiling over rocks.

I hadn't seen Deanna since the night at the plant, had been told she had left town to visit her mother.

It took a bit of convincing, but with Kathy's wooing thrown in, Ralph Crum finally came to believe that the Reverend Wheeler might have had something to do with both Beatrice Hindenburg and Kandy Darling. One of Darling's ex-roommates identified a photo of Wheeler as the man Kandy had been seeing for the past few months.

At the Galaxie Motor Court Inn both the proprietress and the two geeks next to Unit 12 identified a full-color picture of Wheeler as the man who had visited there several times with Beatrice Hindenburg.

Reluctantly, Crum had somebody dust the motel room

and they found both Hindenburg's *and* Wheeler's finger-prints. They didn't find any of Daniels' prints. That was the point that began to sway Crum.

At the Daniels roost on Lost Lake they found Wheeler's prints on the stereo and the toaster, as well as a track from his Chrysler in the muddy yard.

When Ralph Crum made an effort to interrogate Wheeler and found that he had vanished, the district attorney's office put out a warrant for his arrest. He was implicated in two separate murder cases and now he was missing. I never told anyone else what had happened to him—not Kathy, not the cops, not my telephone analyst. They found his car at the plant, but nobody knew what to make of it.

What was the point? The world didn't have to know how Wheeler had died. I got nauseated thinking about it myself. I went back to the plant a day later and searched it thoroughly. I found a pair of rings I recognized as Wheeler's, his wristwatch, the cowboy boots, his jeans and shirt. Anderson had stripped him down to his BVDs and made him stand in the grinder.

The machine was about the size of a double bed, tall, with a funnel-shaped apparatus on the top. Threatening Wheeler with an empty revolver, Anderson must have made him climb into the funnel and sweat. Sam had talked his head off, hoping it would save him. Anderson must have mercilessly switched on the machine and waited for the scrambling minister to get a piece of his anatomy caught in the whirring blades at the bottom. One piece would be all it would take. The blades would pull him in and do the rest.

Then the old man had processed the results the same way he would have processed a hunk of beef.

The suicide-murder ruling in the Daniels case was officially changed to murder-murder, though the case would never be officially cleared.

I squandered my time turning down a couple of teenage runaway cases where the parents swore their children were prostitutes. I also declined to make a secret tape recording of a man's wife making loud love to one of the neighbors in The Highlands so the disgruntled husband could play it over a loudspeaker at his wife's company picnic. I was glad I stayed out of it. A week later there was a shooting at a company picnic out at Lake Sammamish.

When Kathy Birchfield's workload finally slacked off at Leech, Bemis and Ott and she got some time to spend with her old friends, she and I made bleary-eyed appearances at the month-long Seattle Film Festival. She began attending almost nightly with me. Together we indiscriminately viewed everything that wasn't already sold out. The crowds were chatty, vibrant, cosmopolitan—dressing and speaking weirdly enough to hold our interest if the movies were duds. We heard directors and actors tout their latest extravaganzas.

One night after a subtitled horror flick from Bulgaria, Kathy met a gentleman she knew from her business dealings, and as per our standing agreement, she went off with him to share a bottle of red wine and some inspiring whisperings. I skulked home alone.

The next night at a delightfully goofy French comedy about two best friends sharing the same woman, Kathy told me he had been no great shakes and in fact, she hadn't gone home with him, but had abandoned him at the bistro where they had sipped wine for an hour.

After the final credits rolled on the French comedy and

we dutifully clapped in appreciation and began filing out, I heard something strangely familiar. It was a bubbly, effervescent laughter coming from somewhere in the crush behind us.

The echo that had been zinging around inside me for weeks suddenly grew louder.

I whirled and spotted the top of her strawberry-blonde head bobbing in the crowd behind us. She was conversing animatedly with two other women.

Outside on the sidewalk, I pulled Kathy Birchfield to the edge of the building. She gave me a startled look.

"Last night was your turn," I said, scouring the crowd as it thinned out and straggled past. "Tonight is mine."

"You see a friend?" Kathy asked, as she caught a glimpse of Deanna Daniels strolling past, sandwiched between her two chums. "Oh, Thomas. Not this again. Not *her*."

"I'm going to take her home. Maybe you could find your own way."

"Sure, you can try. But I hate to see you get dumped on when all these people are watching."

"Dumped on? I can feel the electricity from here. Dumped on?"

"You need help telling when somebody is giving off signals, Thomas. I'll help you all you need. But you can't tell by yourself. You see, when two people are giving off the right chemistry, it's obvious to almost everyone around. I myself would know if she liked you. You just have trouble reading the signals."

"Let's just go say hi."

Reluctantly, she followed my lead. We caught the trio of women as they were about to bend into a Volvo station wagon, doors winged open.

Softly, I said, "Hello, Deanna."

All three women turned around at once, but only Deanna reacted. She dropped both hands to her sides, sighed and suddenly ceased smiling. Deanna glanced at Kathy, nodded timidly and then focused fully on my face. Under the streetlight she looked better than she ever had.

Kathy looked up at me to see how I was taking my rebuff.

Introductions were made, ponderously, politely, and we all smiled and finally Deanna stepped close, looked up at me and said, "I had to be away by myself for a while."

"Sure."

"I heard you were hurt."

"I'm okay." I winked. "You wanta see my scars?"

"Maybe we should *all* go have coffee somewhere," suggested one of Deanna's companions gaily.

Deanna Daniels slowly turned around and looked at her friends. "No, I don't think so. You'll have to excuse me, but I have some things to talk over with Thomas. I'll get home some other way. Thanks, girls."

"You sure, DeeDee?"

"I'll drive you home," I volunteered, sounding a bit too eager.

Kathy caught the zeal in my tones. She bobbled her eyebrows at me when she thought nobody else was looking and bestowed a slow, sinking, sideways look like a mother eye-scolding a toddler.

Deanna stepped over and grasped my arm possessively. I grinned. First I grinned at Kathy and then I grinned at all concerned. "I'll call you tomorrow, Kathy. Good thing you brought your car, huh?"

"Yeah," she said, gaping in disbelief. "It sure was." Her little yellow two-seater was parked a block away. Deanna and I stood on the sidewalk amid the thinning movie theater crowd and watched her wheel away. She tooted at us and zipped past.

"She's pretty," said Deanna.

"Yeah, I know."

"You two must know each other very well."

"Real well."

"So," said Deanna, giving my arm a squeeze.

"So."

"I'm nervous."

"Me, too."

"I missed you. I didn't . . . Maybe I shouldn't have left, but I had to get things cleared up in my head. I needed a spacer."

"I understand. I was a little on the rotten side."

"No, you weren't. I believe I know exactly what you were thinking."

"Rotten."

"Okay, you were rotten. But you had a certain right to be."

We ended up in a late-night restaurant on Broadway, one of those atmospheric joints with blue and orange lighting, cigarette smoke piped in through the air-conditioning, where they put tiny chairs and tiny tables out on the sidewalk when the weather permitted so the customers could suck exhaust fumes while they sucked Bloody Marys.

Deanna had a Scotch and water and I swigged my usual soft drink.

"Everything is so mixed up in my head," said Deanna Daniels, touching me across the table. I fingered the freckles on the backs of her hands. Wherever she had been during the past two weeks, she had been getting sun. "Sam ran away? Is what the papers were saying true?"

"I'll lay it all out for you, Deanna. Your husband wasn't exactly Mr. Faithful, but he was not cradle robbing. *Sam* was. With girls. Teenagers. But he was too cheap to get an apartment or go to a motel . . . at least not until it was absolutely necessary. At first he took these young girls out in his car. When that got old he used your place at Lost Lake. Then he began using Mark's office. He had keys to the building from years ago. One day he was up there and Mark walked in on him. He probably heard him coming, took Mark's gun and stood behind the door. When Mark walked in they had words. Mark threatened to expose him. So he shot Mark. Then he put the gun in Mark's hand and shot the girl, making it look as if Mark had fired both shots.

"No doubt he had some clever scheme hatched up to get rid of both bodies, but Emmett Anderson walked in about that time and Sam scampered out the back way. I was watching the plant too, but he must have had his car parked around the back by the railroad tracks. He could go out that way and nobody would see him from in front."

"You mean Mark was killed almost on a whim? Because he happened to show up at his own office at the wrong moment?"

"That's right. I'm not ruling out some ulterior motives either, like maybe the fact that if Mark was gone, Sam might have you all to himself. Surely, that crossed his mind.

"He'd been thinking a lot about Mark lately. He

looked like Mark and he wore Mark's castoff clothing and I guess somebody mistook him for Mark a time or two, because he got himself a neat little theatrical beard and wore it when he checked into the motel. And he signed himself in as M. Daniels. I guess he figured it was safer than using a complete alias like Elmer Fudd or something. In fact, it saved him for a while. The detective who followed Beatrice Hindenburg for her father might have tried to blackmail him if he'd known he was the Reverend Samuel Wheeler.

"When I came to your house and got the keys that first morning, somebody called Hung Doan and told him his personal enemies had hired a torch to come in and burn down his livelihood. Only two people knew I was going to be there that morning—you and Sam.

"After I spoke with Kandy Darling she must have got to thinking. She must have known Sam and Beatrice were seeing each other from time to time. And surely Sam had taken her up to Mark's office, too. Maybe she didn't actually figure anything out. Maybe Sam just panicked. But he took her up to your place at the lake, beat her up and then killed her."

"God," said Deanna. "He must have just been a little bully at heart. But how could he preach one thing and live another?"

"Just a hypocrite, I guess."

"What about this other person that got killed? The detective?"

"Teets had followed Beatrice Hindenburg. In fact, he had seen them together in Wheeler's car. But he mistook it for a Cadillac. After he saw me he must have run the plates and decided if the Reverend Wheeler was running around with sixteen-year-old girls like Beatrice, maybe he had a little spare cash. Sam met with him, probably at the closed-down Trinity Plant, and killed him. Later, when Kathy and I went to the plant, Sam locked us in the freezer by jamming the door with a forklift."

"This whole thing is the worst experience of my whole life," said Deanna.

"It wasn't one of my brighter episodes."

"One of my girlfriends told me I should find a cute little beach boy and take some of this insurance money and run off to the Bahamas for three months. You wouldn't want to be my little beach boy, would you?"

"Not my style." She laughed. It was high-pitched and agitated, and several males at nearby tables looked over, wondering how I had captivated this woman. "I might go for a little midnight swim, though."

"A midnight swim? That might be just the ticket. But you're not . . ."

"Serious? Long-term? That sort of thing?"

"Yes."

"I don't know. You?"

"I don't know either."

On the drive to her place, she scooted across the seat and kissed my ear wetly. It resurrected hot memories.

"There's just one thing that bothers me. The police said all of Sam's assets are intact. His wife claims nothing is missing from the house. He's gone, but apparently he didn't take anything with him. Where is he?"

I shrugged. It was one of those suburban mysteries. The *Seattle Times* would run a feature article on it once every five years.

Of course they would never find him. The old man, Anderson, wasn't going to squeal on his own savage vengeance. And besides, his health was failing. I wasn't going to squeal on him. Before the courts could finish him, his own biology would do the job. What was the point in bothering everybody? The courts and police were already swamped. The newspapers already had enough grisly stories. He would be dead in another few months. I didn't have the heart or the righteous indignation to blab it to the authorities—not that they would have believed me, or been able to trace the corpse.

A task force of squeamish detectives wielding electric can openers and forks might get lucky and find part of some bridge work, or a scrap of bone, but I very much doubted it.

Wheeler was in cans, in packing boxes, on grocery shelves, in shopping carts, and in cupboards all up and down the coast. He was gone for good. Before the summer was over he would be spread across the lawns of five western states. I guess that's what they call the greening of America.

EARL EMERSON

Published by Ballantine Books.
Available at your local bookstore.